If You've Got It, Haunt It

Rose Pressey

KENSINGTON PUBLISHING CORP.

http://www.kensingtonbooks.com

KENSINGTON BOOKS are published by

Kensington Publishing Corp.
119 West 40th Street
New York, NY 10018

All Kensington Titles, Imprints, and Distributed Lines are available at special quantity discounts for bulk purchases for sales promotions, premiums, fund-raising, and educational or institutional use. Special book excerpts or customized printings can also be created to fit specific needs. For details, write or phone the office of the Kensington special sales manager: Kensington Publishing Corp., 119 West 40th Street, New York, NY 10018, attn: Special Sales Department, Phone: 1-800-221-2647.

Kensington and the K logo Reg. U.S. Pat & TM Off.

ISBN-13: 978-1-61773-249-2
ISBN-10: 1-61773-249-4
First Kensington Mass Market Edition: December 2014

eISBN-13: 978-1-61773-250-8
eISBN-10: 1-61773-250-8
First Kensington Electronic Edition: December 2014

10 9 8 7 6 5 4 3 2 1

Printed in the United States of America

To my mother, who shared her love of books with me.
Thank you for always believing in me.

Chapter 1

—◆—

*Many vintage clothing pieces
don't have labels listing the size.
Make sure to try on the items when you can
or get the measurements.*

I remember distinctly what I was wearing the day I first came face-to-face with a ghost.

I collect garments for my vintage clothing boutique, It's Vintage, Y'all. Raiding estate sales at the crack of dawn is one of the better ways to find hidden gems. My heart skips a beat every time I see someone wearing an authentic piece of vintage fashion—like the lady who came into my store yesterday in a fifties high-waist silk hoop skirt over a tiered crinoline, or the old photo I just posted on my blog of a rick-rack trimmed, fitted-waist sundress from the forties.

My blog shares the same name as my boutique. I started it right after the store opened and was shocked at how much traffic I received. I get comments and questions from across the nation—

sometimes even around the world. I discuss current trends based on vintage clothing, any new hidden gems I discover, and celebrities I spot wearing vintage.

Some fashions don't deserve to be called vintage though—like those awful polyester suits from the seventies. Those things should never see the light from the darkened corner of a closet ever again.

Not only do I sell vintage clothing, I always dress the part, making the effort to incorporate at least one vintage piece into my outfit every day. I feel more like myself when I'm connected to the past. Maybe that's because my grandmother Pearl had encouraged me to chase my dreams. She was a grand Southern lady who always dressed to the nines and wore a wide-brimmed hat and white gloves in public.

I loved playing in her closet when I was growing up. Everyone remarked how much we looked alike with the same dark hair and brown eyes.

The first day I met a ghost, I was wearing a rayon-linen blend, mid-length Christian Dior, white pencil skirt with a tiny pink floral print and a kick pleat in the back seam. Thank goodness the pleat allowed me to walk normally and not look like a mermaid. I may only be five-foot-two, but I didn't let that stop me from wearing pencil skirts. The skirt was the bee's knees and I'd gotten it for a steal. I paired it with a fifties silk pink blouse, fitted at the waist with turned-up sleeves and a back-notched Peter Pan collar. The tiny buttons were delicately covered with floral-print fabric. I completed the outfit with pink platform cork-heeled wedge sandals that had a soft leather upper with crisscrossed pink straps. They weren't vintage, but totally retro. My purse was a large pink envelope clutch. I'd seen almost the exact outfit in a photo of Jayne Mansfield from 1957.

I was going shopping at the estate sale of the late self-made businesswoman Charlotte Meadows. She'd made her money by buying small pieces of real estate when she was young. The town was all aflutter about her death, not surprising since not only had she passed under highly suspicious circumstances, she was also quite the celebrity around Sugar Creek. Hardly a piece of land in town existed that didn't have her name attached to it in some way. She'd owned or partnered in businesses, land, and homes for miles around—as if she had been playing a real-life game of Monopoly.

According to the headline in the *Sugar Creek Gazette*, she'd died from asphyxiation, strangulation suspected. The thought sent a chill down my spine. Sugar Creek, Georgia, located in the southern part of the state, is a small town more famous for sweet tea and Southern charm than murder, so it was no wonder that her death had caused a stir.

I pulled my attention-grabbing red 1948 Buick convertible up in front of the huge house. Needless to say, most people in town knew me because of my car. The shiny chrome, red and tan leather interior, and tan top were designed to stand out in a crowd. I couldn't own a vintage clothing store and not drive a classic set of wheels.

After shoving the gearshift into neutral and setting the parking brake, I paused to take in the view. Sunrise had brought the first faint colors of day. The entire property was surrounded by immaculately trimmed hedges and a large, ornately-carved fountain bubbled in front. The massive stone steps welcomed visitors to the double oak doors. The outside of the home was white brick with black shutters on the sides of simply too many windows to count. The circular driveway allowed visitors to pull right up to the door.

Entering the house, I was thrilled to see the inside was just as extravagant as the outside. A majestic Victorian staircase swept down to greet me as I walked across the marble floor in the foyer. Intricate moldings edged the ceiling.

A petite gray-haired woman stood sentinel in the entranceway. She acknowledged me with a large smile.

I reached out to shake her hand, surprised I didn't recognize her face. Sugar Creek is a small place, and that's putting it mildly. "My name is Cookie Chanel, from It's Vintage, Y'all. I'm here for the clothing sale. Can you show me where to find it?"

My mother had named me Cassandra, but from an early age, my Granny called me Cookie because of her love for fashion and because it fit so well with Chanel. Of course, that name stuck and everyone knows me as Cookie.

The woman looked me up and down through her cat-eye glasses, then pointed to my right. "They're really picking through that stuff in there. You'd better hurry if you want any good pieces."

By the look of the house, I assumed it was *all* good stuff, though I did have a few items at the top of my wish list. It had taken me several years to train my eye to spot the difference between genuine vintage and knock-off retro. A strong knowledge of fabrics helped me, too. Different types had been invented in specific years.

My jaw just about hit the floor when I entered the living room. So many items were piled up that my eyes had a hard time taking it all in. Clothing, bags, shoes, jewelry, books, and trinkets covered the racks and metal folding tables used for the sale. It was like the time my parents had taken me to Disney World and I hadn't known which ride to take first. *Which rack to start with?*

My wonder was tempered by the disappointment of finding the room explored by over a dozen people. Usually estate sales are kind of a niche event. Clawing through a dead person's belongings is inherently creepy, no denying it. But in Charlotte Meadows's case, I should have expected a crowd. Her magnificent home was famous in the region, and most people probably just wanted to catch a glimpse inside. The gruesome gossip surrounding her death only fueled the mass curiosity.

Sure, it was a beautiful home, but I was just after the clothing and accessories. Rumor had it that Charlotte—who'd been a fashionista in the truest sense of the word—owned a rare Chanel white felt chapeau adorned with a silk black flower pin. I'd have given up my entire collection of Trigère to get my hands on that hat. Other than that, I was keeping an open mind about what I expected to find. The secret was getting to the best stuff first, and it looked like I'd already failed.

I made my way through the crowd, stopping short when I neared the most enticing rack of clothing. A middle-aged woman stood next to a small table with her arms held stiff and straight down at her sides. Her ebony eyes sparked with frustration as she stared my way. Her gaze pinned me, holding me frozen in place.

She was impeccably dressed in a white Dior pantsuit, leopard print heels, and chunky gold jewelry. Her shiny, chin-length mahogany-colored hair looked as if she'd just left a salon. Her outfit must have cost a small fortune. I recognized those leopard print heels from last month's Vogue cover.

Something about the woman was vaguely familiar, but I couldn't place her right away. Maybe she'd been in my shop. Judging by that outfit, I was sure she was after the best clothing, too. She must have known right away that I was serious competition. We seemed to be in a standoff. She positioned her body as if she was ready for a sprint at a track meet.

I glanced toward the racks of clothing, gauging the distance and devising a plan to run and grab. If I wasn't quick I was going to get stuck with one of those aforementioned polyester pantsuits. More often than not, true vintage items weren't at estate sales. The really valuable pieces were few and far between.

The woman stood her ground and our eyes met again. She knew what I was scheming. If she made a move, I'd cut her off at the pass. Maybe she was a shop owner, too, looking for merchandise just like me. She scowled and I wondered if she'd be a hair-puller. I'd narrowly missed being snatched bald in the past. I tried to remain ladylike at all times, but sometimes people made that a very difficult task.

Maybe I could disarm her with some good Southern manners. "Hello." I smiled graciously. I'd act as though we weren't opponents. Kill her with kindness.

"What are you doing?" she demanded.

I glanced from her to the clothing and back again. "Looking through this clothing?"

Honestly, what did it look like I was doing? I'd spotted a lavender Yves Saint Laurent maxi dress from all the way across the room. If I could get it for the price I was thinking, I'd make enough profit to pay the utility bill this month. There was no way I'd let her have it, not when I'd seen it first.

"So you *can* see me. I knew it!" she said with excitement in her voice.

Oh, bless her heart, this lady was a few bricks short of a full load. Did she think she was invisible? I'd never have admitted it, but I was kind of relieved. A crazy person was easier to deal with than a rival vintage store owner who would know the real value of the clothes and fight me every step of the way.

"Yes, I can see you," I said, sorting through the clothing on the rack. I shoved a Chanel number under one arm and gripped it with my elbow.

She studied the Jimmy Choos on her feet. "I've been having a bit of a problem talking to people for the last couple weeks."

Oh dear. I had a serious job to do and this woman wanted to chit-chat over tea and cookies. "I'm sorry to hear that," I said, pulling out a pale yellow cardigan sweater with gorgeous detailed beading all along the front bust. The sweater sported a delicate combination of white rice beads, longer silver tube beads, and faux pearls. It was love at first sight, but the woman was ruining the romance.

"No, you don't understand." She leaned in near to my face.

I backed away and gave her the most evil glare I could manage. When she didn't step back, I glanced around to see if anyone was watching us. Okay, the truth was I looked around to see if anyone could help me escape in the event that this encounter escalated into violence. She'd obviously skipped her meds that morning.

She waved her hand in front of my face to capture my attention again. "I think I was murdered. No, let me rephrase that. I *know* I was murdered. I distinctly remember someone choking me."

"Uh-huh," I mumbled. It clearly called for withdrawal from the situation—Dior be damned. I'd have to signal for assistance from one of the helpers working the sale. I looked around in vain for a possible rescuer.

The woman didn't seem to notice my actions because she continued talking. "Apparently, you are the only one who can see me. You're the first one who's made eye contact or spoken to me since it happened."

I really hated to have the poor woman kicked out of the sale, but she was leaving me little choice. Maybe if I moved to a different rack she would leave me alone. I picked up the yellow sweater again and moved around her.

"I don't like you looking at my clothes." She reached for the sweater, but her hand went straight through the fabric.

I gasped and released my hold on the hanger.

The sweater fluttered to the floor. Again, I scanned the room to see if anyone was watching our inter-action, but the shoppers were wrapped up in bargain-hunting. No one was paying us the least bit of attention.

"How did you do that?" I whispered.

Chapter 2

Heather's Heartfelt Tip
for Getting Rid of an Unwanted Ghost

❧

Have a pesky ghost in your house? First step is simple.
Ask the unwelcome spirit to get lost.

The woman scoffed. "Pick that up before it gets dirty. It's a de la Renta!" She had such command in her voice that I did as I was told.

She hadn't answered my question, so with a shaking voice, I asked again. "How did you do that?"

A red-haired woman in a dull gray dress was walking past as I spoke. She whipped around and looked at me. "I'm sorry? Were you speaking to me?"

"No, I was talking to her." I pointed at the strange woman next to me.

The woman in gray looked in the direction of my pointing finger, then she craned her neck to look behind the racks of clothing. "I'm sorry, but I don't see anyone."

"You don't see this woman standing next to me?" I pointed again.

She frowned as she shook her head. "No."

Before I could say another word, she hurried away. I'd just received the same type of look that I'd been giving out for the last five minutes—the look that said *You should be committed.*

I'd been working a lot lately. Ever since I'd opened the shop and started my vintage clothing blog—it had become popular almost overnight— things had been a tad overwhelming, but I'd never thought the stress had reached hallucination level. Perhaps I needed to take a spa day . . . or ten. A vacation to a luxurious resort sounded like just the right medicine. The problem was I couldn't afford it. I'd sunk my entire inheritance from my beloved granny into opening It's Vintage, Y'all. The only vacation I could manage was a glass of sweet tea on my patio overlooking the shopping center parking lot.

I went back to the clothing. My plan hadn't changed, mostly because I couldn't come up with a better one. I'd act as if nothing was odd or out of place. If I did that, maybe it would be so.

"See, I told you that you were the only one who could see me," the crazy woman said around a chuckle. "Aren't you the gal who owns the vintage clothing shop? Cookie Chanel? You know, you look so much like your grandmother did at your age, it's uncanny. You have the same dark hair and big brown eyes."

I froze with my hand on a cream-colored Armani blouse. In that moment, it all came flooding back to me. When Charlotte Meadows had been murdered several weeks ago, I'd seen her picture in the paper. With a hollow feeling, I realized the woman in the picture was the same one standing next to me. She was Charlotte Meadows! This couldn't be happening!

My heart pounded in my chest and sweat broke out on my forehead. I was having a panic attack, that was all. I'd take a few deep breaths, count to ten, and the situation would be over. If I ignored her, everything would be business as usual.

Still sweating, I sorted through the rest of the rack and moved on to the next one. Charlotte followed closely behind, invading my personal space like a tick stuck on a dog.

I pulled out a fifties beige Schiaparelli cashmere sweater with silk embroidery and beaded overlay. "Oh, you don't want that sweater," she said.

"I don't?" I tried to avoid eye contact.

"No, you don't. I ate some bad shrimp once while wearing it. Of course, I had it dry cleaned, but some stains never really come out."

I rehung the offending item in a hurry and picked up a burgundy blazer.

"You don't want that one either," she said.

"More shrimp?" I asked.

"No. I met my ex-fiancé while wearing that one. It has bad vibes now." She shivered.

"Then why did you keep it?" Despite my better instincts, I felt myself getting pulled into conversation.

She flashed me a look of incredulity. "For sentimental value of course."

"Of course." I rolled my eyes. "Are you going to comment on every piece of clothing here?"

She shrugged. "If need be, yes."

I couldn't believe I was talking to the woman.

She couldn't possibly be a real ghost. I'd watched plenty of ghost-hunting shows and viewed every paranormal movie I could lay my hands on. From what I'd seen, ghosts just didn't start holding conversations with people. They lingered in corners as shadows or materialized as mists or knocked paintings off walls. When I was young, Granny gathered the cousins around the fireplace and told us ghost stories. She spoke of seeing haunts, but she'd never talked to one. If she had, she never told me about it. Granny's stories had sparked my fascination with the paranormal.

The only people who talked to ghosts were psychics, right? Immediately, I thought of my friend Heather Sweet. She had been my best friend in high school, and she owned the occult shop next door to mine. Maybe she'd be able to talk with Charlotte Meadows. Regardless, the whole situation was completely insane.

I grabbed a few items at random and made my way toward the woman in charge of collecting money. I prayed that I hadn't picked up anything in polyester or spandex in my haste to get out of there.

"I know this is crazy, but it's real!" Charlotte exclaimed in irritation.

"I'm not listening to you," I said over my shoulder.

"Why aren't you paying attention to me? I know you can see me and I know you heard me." She moved in front of me and I hurried around her.

"You were just talking to me a minute ago." Charlotte walked beside me, matching my pace.

"Yeah, well that was before I decided I'd gone

insane," I whispered. "Now go away. See you later, alligator."

"Like I said, I know this sounds crazy, but it's real. How do you think *I* feel? I'm the one who's been murdered. I'm the one who's dead. I need you to find out who killed me."

Chapter 3

Cookie's Savvy Vintage Fashion Shopping Tips

❖

Prior to the sixties, seams had a "clean finish,"
meaning they were pressed open and the edges were left raw.
Genuine vintage items display old-fashioned handwork
and time-consuming touches.

The woman collecting money frowned when she looked up to see me talking to myself. I gave her a tight smile and shoved a couple crumpled twenties into her hand before heading toward the door. In my hurry to get out of the house, I tripped on a rug halfway down the hallway and landed on my hands and knees with a thud.

"Oh dear, are you all right?"

I looked up from the floor to see a stranger reaching her hand out to me.

The woman's bright auburn hair glinted under the light of the chandelier. Her brilliant blue eyes stood out beneath her long eyelashes, and her face held a curt expression. Flattering her slim figure, she wore a classic black suit with a crisp white shirt and black heels. The scent of jasmine surrounded her.

Charlotte stood next to us with her arms crossed in front of her chest. "That's my ex-business partner, Marie Vance. She is a little flighty. A strange bird, bless her heart."

"Hello, dear, I'm Marie. You have some beautiful clothing." She pointed at the items clutched in my arms. "Charlotte loved fashion. She was a real fashion leader in town, so I'm not surprised to see such a good turnout for her sale. Did you happen to know Ms. Meadows?" The falsest of smiles twisted the corners of her mouth.

I wondered if it would crack her face right down the middle. I looked over at Charlotte and she shrugged.

"Um, no, I didn't. I'm Cookie Chanel. I own It's Vintage, Y'all over on Main Street." I gestured over my shoulder.

"Oh yes, I've been meaning to stop in there," Marie said.

Well, at least one good thing might come out of this bizarre experience. Maybe I'd get a new customer.

"Will you sell the clothing you bought here today at your place?" Marie asked.

I looked down at the items in my arms. I wasn't even sure what I had. I could have picked up a pair of men's briefs as far as I knew. "Yes, I'll probably place them in my boutique."

"Have you already purchased the items?" she asked.

I sure wasn't stealing them if that was what she was implying. "Yes, I have."

"Well, I'm sure they would give you your money back since you haven't even left the house with them yet." She pointed at the woman collecting money.

Charlotte shook her head. "I told you she was a kook. That's why we aren't partners anymore."

I didn't tell Charlotte, but that clearly wasn't the only reason, or even the *main* reason that they weren't partners anymore.

"Actually, I don't want to return them. But thanks for letting me know." I offered a huge smile.

"I just hate to see the things go to a bad home. Charlotte took care of her belongings so well," Marie said.

She thought that I wouldn't take care of the clothing? My whole *life* was clothing. Her remark was more than insulting.

Charlotte clucked her tongue. "She's right about that. There's a reason I partnered with Marie in the first place. She knows class when she sees it."

Marie folded her arms in front of her chest. "I'm trying to discourage anyone from buying anything here. It's very important. What can I do to convince you to put the items back?"

The day was getting more bizarre by the minute.

"I'm sorry, but I've already purchased the items. If you'll excuse me, I'm late for an appointment." I rushed toward my car before she had a chance to rip the clothing from my hands. I needed fresh air and to get away from these strange women—dead *and* alive.

"I'm lost. You have to help me," my new ghost friend said as she floated beside me.

I hurried my steps to get away from her, but it

was no use. She kept pace with me to the curb where my Buick glinted in the sun.

"Aren't ghosts supposed to be stuck in one spot? Don't you want to haunt your house for when new people move into it? Just think of all the pranks you can play on them," I said, fumbling to get the car key in the lock.

"You know, I never gave much thought to ghosts or the paranormal. I guess I always assumed that a ghost was forever doomed to stay in one building." She clicked her tongue. "But apparently that's not the case."

"Apparently," I said.

"Was my story in the newspapers? Did they use a bad picture? I hope they didn't use that god-awful photo I had taken in the mall last summer. I don't know what I was thinking going to that place."

I sank into the car's luxurious leather seat, which was still supple, thanks to a lot of rubbing with saddle soap. Charlotte got into the passenger seat by simply passing through the door. I had to admit that was a nifty trick.

As we pulled away, I spotted Marie Vance through my rearview mirror, chatting with a man on the front steps of Charlotte's home. He wore a dark suit the same color as his shiny black hair.

Charlotte looked over her shoulder. "Marie must have a new man in her life. I've never seen him before. He won't last long, just like the others. She'll eat him alive."

"She sounds pleasant," I said.

Charlotte looked back at her house. "It's hard to leave my home." Her voice cracked.

"I'm sure it is," I said softly, thinking of the

sadness I'd felt when my parents had sold the house I'd grown up in and moved to Tybee Island. The small two-bedroom house I rented seemed cheerless in comparison.

I felt sorry for her and, perhaps foolishly, decided not to remind her that she didn't have to leave it.

After briefly contemplating heading straight to the nearest mental illness facility, I pointed the Buick in the direction of my shop. I had time to finish a few projects before I opened at nine. I hated being late.

"I can't believe they are selling off my items." Charlotte stared out the passenger side window.

I turned up the radio, trying to block her out and pretend I wasn't driving a ghost around town. Big band music streamed from the speakers as I navigated the historic downtown area of Sugar Creek. It housed eclectic boutiques, antique shops, and cozy cafés. Cars moved at a lazy pace as I drove around the courthouse that dominated the town square. Brick and stone buildings lined the streets, some dated back to the late 1700s. Sugar Creek's economy thrived, thanks to the tourists who came to enjoy the historic downtown and the whiskey distilleries on the edge of town.

After several years of working as a fashion buyer at Saks in Atlanta, I'd moved back home a little over a year ago to open my boutique. There was a memory for me on every corner in Sugar Creek— some painful and some joyful. Sometimes I drove by my parents' old house and wondered how different my life would have been if they still lived in it.

A huge banner announcing Sugar Creek's Spring Fling hung high across the main intersection of town. The annual festival held in May had been in the works for months. I sure wasn't going to let a ghost ruin that for me. I'd put too much time and effort into helping organize the event to let a pesky ethereal spirit stop the festivities.

I was on the organizing committee with four other women. Since I was the youngest of the group, they thought I'd bring a fresh vibe to the event, but they wouldn't take me seriously if they knew I was talking to a ghost. The festival had everything from food to bands. We'd even gotten Brothers J, my favorite bluegrass band, to play in the gazebo in the park.

I pulled up in front of my shop, cut the engine, and let out a deep breath, trying to clear my thoughts. It wasn't an easy task with Charlotte piercing me with her sharp gaze.

Magnolia blossoms perfumed the air. It's Vintage, Y'all had a prime location on the main artery of town, nestled among the many historic buildings. Wide sidewalks lined the streets vivid with color from the large pots of geraniums and petunias located next to the park benches. Many different businesses made their home along Main. Everything from the coffee shop on the corner, barbershop a couple blocks away, to the antique store around the corner.

Down a few blocks from my place was an old cemetery with Spanish moss-covered oak trees concealing its entrance. I'd never liked walking by there at night for the silly fear of seeing a ghost. Now I had one sitting next to me.

My boutique was a cottage-style building painted a soft lavender color with white trim. The front windows stretched all the way to the floor, allowing maximum space for displaying the clothing for sale inside. I'd recently restyled the storefront windows to herald the arrival of spring in Sugar Creek. Paper pompoms along with streamers in different shades of fuchsia, turquoise, and yellow hung from the ceiling. Apothecary jars with candy in matching colors were located on display tables next to the mannequins.

In one window, I usually featured dresses. Currently, I was showcasing a sundress in mid-length cotton with a green, pink, and rose-colored floral print. It gathered into a drop waist and fell in soft folds with a center back zipper. It wasn't from any special designer, but the semi-full skirt was just so stunning. The other mannequin followed the same color scheme in a pink and emerald floor-length, couture cocktail dress with a princess-seamed bodice and three-layered skirt. It was a fifties number by Suzy Perette, whose designs I've always adored.

In the other window, I'd dressed the figures with pedal pushers and halter tops also from the fifties.

A shabby-chic WELCOME sign greeted customers at the front door and the IT'S VINTAGE, Y'ALL sign dangled above the door.

Instead of heading inside, I walked right past the store and stepped into the occult shop next door. Of course, Charlotte walked right in beside me.

If anyone could get rid of Charlotte, it was my best friend Heather.

Chapter 4

Heather's Heartfelt Tip
for Getting Rid of an Unwanted Ghost

If asking the ghost to leave doesn't work, show the spirit
all exit locations. Remind the ghost that you're not
afraid to have the home exorcized if needed.

Magic Marketplace was housed on the ground floor of an old brick building that dated back to the mid-eighteen hundreds. Three additional businesses shared the space on the other floors. The walls were painted a watered-down shade of chocolate and the hardwood floor wasn't without its dents and scratches. They only added to the ambiance.

"Oh, it stinks in here." Charlotte waved her hand in front of her nose.

"Be quiet," I whispered.

The smell of spice and incense lingered in the air. Lining the shelves like little soldiers were mysterious-looking bottles of potions and herbs for every imaginable spell in the book. And speaking of books, there were tons of those, too.

I thought the store was empty until Heather

popped up from behind the counter. Her verdant green eyes held a wild look. A disappointed frown spread across her heart-shaped face as she blew her blondish-brown hair out of her eyes.

"Hey, you. Are you having problems?" I asked.

She brushed her hair off her forehead. "I've misplaced a book. I know I set it here the other day." She waved her hand. "It'll show up eventually. How'd the sale go?"

My shoulders slumped. I closed the distance between us in two giant steps. Charlotte moved effortlessly alongside me.

"What in the heck happened to you? You look like you've seen a ghost," Heather said.

My mouth dropped. A sense of relief washed over me. Thank goodness, she could see Charlotte, too. I'd done the right thing by coming to an expert like Heather.

Heather's voice raised a level. "Speak to me, Cookie. You're scaring me."

"I knew you'd be able to help. You can see the ghost too, right?" I asked, gesturing toward Charlotte, who frowned in response.

Heather's mouth fell open. "Get out. You really saw a ghost! What did you see? A misty form? A shadow zip past? Did you feel an unexplained cold breeze?"

"Not exactly," I answered. "More like a woman wearing an impeccable suit—"

"Aw, thank you," Charlotte said. "Death is no excuse for letting oneself go. It makes me feel good to know that someone noticed."

"She did have on a tad too much makeup,

though," I added when Charlotte had finished her little speech.

Charlotte glared at me. If looks could kill, I'd be joining her in the afterlife immediately.

I stared at her, then turned back to Heather and gestured toward Charlotte again with a tilt of my head.

Heather stared at me as if I'd lost my mind. "Do you have something wrong with your neck?"

"Don't you see her?" I whispered. "She followed me here."

Heather scanned the room. "Who is she?"

"Remember the woman who was strangled a few weeks ago? Charlotte Meadows?"

"Yes! She owned half the real estate in Sugar Creek."

I snapped my fingers. "That's the one."

Charlotte slapped her hand on the counter, making no sound. "I worked my butt off around this town to achieve that level of success, then some bastard came along and robbed me of my life. I sacrificed having a family for my real estate company, and look what happened." A faint tremor sounded in her voice as if the emotion had overwhelmed her.

Heather stacked a few books onto the counter. "It's such a shame what happened to her. They don't seem to have any clue who murdered her."

"See, that's exactly why I need your help," Charlotte said.

That *was* incredibly sad. I completely understood her loneliness for family. I still had hope for the future, right? I still hoped to create a family of my own someday, although that possibility was growing slimmer by the day. Sugar Creek wasn't exactly a hotbed of eligible bachelors. It was too late for Charlotte. Not too late for me . . . I hoped.

My last relationship had ended when I realized my boyfriend was a cheating rat. Plus, he'd never wanted me to pursue my dreams. Clark had wanted me to give up the idea of opening my own boutique. He'd given me the ultimatum of the shop or him. Of course, when I found out he was cheating, I didn't have to make that decision. I would have chosen the shop even if he hadn't been a two-timing snake in the grass.

Heather grabbed my arm. "Here, have a seat and tell me what happened."

I held on to the counter as I inched my way over to the stool and plopped down. Charlotte leaned her hip against the register, crossed her arms over her chest, and watched as I explained what had happened at the estate sale.

"So, you're saying she's here right now?" Heather looked uneasy as she glanced over her shoulder.

"Well, isn't she a smart one," Charlotte quipped.

I gestured with my thumb. "She's right there, listening to every word we say. I knew if anyone would understand, it would be you."

Heather's expression was somewhere between a grin and grimace. "Yeah," she said less than enthusiastically.

"Can you tell her to go away?" I asked.

"She can tell me, but it won't do her any good," Charlotte retorted.

"Here's the thing." Heather paused and gave me a sheepish grin. "I'm not sure how to put this. Thing is . . . I can't actually see her." She paused again. "The truth is, I can't really communicate with spirits. I'm not psychic . . . I'm just a big fat phony."

Chapter 5

Cookie's Savvy Vintage Fashion Shopping Tip

*Check the item's armpits and collar
for hard-to-remove stains.*

My voice rose. "Are you serious?" I couldn't hide my disappointment. I'd expected to trust the one friend who I'd thought told me everything. Why had she felt like she couldn't be honest with me?

"I can't talk to spirits," Heather repeated.

"Why didn't you tell me this? I thought we were friends?" I asked, hurt.

Heather looked defensive. "We are friends." She studied her shoes. "It's not like you ever asked much about my psychic skills, anyway."

Okay, maybe I'd been a little busy with the shop and my blog, but it never occurred to me to ask if her skills were real. With a sinking feeling in my gut, I realized it made a heartbreaking sort of sense that she wouldn't share such a secret with me. It was the kind of thing hard to tell even your best friend.

"But talking to spirits is your job! You've got a

sign out front that says PSYCHIC MEDIUM. I think that implies that you can talk with ghosts."

Charlotte rubbed her temples. Considering ghosts probably didn't get headaches, I figured that was her way of letting me know she was losing her patience.

Red colored Heather's cheeks, but she didn't offer an explanation.

"I tell everyone you're an expert," I said, unable to keep the disappointment out of my voice.

"I know a lot about spells—which herb or potion works the best for which formula. Just because I can't talk to spirits doesn't mean I'm not good at the other stuff." Heather folded her arms in front of her chest as if giving herself a comforting hug.

Picking up a voodoo doll from the counter that looked a lot like Heather's ex-boyfriend, I said, "Well, no . . . it doesn't mean that."

"Don't tell anyone, okay?" she asked.

Charlotte harrumphed.

I forced my lips into a small smile. "I won't say a word."

Heather straightened the stack of books that had been scattered across the counter. "Besides, I never give anyone bad news. I just keep things general. You know, give them positive motivation. When you think about it, I'm like a psychologist. I'm helping people."

"Oh dear heavens. I've heard it all," Charlotte said.

"If you can't see her or talk to her, then what am I going to do? Why can *I* see her?" The strain in my voice increased with every word.

"Maybe you're the one who's psychic. That is so wonderful! I'm jealous." Heather's eyes lit up. "Hey, maybe you can do readings now. We can showcase you in the shop." She tapped her lip with a bright pink, plumed, fountain pen in contemplation of my new psychic profession.

"I am not psychic. Don't you think I would have known that by now?" I glanced over at Charlotte.

"Y'all are putting on quite a display. I haven't seen this much confusion since they installed those self-checkout lanes at the Piggly Wiggly." Charlotte studied the large emerald ring on her finger.

I scowled.

"Is she talking to you? What is she saying?" Heather asked.

I swallowed a bad-mannered comment about Charlotte. "She's amused by our dilemma."

Heather clapped her hands together. "Hey, I have some books that can probably tell us how to get rid of her."

I straightened. "That's a good idea."

Charlotte laughed. "It won't do any good. I'm not going anywhere until you help me with this injustice."

I placed my head in my hands. "She says she's not going anywhere until I find her killer."

"Whoa. How are you supposed to do that?" Heather bounced over to the shelf and pulled off a book.

She had opened the shop several years ago. She'd moved from dead-end job to dead-end job until she'd finally found her calling with this place. She knew spells and tons about ancient religions, so she was an expert in that sense. Her mother was a self-proclaimed witch, so Heather had grown up reading her mother's collection of occult books. When I was ready to open my shop, she told me the space next to hers was available, and I was happy to rent it so we could be neighbors as well as best friends.

I'd been trying to convince her to start a blog like mine. I knew how much she could help people with spells or any number of occult topics. She loved to share her knowledge, but for some reason she couldn't be persuaded to embrace the online world. A spooky Facebook page would have really helped her get more customers in the door.

Suddenly, I realized that maybe it was because she'd felt like a big fat phony. I needed to remind her that her lack of psychic abilities wouldn't affect her knowledge of all things occult.

She brought the book back to the counter and plopped it down in front of me. It didn't look like it held ancient wisdom on banishing spirits. It was entitled *Cleanse Negative Spirits From Your Life.* With a fleeing ghost in a white sheet on its front cover and a smiling author photo on the back, it looked much like any other hardback you might see on the shelf at Barnes & Noble.

She opened the cover. Her index finger scrolled down as she scanned the contents and then flipped to a page in the middle. "It says the easiest way to get rid of a ghost is to ask it to leave."

I frowned. "Don't you think I haven't tried that already?"

"Did you use a firm voice? The book says you have to use a firm voice."

I inhaled a deep breath and slowly let it out then

turned to Charlotte. With a firm voice, I said, "You can't stay here. You have to leave. Be gone. Go into the light." I pushed the air with the palms of my hands as if giving her a visual on how it was done.

Charlotte chortled.

"Yeah, she's laughing," I said.

"She's a nasty one, huh?" Heather's eyebrows drew together into a scowl as she looked in the general direction where she thought Charlotte was standing.

Charlotte pointed at Heather. "Hey, at least I'm not the fake psychic."

"What is she saying?" Heather asked.

I picked up a pyramid-shaped green gem from the display table and pretended to study it. "Um, she called you a fake psychic."

"Oh, is that right? That does it. She's out of here." Heather gestured toward the front door.

It was the first time I'd ever seen two people argue with each other when they couldn't even talk to each other.

Heather flipped to the next page in the book.

I smirked at Charlotte. "What else does it say, Heather?"

"It says she may not know she's dead. You have to tell her." Heather glanced around, looking for Charlotte again.

Charlotte paced in front of us, her heels making no sound on the floor. "Have you lost your cotton pickin' mind? I know I'm dead. Reminding me is just cruel."

I waved my hand. "She knows."

Heather looked back at the page. "Okay, it says to ask her what she wants."

"I told you. She wants me to find her killer."

Charlotte took a deep bow in a mocking motion. "Thank-you! Now if you could cut out the nonsense and get on with it, I would appreciate it."

I blew a strand of hair out of my eyes. "It's no use, Heather. Nothing in that book is going to help."

"What are you going to do?" She closed the cover.

"Find a way to get rid of her."

Chapter 6

Heather's Heartfelt Tip
for Getting Rid of an Unwanted Ghost

❦

Set house rules. Ghosts want to haunt on their own terms.
It won't take long for the specter to grow tired of
following your orders and leave.

I'd had a ridiculous notion that Charlotte would
stay at Heather's occult shop after I left. It was a
shop for fans of the paranormal. She'd feel right at
home. Silly me. As I walked through the door of
It's Vintage, Y'all, Charlotte followed right behind
me like an annoying, talking shadow.

"You have a nice shop. And good taste, I must
say. Is that your grandmother's wedding gown over
there? Oh, she looked so pretty in it. I remember
her wedding photo displayed prominently on her
living room wall."

"Did you know my grandmother?"

"Oh yes. We went to finishing school together.
We learned how to write beautiful thank-you notes
and how to set a proper table for a dinner party. Of
course, our favorite lessons were about how to dress

for special occasions. I can see you've inherited Pearl's fashion sense."

Well, it was about time Charlotte started being more polite. She'd definitely attract more flies with honey than vinegar.

"I'm glad you think so." Searching my memory, I could recall my granny talking about her friend Charlotte . . . but I never realized she was talking about *the* Charlotte Meadows.

I'd tried to keep the same theme on the inside of my shop as on the outside. I'd recently painted the walls a lovely shade of lavender. Black and white drapes adorned the windows and crystal chandeliers hung from several positions throughout the shop. I'd placed chintz-covered armchairs around the space and a matching fainting couch rested by the dressing rooms. It was definitely old Hollywood glamour.

"Haven't you been inside before?" I asked.

"No. I figured all your stuff was clothes from people in town. I like to be unique. I can't be seen in something someone else from Sugar Creek has worn first." Charlotte stood in front of a mannequin, studying my work.

As I went through my morning routine of opening the store, Charlotte trailed me, yammering on about how to find her killer. I tried to tune her out by focusing on my paperwork, humming along to "Don't Sit Under the Apple Tree" by the Andrews Sisters, but it wasn't working. I'd subscribed to satellite radio so that I'd get the forties and fifties channels. Thank goodness for that invention.

The bell on the door jangled and a customer entered. I smiled and acknowledged her. She returned the pleasantries. Would she respond to Charlotte, too? No such luck. Like everyone else, she didn't appear to notice my ghostly companion.

As the door was closing behind the customer, a streak of white fur zipped through the opening, ran across the floor, leaped onto a table near the register, then made a final jump onto the counter. The cat plopped down and began licking her delicate paws in drawn-out strokes. With her gorgeous long white fur and dainty movements, she reminded me of a movie star.

The kitty stared at me throughout her grooming process. Something in her deep green gaze was unnerving. It was as if she knew me. If I didn't know better, I'd think that she was trying to talk to me through her expressions.

"Excuse me. Is this your cat?" I pointed toward the fancy feline.

The woman looked over from the rack of clothing she'd been perusing. "No, it's not my cat."

"It must be a stray," Charlotte said.

The cat glanced over at Charlotte as if to say, *Good assumption.*

"She can see you," I said.

The customer acknowledged me with a grin from across the room. Clearly, she thought I'd been talking to her.

"Where do you think it came from?" Charlotte asked.

The cat continued to lick its paws while keeping her eye on me.

"I don't know," I said.

Charlotte moved closer to the customer. The

woman shivered as if she'd noticed a cool breeze, but continued shopping.

"You don't have a lot of business," Charlotte stated.

"Well, I just opened," I said.

"Yes, I was waiting until you were ready for business," the customer acknowledged.

I needed to watch what I said. When I talked to Charlotte, it looked as if I was talking to myself.

The browser walked out, probably tired of listening to me have a one-sided conversation.

"Great. You just lost me a customer." I pointed at the door.

"You really need to work on your marketing plan," Charlotte said.

"Thank-you for that astute observation. I'm on it, okay?"

"It looks like you could use some help. Apparently, your plan isn't working." Charlotte prowled through the store as if she hadn't just insulted me.

"I'm doing okay. It just takes a while for a new business to get on its feet."

"Apparently, it takes some longer than others. How long have you been in business?"

"A little over a year," I answered.

"It's make-or-break time. Most businesses never survive past the one-year mark," she said.

I reached out and stroked the cat. She meowed in approval. "Well, the kitty likes me, which is more than I can say for you."

Charlotte scoffed. "Hey, I never said I didn't like you."

"I don't think you had to. It's in your actions."

"You need to cut me some slack. After all, I was

murdered. I've kind of had a few bad weeks," she said with a furrowed brow.

She had me there. It couldn't have been easy for her to adjust to the afterlife—not being able to interact with people, not being able to eat chocolate.

Just as I was feeling sorry for her, she said, "I wouldn't have paired those red pants with that zebra-print blouse." She pointed at the display I had in the corner of the room.

The cat meowed as if in agreement.

I had two critics. "Look, if you are going to continue to critique my work, you'll have to leave." I placed my hands on my hips. "And that goes for you too, Fluffy."

Charlotte sauntered over to another mannequin. "Fine. If you don't want my expert advice, that's your loss."

"Well, I *don't* want your advice." I busied myself behind the counter, straightening rows of Art Deco jewelry displayed on a black velvet cloth under a showcase light.

Great. I was talking to a ghost as if it was a normal thing. Brush my teeth, eat breakfast, go to work, and converse with the afterlife—all part of an ordinary day.

The cat stretched and meowed.

"Oh, are you apologizing?" I inspected her neck, but didn't see a collar. "Where did you come from?"

She looked at me with that same peculiar expression and tilted her head. Her bright green eyes sparkled in the light. If I hadn't known better, I'd have said she winked at me.

Chapter 7

Cookie's Savvy Vintage Fashion Shopping Tip

Thrift shops, flea markets, yard sales, and estate sales are all great places to find vintage fashion.

During my lunch break, I went to Pets Please, a paradise of pet-related paraphernalia located around the corner on Clay Street, and picked up a few essentials for the cat. I told myself she could only stay until I could find her owner, although she didn't seem to care if I ever located her home. When I left, she'd been stretched out in the sunshine at the front of the store and acted as if she didn't have a worry in the world. She was still there when I returned.

After helping the last customer for the day purchase a lovely, strapless, pink tulle and lace fifties prom dress that would never go out of style, I flipped the sign to CLOSED, and said, "Okay, kitty, I'll be back to get you after my meeting."

The cat purred and opened one eye to look at me. After a hot second, she got bored and closed her eye again.

"What are you going to name her?" Charlotte asked.

"Before I name her anything, I need to find out if she has a microchip. Someone has to be looking for a cat as beautiful as she is."

"Okay. What if she doesn't? Then what are you going to name her?"

"Hmm. I'd like to name her Wind Song. After my grandmother's favorite perfume." I smiled.

I'd dreamed of a life on the big screen when I was young, but I'd given up on that fantasy years ago when I discovered I could more realistically have a career in fashion. Clothing was much more my calling. My acting skills weren't that great anyway, so Hollywood wasn't missing much by losing me.

"It suits her. Now she just needs a diamond collar," Charlotte said.

With Charlotte following me, I left the shop and locked the door behind me. I climbed behind the wheel of my Buick and headed for the final committee meeting before tomorrow's big event. Last minute details about the clowns, jugglers, and face painters for the kids still needed to be sorted. The festival board of directors, which consisted of Blanche Dickens, Cindy Johnson, Dixie Bryant, Annette Hayes, and me had just a few loose ends to tie up.

I was in charge of the vendor booths on the north side of town. The other businesses in town usually offered booths in front of their storefronts, while handcrafted items from artists across the state were set up in the nearby church parking lot.

Blanche was the head of the committee. She

had wanted to handle all aspects of the event, but she'd soon realized that sometimes it was necessary to delegate.

She owned the pet store around the corner and had given me valuable advice when I'd opened my place. She made running a business look effortless. Her strength never ceased to amaze me, even if she was a bit pushy at times. When her husband ran off with a woman half his age, she'd picked herself up by her sandal straps and started her life over. Plus, she hadn't let the gossip around town get her down.

I could allow her to take charge of the festival, though when it came to my store, I was a total control freak.

The meeting was being held in a lackluster, red-brick building on the edge of historic downtown at Maple and Main streets. Sugar Creek had the Norman Rockwell vibe with brick storefronts lining the streets around the courthouse square. Ornate lampposts and pots of flowers dotted the sidewalks. We drove past a horse-drawn carriage on our way there.

Charlotte complained about the estate sale for most of the ride, but finally switched back to her favorite topic. "I'm telling you there has to be a way to find my killer. Someone had to have seen something." She looked out the window, watching a world that was very much still alive.

"I wouldn't be so sure about that. After all, even *you* didn't see your murderer," I said as I turned the steering wheel. The Buick had been built before the days of power steering, so it took some effort to maneuver it. My arms had become more toned since I'd inherited the car, so that was a plus.

"Right," Charlotte murmured, but her mind seemed to be elsewhere.

"Don't you know who might have wanted you dead?"

"I don't know. That's why I'm asking for your help."

"Asking me for help in solving your murder is like asking me to help you solve a math problem. Math was not my favorite subject."

She didn't acknowledge my comment, but changed the subject. "How you put up with these committee women is beyond me. They're nothing but a bunch of hens. Yak, yak, yak. All they do is talk." Charlotte mimicked with her hand.

The fuzzy dice swung from the rearview mirror as I maneuvered the large steering wheel and turned onto Maple. "Yes, I can see where nonstop talking would definitely be annoying." I glanced over at her.

She scowled.

"You don't have to come to the meeting with me," I said.

"What else would I do?" She studied her manicured fingernails.

After turning into the small parking lot, I pulled into the nearest available space. "Haunt someone else?" I suggested.

"Fat chance," she quipped as I got out of the car.

Of course she went inside with me. It was too much to hope that she would wait in the car. When we entered the meeting room, no one looked up.

The other members had already arrived, making me look like a straggler even though I was early.

A long conference table sat at the back of the room with metal chairs placed in neat rows in front. To the right was another small table with refreshments.

Blanche noticed my presence and quirked a finely sculpted eyebrow as if to say, *Finally, you're here.* She had a tendency to be a tad high-strung. Short and pleasantly plump, she wore a blond updo that would definitely be classified in the big hair category. My friend Binky at the Rexall had told me that Blanche went through two cans of hair spray a week to achieve that look.

"Hurry up, Cookie. We need to get this done." Blanche motioned for me to join the group.

"She always was a highfalutin, bossy one," Charlotte said.

I couldn't argue with that. Blanche was certainly on the assertive side. One time, she'd even tried to tell the police how to investigate a string of burglaries around town. In her defense, I should add that the criminal had been arrested because of her tip.

"Oh, Cindy is here. That just dills my pickle! We had a falling out recently," Charlotte whispered.

As if anyone other than me could actually hear her.

I followed her ghostly gaze to see Cindy Johnson. She had married Bill Johnson right after they'd graduated high school. He owned the Ford dealership in town and she spent her time with charitable events and causes. They had divorced last year. She still wouldn't divulge the details of what had brought on the breakup. The gossip going around was that he'd cheated. Always looking for details, the busybodies in Sugar Creek were still circling her like vultures.

Why hadn't Charlotte mentioned knowing Cindy? If they knew each other, Charlotte would have known Cindy was a committee member. I'd have to find out what had sparked their argument.

I took a chair in the first row and Charlotte sat right beside me. She folded her arms and leaned back in the chair, glaring at Cindy.

"There are just a few matters to discuss . . ." Blanche began.

My thoughts wandered. The meetings were always on the boring side, but then again, what meeting wasn't? I looked around. Cindy had her blond hair cut in a chin-length bob. She wore a red and white striped scarf around her neck and a navy blue suit . . . definitely not vintage.

"She'd look better if her suit wasn't so drab," Charlotte said, as if she'd read my thoughts. "That woman has skeletons in her closet, if you ask me. She pretends to be goody-goody, but—" Charlotte clucked her tongue.

"Has everyone paid for their booths?" Blanche's gaze traveled over to me.

I snapped out of my thoughts and away from Charlotte's gossip. I held up my hand. "Paid in full."

Blanche didn't respond to my answer. She moved on to the next point of discussion. "Let's hope the parking runs smoothly and the appropriate streets are blocked off."

As I listened to her bark out more orders, a noise behind me captured my attention. I glanced over my shoulder. A man stood at the exit. At first, I didn't recognize him, then it came back to me. He had been speaking with Marie Vance outside Charlotte's home this morning. He didn't meet my stare.

Charlotte looked over her shoulder. "Isn't that Marie's new boy toy?"

"I don't know," I whispered back.

Talking stopped and all the women focused on the man.

"May I help you?" Blanche asked, clearly irritated by the interruption.

"Oh, he's here to see me." Cindy jumped up and headed toward the man, her kitten heels clicking on the linoleum floor. "If you'll excuse me, I'll be right back."

We watched as Cindy stepped outside with the man.

"Well, that was strange," Charlotte said. "Is he dating both women?"

That was a big assumption. "How do you know he is dating either woman?"

"I don't. I just guessed."

"Who was that?" Blanche asked all of us.

No one knew.

I was sure that she wouldn't allow Cindy to talk to a stranger and not include her in the conversation. She'd probably corner Cindy after the meeting and ask a million questions.

After a couple minutes, Cindy returned, clicking her heels more forcefully than before.

Charlotte fidgeted in her seat beside me, probably wondering the same thing as me. Who was the mysterious man and why were Cindy and Marie talking to him?

Once the excitement of the stranger had died down, Blanche declared the meeting adjourned, lifting her hand and bringing it down as if banging an imaginary gavel.

I was anxious to pick up Wind Song and get home. It had been a long and bizarre day. Not to mention that I was starving. I reached out and grabbed a can of Diet Coke and a potato chip from the refreshment table. They were my favorite— Miss Parker's Sweet 'n Sour Potato Crisps. The brand was only sold in the South.

Charlotte wiggled her finger. "You know, those diet drinks won't matter if you continue eating potato chips."

"I like potato chips," I said through gritted teeth.

Charlotte wiggled her finger again. "They're your hips."

I glanced down at my bottom half. Sure, I had curves, but I figured they were just the right amount. My frame was naturally petite and I had an hourglass figure.

"Will you stop talking," I whispered. "You're going to get me into trouble. Here comes Annette. Be quiet."

"She can't hear me. What difference does it make?"

Annette Hayes wore her gray hair in a sassy short cut. I'd forgiven her for rarely wearing vintage because she always looked fabulous in her clothes. Her outfit featured buttercup-colored trouser pants and a white, cotton, eyelet lace blouse.

Every time I saw her I couldn't help but smile. I'd spent many hours in her antique shop, learning to care for and appreciate the treasures of previous generations. Her store had whisked me away to the past and made me dream of having a shop of my own. She was as close a mother figure as I had, since my parents had moved to Tybee Island, although I doubted she realized that. I knew she wouldn't have signed up for the job. One thing was for sure, we shared a love for old things.

She touched my arm. "You seem distracted. Is everything okay?"

I glanced around to make sure no one was listening. "Do you believe in ghosts?"

Her eyes widened. "That's an odd question. I thought you would ask me something about the festival. But to answer your question, yes, I suppose I think it's possible. Why do you ask?"

Before I could answer, Cindy approached. I felt Charlotte tense beside me. The first chance I got, I'd have to stop in Annette's shop and tell her about Charlotte's ghost. I wondered if she'd believe me.

"What are y'all talking about?" Cindy flashed a wide smile.

"Tell her I'm still madder than a wet hen at her. Tell them I'm here," Charlotte urged.

Should I tell them about her snarky comments?

Dixie Bryant joined us, her warm hazel eyes magnified by the oversized white-rimmed glasses she wore. "Hi, Cookie. You need to stop by the café for a piece of red velvet cake." She patted my shoulder. She was a petite bundle of energy who always

reminded me of a pixie, as though the first letter
of her name could be either *P* or *D*.

"Bless her heart. Her cake is dry. It's like eating
a sponge," Charlotte said with a scrunched-up face.
"And you'd better bring the Tums if you go anywhere near her chili. That stuff set my stomach on
fire. She's as sweet as a Georgia peach, though."

Dixie owned Glorious Grits around the corner.
She was a sassy brunette with a collection of jeans
that consisted of almost every known designer. It
wasn't often that I saw her out of her green polka-
dotted café apron, but the bright red silk blouse
she had on set off her complexion nicely. She was
constantly trying to add inches to my curves with
her cakes.

"I'll stop by real soon," I said with a smile.

Blanche was shuffling through papers like a
bubbly teenager frantically planning junior prom.
She called Dixie and Annette back over.

Charlotte walked to the door and waited for me,
tapping her foot impatiently. Cindy looked in the
direction of the door. For a second, I wondered if
she could see Charlotte, too. Or maybe she sensed
her? But knowing Cindy, if she'd seen Charlotte's
ghost she wouldn't have kept that fact to herself.

"I'll talk to you tomorrow, ladies," I said with a
wave. Turning to Cindy, I said, "Well, I'd better get
home. I have a ton of work for the store."

She studied my face. "Sure, I'll probably see you
tomorrow for the big day."

"Thank goodness you didn't make me endure a
conversation with her," Charlotte said as we headed
toward the parking lot. "Now, are you going to help
me find my killer?"

"I think you should just trust the police. I'm sure they're doing all that they can to find out who murdered you."

She brushed off my comment with a wave of her hand. "Oh, please. They have other things to worry about than solving my case."

"Like what?" I asked.

"Eating doughnuts." She smirked.

"That's not very nice."

"Well, I'm not happy with them. If they were any good, they'd have my killer under arrest by now."

As I headed down the sidewalk, the man who had been talking with Marie and Cindy was walking straight toward me. He took a quick drag on his cigarette, then tossed it on the ground and stomped it out. He was only a couple steps away when he said, "Are you friends with the women in that meeting?"

I thought about telling him to mind his own business, but I was curious about his question. "I'm on the planning committee for the town's spring festival."

"Then you know Cindy Johnson." His dark eyebrows shot up.

"Yes, I know her." I looked toward my car, hoping for a chance to slip away. "Why do you ask?"

"My name's Edward Andersen." He pulled a card from his pocket and handed it to me. Besides his name, the card read PRIVATE INVESTIGATOR. PRIVATE AND CONFIDENTIAL. STATE LICENSED AND INSURED. His phone number was listed underneath.

I studied his face. "What do you want with Cindy?"

"I'm looking into the death of Charlotte Meadows." His mouth took on an unpleasant twist.

Charlotte released a little gasp.

"Who hired you?" I asked.

"I'm afraid I can't release that information."

I stepped around him toward my car. "I don't know anything about her death. I barely knew her."

"Ask more questions," Charlotte urged. "Find out what he knows."

How was I supposed to ask more questions? He had already walked away.

"You'll call me if you think of anything?" His voice carried across the parking lot.

Charlotte walked so close that she was practically attached to my side. "I can't believe someone hired a private investigator. And I can't believe that you didn't ask more questions. You have to find out what's going on."

"Like I said, it's up to the police. Not me."

"Well, they're not doing enough." Her voice raised a level. "Speaking of which, there's one of the detectives who's supposedly investigating my death. He's clearly not very good at his job." She pointed across the parking lot toward an official-looking black Crown Victoria.

I realized that the detective had been watching my exchange with the private investigator. When I glanced over my shoulder, Andersen was gone. He hadn't wasted any time getting out of there. I was the one stuck with the police watching me.

As I shoved the key into the lock and opened the car door, Charlotte continued, "That's Detective Valentine. He's been poking around my house."

The man had short dark hair and tanned skin.

He wore a red T-shirt exposing his muscular forearms. I'd never seen him before. Was he new on the force?

"He doesn't look like a policeman. I don't see a gun," I said as I surveyed him.

The detective quirked his eyebrow. My stomach took a dive and my heart rate sped up. Why was I nervous? So what if the detective seemed interested in what I was doing. He couldn't possibly know I was talking to Charlotte. She was a ghost. He couldn't see her. No one could, except me.

I jumped into my car as if I'd done something wrong, not quite sure why I was rushing. I wasn't guilty, but I was sure acting suspicious. With a slight tap on the gas pedal, I backed out of the space, then headed for the exit. Not too fast, though. I didn't want to get a speeding ticket. I glanced in the rearview mirror. The detective was still interested in my movements.

"Why was he staring at me?" I asked, turning on the radio to my favorite oldies station. Just like in my shop, I'd had satellite radio added to the car's audio system, as well as modern speakers, so I could always listen to the sounds I loved. "Bye Bye Love" by The Everly Brothers spilled from the speakers as I pulled out of the lot.

"Maybe because you acted as if you'd killed someone," Charlotte offered from the passenger seat.

"I wasn't acting nervous. Was I?" I tapped my fingers against the steering wheel.

"No, not at all." She rolled her eyes. "Anyway,

thank goodness that pointless meeting is over. Do you always hum along with the music?"

I turned down the radio even though "Moonlight Serenade" by the Glenn Miller Band had come on. "Do you want to tell me what was going on between you and Cindy Johnson? Why are you so hard on her?"

"I was involved with her charity."

Using my muscles, I navigated the steering wheel around a curve. "Oh, yeah. It's called Speak Out."

Cindy was the president. The charity worked to end violence against women and children.

"I was supposed to donate money to the cause, but I changed my mind at the last minute," Charlotte said.

"Why would you do that?"

"Cindy was up to no good." Charlotte drew her lips together in a grim line.

"Like what?"

"Marie told me that Cindy was being accused of stealing money from the charity, so I poked around and found proof. I have the documents to prove it. Well, at least, I did have them."

Well, that certainly would put Cindy on the suspects list. She seemed so sweet and helpful to others, how could she have murdered Charlotte?

I'd never had a cat, so I wasn't sure how many scratches I'd end up with when I tried to put Wind Song in her new carrier. I set the carrier on the floor and knelt down to open the door. To my surprise, the feisty feline marched over and walked right in. The look on her face said, *I'm ready to go home.*

Charlotte stood next to the carrier. "I've never seen a cat readily stroll into a carrier before."

I fastened the latch. "Something tells me this is no ordinary cat."

"Now that the cat's ready, let's get out of here. It's been a long day. I'll meet you in the car." Charlotte disappeared out the front door without bothering to open it. She could walk through anything she wanted.

Having read up on the subject of ghosts, I found it fascinating to see the phenomenon firsthand. What other things could she do?

With cat carrier in hand, I left the shop and locked the door behind me. "Why use the door?" I mumbled. "If you can walk through anything, of course you should take the shortcut and use the wall."

"Old habits die hard."

When we arrived back at my place, I pulled into the driveway and shifted the car into park. I lived in a small, white, two-bedroom, cottage-style home that overlooked the parking lot of a shopping center. A magnolia tree bloomed in the front yard. I had a small lawn in the front and back where I meant to add flowers but never got around to planting any.

"This is my house," I said.

"I gathered as much." Charlotte scrutinized my humble abode.

It wasn't much, but it was home, and it was all mine. Well, as long as I paid the rent, it was mine. The prospect of home ownership was alluring, but having put my life savings into opening my boutique, I was far from ready to plop down a down payment on a place of my own.

I climbed out from behind the wheel, grabbed Wind Song's carrier, and walked up the front path toward the small porch. Flower pots with pink petunias flanked the door and my welcome mat had a pink flamingo. As I shoved the keys into the lock, my retro Heartbreak Hotel keychain tapped against the door. My only plan was to wait Charlotte out. How long could she handle hanging around with me? She'd get bored after a while and go back to her old haunt.

I placed my purse and keys on the art deco chrome and glass table next to the front door, then set Wind Song down and opened the carrier. She pranced out without even acknowledging me and jumped up on the small table to look around the room. I hoped she liked what she saw.

No surprise, my décor consisted of a lot of vintage items. The place had a distinct fifties flair. On the far living room wall was a silver sunburst clock. A kitschy fifties-style plaster peacock wall hanging was displayed on the opposite wall. I did have new items, like my cream-colored sofa, although it had clean lines like the sofas seen during that period. When I found this place, I knew the simple one-story floor plan was perfect for me.

I waved my arms. "Well, this is it. Not as nice as your place. I bet you miss your house. You'd probably rather go home than hang around my cramped little space, huh?"

Charlotte laughed. "Nice try. I wasn't born yesterday. I didn't even die yesterday, so you'll have to think of something more clever than that to get rid of me."

I blew out a deep breath. "Fine."

Normally when I had guests, I'd give them a tour of my home and offer a choice of food and beverage—the usual hostess stuff. But I couldn't do it. Ghosts can't eat or drink. Besides, I didn't want Charlotte to get too comfy. The more ill at ease she was, the better chance that she'd leave. I wondered if she needed to sleep. I guessed night-time was when the ghosts usually did their haunting thing.

"Don't think that you have to entertain me." Charlotte took in the whole room. "Just go about your business."

"I have to write a blog post." Why was I telling her that? It wasn't like I needed permission.

"I'll wait." Charlotte sat on the leather chair by the window, crossing her legs and leaning back onto the cushion.

That was what I was afraid of.

I went to the kitchen and placed food and water on the floor for Wind Song.

The elegant cat approached slowly, sniffed the food, then took a nibble. She looked up at me and I could have sworn that her expression said, *Are you kidding me?* Apparently her hunger was stronger than her objections, for she settled in to eat with enthusiasm. Her tail swayed with each bite, the white fur moving like a fancy fan.

Before sitting down to write, I whipped up dinner. I didn't consider myself the best cook, but I had a few meals that were my specialties. One of them was oven-fried chicken. It had all the flavor without the added fat. Of course, my granny would have said that was impossible. I marinated the chicken in buttermilk then added a light coating of flour and spices. While it was baking, I prepared a side of cornbread and lemon-mint snap peas and lima beans for the oven as well.

I grabbed my laptop from the kitchen counter and positioned myself on the sofa in the living room. The large windows in the room allowed ample sunlight, making the room cheerful.

Depending on the schedule of the store, I tried to post every day. I put up as many vintage photos of clothing as I could find, too. I liked seeing the clothing as it was worn originally—and then matching up the vintage photo with an image of someone wearing the same outfit with a modern twist.

Sometimes I shared photos of myself wearing vintage clothing from my own collection—Granny's personal clothing that she'd kept over the years.

I'd been consulted to authenticate items, select period-authentic garments for photo shoots and even a couple low-budget movies. I had my fingers crossed that I'd move up to the big-budget productions soon. Maybe I'd make it to Hollywood, after all.

Vintage clothing stores had become increasingly popular over the past fifteen years, and for that I was grateful. Obviously, I was a big fan of vintage and glad that more and more people were seeing the advantages to wearing classic garments from earlier eras. Since styles often came back around, it was easy to see how people would seek out looks from the past that were trendy again.

I didn't just want to cater to serious vintage clothing collectors or people wanting something for a Halloween costume. I wanted to draw customers from every level of fashion awareness who wanted to have fun with older items. I even had teenagers coming in for prom dresses and fashion-conscious shoppers looking for the originals that inspired the latest trend.

I tried to put together a collage of Oscar outfits from decades past, but I didn't get very far. Charlotte was pacing around the house with increasing agitation until it became clear that I wouldn't get any more work done.

Dinner was ready, so I grabbed my plate, and then returned to my work.

"You shouldn't work while eating dinner," Charlotte said.

"I like to call it multitasking."

After closing my laptop, I stood and stretched. "Well, I'm going to bed. Good night."

I placed my dirty dishes in the washer and headed toward my bedroom.

"Are you going to help me find my killer?" Charlotte closed the distance between us. Her movement was swift.

I hadn't been watching, but I was pretty sure she had glided over to me.

"I think I've had enough of this conversation." I headed down the hall toward my bedroom.

Charlotte followed. "Look, I can help you if you help me."

"What do I need help with?" Despite myself, I was curious.

"You clearly need customers and I can get them for you." She straightened her shoulders and made direct eye contact.

I lifted my chin and marched away. "I am doing just fine. Thank-you."

I shut my bedroom door, but Charlotte walked right through the wood.

At one time, my bedroom had been a refuge, with the delicate antique floral embroidered quilt covering the bed and the romantic vintage lace curtains. An antique crystal vase filled with sweetheart roses sat on the nightstand. I'd bought them for myself. The room was no longer my safe haven now that Charlotte had invaded the space.

"Don't get so defensive. I know how hard it is to run a business. My real estate agency didn't become successful overnight. You've been working on that blog all night. Do you sell clothing online?" Charlotte asked.

"No." I just hadn't found time to set up a retail presence online.

"Mistake number one."

"I'm not listening to any more of your badgering." I pulled my favorite pajamas out of the closet. They were bright pink with images of retro shoes on them. Pajamas were one item that I didn't mind buying new. It was hard to find old pajamas that were in good enough shape that I would want to wear them. With dresses, it was different. A woman might spend a lot of money on a classy outfit, only to wear it once or twice. But when a gal likes her pajamas, she would wear them until they fell to pieces.

"Do you mind giving me some privacy?" I said to Charlotte.

She leaned against my dresser. "You haven't got anything that I haven't seen before."

"Yeah, but it's my stuff and I don't want you to see it. Now turn around." I motioned for her to face the wall.

"I'll make your life miserable until you say yes," she said from over her shoulder.

I pulled the top over my head. "Yeah, right. I'd like to see you try."

I flipped off the light and jumped into bed, pulling the covers up close.

"I'll make it my mission to find every pet peeve you have and bug you with every single one of them." Charlotte stood beside my bed.

I couldn't see her, but I knew she was there. With any luck, she would be gone in the morning.

I woke at two AM to the sound of a dripping faucet.

Charlotte was hard at work trying to pinpoint my pet peeves. She'd found the first. The rhythmic sound of the water hitting the basin drove me insane. I grabbed my pillow and tried to drown out the noise, but it was no use.

"Ah-ha! I knew that would get you!" she exclaimed. "What's next? Maybe I should sing you back to sleep."

"Okay, okay! I'll help you find your killer. Please just let me get some sleep." What did I have to lose?

She wouldn't leave me alone, and my business was struggling anyway, so how much worse could things get? It would be worth the hassle if it would get her off my back. The most important reason though was because I knew my granny would have wanted me to help her friend.

Chapter 8

Heather's Heartfelt Tip
for Getting Rid of an Unwanted Ghost

If you decide to cleanse your home by burning sage,
make sure to have a fire extinguisher nearby.
Trust me, I learned this one the hard way.

I woke the next morning with the sun splashing across my face and robins chirping outside my window. It was a beautiful spring day. I smiled and stretched as I opened my eyes.

Then I saw Charlotte sitting at the foot of my bed and remembered.

"I'm glad you're awake," she said. "I made a list of all the things we can do to help your marketing. Well, I made a mental list, considering I can't use a pen. Unfortunately, I haven't figured out how to pick things up." She wiggled her fingers for emphasis. "So get up, have some breakfast, get dressed, and let's get started. This is going to be a beautiful day."

"Oh great. You're a morning person." I noticed Wind Song was stretched out beside her. The cat's eyes were closed and her tail moved gently back and forth.

I climbed out of bed and tackled my morning routine—ten minutes of stretching and ab crunches, followed by ten minutes of yoga and meditation, followed by a dish of Greek yogurt topped with granola. My outfit of choice for the day was a fifties cotton full-circle dress with an allover black and ecru check pattern. Seven white pearl buttons dotted the bodice and delicate white lace adorned the waist and bodice. I wrapped a red patent leather belt around my waist and slipped into matching red pumps. I was glad to find that my belt still fit in its usual notch.

When I was dressed, I called to Wind Song. "Come on, little tiger. It's time for us to go to work."

The elegant feline jumped down from the couch where she'd been curled up on a maroon velvet pillow that complemented her white fur beautifully, sauntered over to her carrier, and climbed into it. She looked up at me, seeming eager to get to the shop. Again, she'd jumped at the chance for a ride in the carrier. What a strange but fascinating creature she was.

After the ride to the boutique spent listening to Charlotte complain about having her items sold off, I was ready to buy a pair of earplugs.

Hundreds of tourists had packed into town for the Spring Fling and I had high hopes they would bring a lot of business to the booth I would set up in front of the store. Not to mention that I was relieved that all the planning was over.

Finding a parking space proved to be difficult,

but after driving down a few streets I found a spot in front of Holly's Hair Salon. As I got out of my Buick, heavenly food smells carried through the air. The street was lined with canopied stands of every color selling everything from funnel cakes to crawfish étouffée. I stopped at the Ladies' Auxiliary booth located under the cover of a Spanish moss-covered oak tree and indulged in the best lemonade and peanut butter fudge that I'd ever tasted. I happened to be a lemonade freak. As for fudge—don't get me started.

Charlotte stood nearby, arms crossed, scowling in disapproval. "If you want to look good in your clothing, you'll have to watch your diet."

I licked a bit of fudge from my fingers. "Oh, right. I'll be sure to remember that."

After setting my tables and racks of clothing along the sidewalk under the shade of a canopy, I stood back to admire the display. Since summer was around the corner, I'd displayed shorts, halters, and swimsuits from different decades.

"Cookie, over here," a sweet voice called out from behind me.

I whipped around to see my parents marching toward me. The smiles on their faces brought tears to my eyes. I ran over and threw my arms around my mother Margaret. She was different from me in many ways. Her idea of fashion was long loose flowing skirts and Birkenstock sandals. She wore her long blond hair in a braid most of the time.

"I've missed you, sweetheart," she said, pushing back tears.

"I thought you'd never get here." I reached for my father Hank.

My father wrapped his arms around me. He was a casual dresser. His outfits always consisted of khaki pants and polo shirts. His once dark hair was completely gray. He said it made him look distinguished and I had to agree.

"Are you here alone?" My mother played with the long beaded necklace dangling around her neck.

"I have help for the day. Blanche's niece Brandy is manning the dressing rooms," I said.

My mother scowled. "Do I know Brandy?"

"Of course you do. Little Brandy who wiped chocolate ice cream on your white dress. She's a senior in high school now."

My mother grinned. "Oh my. I remember her now. How time flies."

"What are y'all doing today?"

"Your mother wants to check out the craft booths. I'm here for the food," my dad said.

"Don't forget to listen to the music in the park," I said.

"Will do."

My mother touched my hair. "Are you getting enough to eat? Did you like the Chia seeds I sent?"

I hated them, but I didn't tell her that. "Absolutely."

My father patted my shoulder as if he fully sympathized. I was sure he'd tried the seeds and much more.

"Your father and I are going to look around. We'll be back soon." The bangles on her wrist clanged together as she waved.

"How long are you in town for?" I asked as they walked away.

"We're driving back to Tybee Island tonight. You're father claims he can't miss the big PGA golf tournament at the club tomorrow. He has tickets."

I wished they could stay longer, but maybe it was for the best since I had an unwanted visitor around.

I glanced up to see Heather headed my way, carrying a thin rectangular box. She wore a white maxi dress with a crocheted bodice. Wooden bracelets covered her wrists.

"Is your ghost friend with us today?" She looked around for Charlotte.

"I'm afraid so. Did you think I was kidding when I said she wouldn't leave?"

Heather tucked a strand of hair behind her ear. "I don't know what I thought."

"Well, it's not like she really has anywhere else to go that is so important." I looked down at the strange item Heather was holding. "What is that?"

"It's a Ouija board," she said with a smile.

Anxiety danced in my stomach. "No way. I don't want that thing anywhere near me. I've watched those ghost-hunting shows. They're always warning people not to use them. Besides, I already have one ghost. Why would I want more?"

Heather hugged the box to her chest. "I guess you're right, but maybe it would help us communicate with her."

"Help *you* maybe. I'm not having the least problem talking with her. As a matter of fact, she won't shut up."

Heather placed the Ouija board down near the steps and we got to work setting up our items for the festival. We situated our booths next to each other on the sidewalk, which only made sense because our shops were next to each other. But the best part was we could sit together and people watch. Charlotte was perched behind me on the front steps of the shop—I wasn't about to find an extra chair for a ghost. With the sun shining brightly, I was thankful for the shade of the canopy.

Wind Song sat between us on the sidewalk watching a butterfly that was busy in the pot of geraniums.

A horse-drawn carriage clomped past with a couple tourists in back. They smiled and waved as they rode by.

I glanced over my shoulder and noticed that the Ouija board had been moved. It was beside Wind Song. "I knew it was bad to have that thing anywhere around."

"What do you mean?" Charlotte asked.

"Did you move the board?"

She held her hands up. "I'm a ghost, remember? I can't move things. I'm dead."

"Well, what about all those ghosts who haunt places and throw objects? They do it all the time."

"That involves a skill level of haunting that I have not obtained yet," Charlotte said, looking somewhat abashed.

"Thank heavens for small favors."

Before she could utter a bon mot, Heather returned with her arms full of books. Charlotte mumbled under her breath, but I ignored her.

"Did you move that board before you left?" I asked.

Heather shifted the books in her arms. "No, I haven't touched it."

"It's been moved over here beside the cat." I picked up the board and handed it to Heather.

Wind Song meowed.

"You must have forgotten and moved it?" Heather phrased it as a question, but I knew she didn't believe it.

I contemplated her suggestion. I was stressed, as evidenced by the ghost I was talking to, but I was certain that I hadn't moved that board. Then again, a seed of doubt sprouted in my mind. Maybe I'd been so distracted that I hadn't realized what I was doing.

"Well, even if I did move it, I don't like the thing. It gives me the creeps, so by all means, take it back." I motioned for her to get rid of it.

Heather tucked the board under her arm and Wind Song meowed again. "I think she likes the thing."

I hated to admit it, but I was beginning to think maybe Heather was right.

Charlotte groaned. "Oh, for heaven's sake, here comes that woman. She is so talkative that she gives my headache a headache."

Blanche Dickens yelled from across the street, "Cookie. I need to speak with you." She wore a bright yellow cotton blouse and white pants. Her blond hair was in its usual updo.

Approaching, she said, "Cookie, Mrs. Henderson's booth is a mess. I thought you talked with her about what was appropriate to sell at the festival."

I pushed back a groan. "Well, I would talk with her, but I have to watch my booth. I can't leave the clothing unattended." I gestured around.

Blanche twisted her hands together. "Oh dear. What am I going to do? She won't listen to me."

"I can watch the things for you," Heather offered.

I shot her a glare.

A pleased smile curved Blanche's lips. "Perfect. Now will you please go get rid of that picture she painted of a couple smooching with not a stitch of clothing on their bodies?"

"I'll take care of it." I shuffled off toward the church parking lot.

I weaved through the crowd, passing the funnel cakes and lemonade. It took a lot of willpower not to stop, but I knew Blanche would have a hissy fit if I didn't talk with Mrs. Henderson. I was the only one who seemed to be able to get through to her. She just ignored everyone else as if she lived in her own little world. The retired art teacher had always been a bit eccentric.

I decided to take a shortcut through the narrow cobblestone alley that connected Main Street with Elm.

"What are you going to do? Buy the painting?" Charlotte asked as she kept up my pace.

I scoffed at her suggestion, but the thought had crossed my mind. I could buy the darn thing, then toss it in the Dumpster in the alleyway on my way back to the boutique. Blanche Dickens would never know.

I didn't have a chance to make it to the offending artwork. I turned next to the coffee shop to enter the alley and stopped dead in my tracks. Charlotte froze next to me.

Amid the trash cans outside the back doors of

the Main Street shops, a man lay facedown in the alley. His arms were flung out above his head and his legs were slightly twisted to one side. He wore a dark suit, which looked a little out of place for a spring festival. Most everyone wore shorts and T-shirts to beat the heat. The once comforting smell of funnel cakes and hot dogs wasn't so soothing anymore. Uneasiness weaved its way through my mind. The brick walls of the nearby buildings seemed to close in on me.

A surge of panic ran through me as my thoughts drifted back to the private investigator I'd met after the festival meeting. I couldn't see this man's face, but judging from his clothes, it was the same person.

"Do you think he's okay?" Charlotte asked.

I ran over to him and knelt down. "Sir, are you hurt? Do you need help?"

I poked at his shoulder, but he didn't answer. When I saw his face, I knew for sure it was Edward Andersen.

"I do believe he's expired," Charlotte offered.

It looked as if he'd been attacked from behind. Blood had pooled under his body. A card lay beside him on the pavement. I reached down and picked it up. It was from Cindy Johnson's charity. I flipped the card over in my hand. *9:00 AM* was written on the back. I looked at my watch. It was just after nine.

Had he had a meeting with someone? A meeting with the murderer? Would this man's ghost find me, too? I concentrated on remaining calm, breathing in and out, pulled out my cell phone, and dialed 911.

"Nine-one-one. What's your emergency?" the woman asked.

I pulled together my courage and said, "There's a man in the alley by Elm and Main. I think he's dead."

"He's definitely a goner," Charlotte said.

"Is he breathing?" asked the emergency operator.

"No, I'm sure he's not."

"The police are on their way." Her voice was calm and professional.

I ended the call. "It must have just happened." I scanned my surroundings for any sign of movement.

"Are you okay?" Charlotte asked with a new softness in her voice.

I wiped my forehead. "I'll be fine." Though I wasn't sure I would be. My legs felt like they were about to give out.

The sirens sounded first, then the flashing lights appeared. The first officer on the scene didn't seem to be in a hurry. It was as if he knew the man was already dead. It didn't take long for a crowd to gather once the police arrived.

I leaned against the wall, wishing I could be somewhere else, anywhere else. The thought that passing through this alleyway wouldn't be safe had never crossed my mind. As a teenager, I'd traveled this path many times on my way from the antique shop to the diner.

"Oh yeah. He was murdered," Charlotte said, shaking her head in pity.

"Murdered?" I said out loud without thinking.

Blanche Dickens pushed through the crowd and stood beside me. Her blue eyes widened, giving her the look of a startled kewpie doll. "Do you think he was murdered?" she whispered.

"I-I don't know," I stammered.

"Who would do such a thing?" she asked.

Charlotte appeared next to Blanche. "How the heck should you know?" She was taking advantage of her new paranormal skills.

"I don't know," I said, answering Blanche's question.

Gentle pressure glided across the bottom of my legs and I looked down. Wind Song weaved around my legs, then looked up at me and meowed. How had she known where to find me? She must have followed me to the alley.

Charlotte cleared her throat and recaptured my attention. She pointed. "Look who it is. The detective from last night."

I followed the direction of her pointing finger. The handsome Detective Valentine was heading my way.

Chapter 9

*Use padded hangers for your items
and acid-free tissue paper for storage.*

Detective Dylan Valentine stopped in front of me, taking a pen and notebook from his pocket. "Hello, Miss Chanel. I understand that you discovered the deceased, is that right?"

I inclined my head at an attempt to respond, but no words came from my mouth. Thoughts jumbled through my mind. If only I hadn't decided to take a shortcut through the alley. I bet that the dead man would say the same thing if he could. Since I'd been in a hurry to speak with Mrs. Henderson, I'd taken the most direct route. If only I'd gone the long way around through the masses of spring festival gatherers. What if I'd been a little earlier? Would I have stumbled upon the murderer? Would I, too, have been a victim?

I swallowed hard as I glanced over at the scene of the crime again. The police had draped a white sheet over the body. That was about as final as it got. The cat meowed and pawed at my leg. Was she hungry? If so, her demand for food had come at the worst possible time. She'd have to wait.

I assumed the detective watched me from behind his mirrored aviator sunglasses, making the odds of me knowing the right thing to say to him unlikely. I knew he was waiting for me to offer some details, but honestly, what could I tell him? I'd found the body . . . end of story.

"Can you tell me what you were doing at the time?" His velvet-edged voice was full of compassion.

I tried to steady my trembling hands. "Yes. I was walking through the alley and there he was, just like that." My eyes widened as I glanced at the body.

Detective Valentine took off his sunglasses, revealing his intelligent blue eyes. "You were speaking with this man last night. Do you know him?"

I'd hoped that he'd forgotten that he'd seen me speaking with the private eye.

"Oh, this could get interesting." Amusement filled Charlotte's voice.

It was like the air had been knocked out of me. I couldn't lie and say that I hadn't spoken with the man because the detective had seen me.

"Yes, I spoke with him. But I don't know him." I rushed my words.

Detective Valentine watched the activities around us. His relaxed demeanor made me uneasy. "What did he want?"

My thoughts were so jumbled. Surely, I'd put my foot in my mouth.

"Just tell the truth," Charlotte pushed as if she'd read my mind.

A rush of fear ran through me as the full scale of the chilling scene hit me. "The man said he was a private investigator. He wanted to know if I had information about Charlotte Meadows. He's probably investigating her murder." That seemed like a safe assumption to me. I glanced over at the sheet-covered body. "Well, he *was* looking into the murder. He's not doing anything now."

A glimpse of quiet strength flickered in the detective's blue eyes. "What do you know about Charlotte Meadows?"

I gave Charlotte a warning glare. Of course, Valentine couldn't see her, so he probably wondered what I kept looking at.

"I don't know anything about her." The more I talked, the bigger hole I dug for myself.

Hooking his pen inside his notebook, he said, "Thanks for the information." He pulled a card from his pocket and handed it to me. "If you think of anything else, please don't hesitate to call me. Another officer will be over to speak with you shortly."

By that, I knew that I wasn't leaving the scene any time soon.

The detective walked over to a group of officers. They spoke for a while and then glanced over at me.

I wished I could disappear. The crowd that had gathered around the scene watched all of us. I felt as if I was on a stage, but unfortunately my performance wasn't a good one.

"That detective is a handsome man," Charlotte whispered next to my ear.

I jumped and clutched my chest. "Don't do that. You scared me."

Charlotte flashed a sweet smile as if it was no big deal that she'd almost caused me a heart attack.

Heather gave a halfhearted smile as she approached from the crowd. "Are you talking to the ghost again?" she whispered.

I motioned toward Charlotte with a tilt of my head. "Yes. She's too chatty."

"What did the police say?" Heather asked.

A strand of hair had slipped out of my flower barrette. I brushed it out of my eye and tucked it behind my ear. "He wanted to know why I'd spoken with the dead man."

Her mouth dropped. "Why did you speak with him?"

"Well, he spoke with me first. I don't know what he wanted to know about Charlotte, but it's more than a little odd." Police officers traveled back and forth past us, but I didn't think anyone was listening to our conversation. I gestured toward the body. "The guy was obviously looking into Charlotte's death, and then he turns up dead? That's not a coincidence."

Heather fidgeted with the bangle bracelets on her wrists. When her nerves kicked in she couldn't be still. "I wish I could say it was a coincidence, but I have to agree with you."

"Well, look at you two sleuths. Why don't you do something to help me instead of just talking about it?" Charlotte swept her arms from Heather to me. "I'm in a bit of distress over here."

"The ghost is talking again. I have to ignore her," I said, glaring at Charlotte.

"Does Charlotte know that man?" Heather asked.

"I've never seen him a day in my life . . . or

former life. Well, whatever. You know what I mean," Charlotte said.

"She doesn't know him," I said.

Heather's forehead furrowed. "What if Charlotte's killer felt the private eye was too close to solving the crime?"

I blew the hair out of my eyes. "That's what I'm thinking."

"This doesn't look good for you," Charlotte said, pointing at me. "People are staring."

"They're just interested in this macabre scene, that's all," I said, trying to convince myself that she wasn't right.

She moved closer to Detective Valentine, looking him up and down and following him as he stepped over to the body. He peered under the sheet. Charlotte kneeled down beside the detective and the body. I guess being next to a dead body was no big deal to her.

"Someone did a real number on that guy. What was his name?" Heather asked.

"Edward Andersen. At least that was the name on the business card he gave me." I had stuffed the card in my purse, thinking I wouldn't need it. I took it out to give it another look.

"Do you think he was murdered? Or was it just an accident?" Heather asked, craning her neck to read the card.

"I'd like to say it was an accident, but from what I saw, I don't think so."

Charlotte popped up beside us again. "Well, he certainly didn't do that to himself." She tsked. "Such a pity that he had to check out so soon."

"So someone killed him?" Heather whispered.

"Yes, I think he was murdered," I said.

The last thing I needed was to be involved in another murder investigation. But as much as I wanted to stay out of it, I couldn't help but wonder if the death of Edward Andersen was connected to Charlotte's murder. I needed to get out of this crowd so I could ask Charlotte questions without causing the whole town to think I should be committed.

Once the coroner had taken away the body, the crowd thinned out. I was still waiting for the police to tell me I was free to leave.

Blanche Dickens stared at me from across the way. Her lips were curled in a look of frustration—a cross between a grimace and a scowl. I thought she would have forgotten about Mrs. Henderson and her naked portrait, but apparently she still wanted me to get rid of it.

She hurried over, placing her hands on her hips as she stood in front of me. "Cookie, now that this disaster is over, can you—"

"I'll talk to her as soon as the police let me go." The words slipped out before I thought about what her reaction would be. I regretted that lapse in judgment.

Blanche leaned in close as if I was about to share a secret. "Why won't the police allow you to leave?"

There was no point in postponing the inevitable. She would find out the truth soon.

"Well, I discovered the body, Blanche. They just want me to tell them if I saw anything unusual." I knew her imagination would run wild.

Blanche clutched her chest. "Oh, dear. This is dreadful."

"Yes, it's a terrible situation." Maybe she would let me off the hook after all.

She scanned the police action. "Well, do go as soon as possible, okay?"

So much for letting me off the hook. Blanche had recovered from her shock quickly. All she wanted was that hideous portrait removed. I couldn't say that I blamed her—it was ugly—but there was a time and place for everything.

After a few more minutes, a young blond officer told me that they didn't have any more questions for now, but they might need me later. I hoped they wouldn't.

Detective Valentine was talking with another officer. He noticed me, though, because our eyes met. He offered a grin, but I turned and headed away from the alley. I'd put Wind Song in the shop, then I'd go deal with Mrs. Henderson.

My parents had slipped my mind and I wondered if they'd seen the commotion. It would have been hard to miss the crowd and sea of uniformed officers. The thought had barely entered my mind when I spotted my mother's panic-stricken face.

"Sweetie, what happened?" she asked as she approached.

My father was only steps behind her with the same worried expression. It wasn't easy to convince them that I was perfectly fine. It wasn't every day that someone discovered a dead body, but if my parents had taught me anything, it was to be tough. As my grandmother had always said, "Suck it up, Buttercup."

"You promise you'll call if you need anything?" my father asked.

Wind Song pawed at my foot.

My mother noticed the cat and asked, "Is that your cat?"

"Apparently she is my cat," I replied. "Mom, meet Wind Song. Wind Song, this is your grandma." My mother gave the cat a friendly tickle on her ears.

After a final hug, my parents weaved through the crowd toward their Volvo. Seeing them go made my heart sink. As soon as I had time, I would visit them at the beach. I could use a vacation.

I picked the cat up, and she snuggled against me without objection. Clutching her, I hurried away.

After setting the cat on a soft cushioned chair in my shop, I said, "Wind Song, it's too dangerous out there for you."

She meowed in protest, but I closed the door and locked her in, anyway.

I made my way past one of the front windows, surprised to see she had already jumped up beside the mannequin. Her gaze was locked on me and she followed my every move with her eyes. The Ouija board was on the floor beside her. That was strange. I didn't remember leaving it there.

Chapter 10

Heather's Heartfelt Tip
for Getting Rid of an Unwanted Ghost

❦

You can try a broom to sweep the spirit away,
but I've never had much luck with this method.
At least your floors will be clean, though.

The fact that a dead man had been found in historic downtown Sugar Creek put a damper on the Spring Fling festivities. Most of the tourists cleared out and went home and I couldn't say that I blamed them. Mrs. Henderson gave me a hassle with the portrait, but she relented and loaded it back into her van. Her work of art wasn't one of those abstract things, either. It showed the human anatomy in full detail. I was sure a few parents in the crowd wouldn't want to deal with the questions that the painting sparked.

After loading Wind Song into her carrier, I closed the shop for the day and headed home. I was ready to have a light dinner, hunker down between the sheets and sleep. Maybe tomorrow things wouldn't seem so crazy. But as long as Charlotte was still hanging around that probably wouldn't happen. She was in the passenger seat during the ride home and it looked as if she wasn't going to leave my side any time soon.

Preparing dinner of blackened catfish and fried green tomatoes aided in distracting me from the tragic event. My kitchen had warm cream-colored cabinets and a soothing yellow hue on the walls, so it felt as if the room was embracing me in a big hug. For dessert, I made bread pudding with bourbon sauce. I'd save some for Heather because it was her favorite. Charlotte sat across from me as I ate dinner. She was in a talkative mood. Once I finished, she even walked along beside me as I cleaned the kitchen.

After getting Charlotte to stop chatting about clothing and everything else under the sun, I headed to bed. After curling up under the covers, I had a hard time sleeping. Instead of drifting off to dreamland, I tossed and turned, looking at the clock every ten minutes.

Wind Song slept fine, curled up in a ball at the end of my bed. She looked like a princess with her gorgeous white fur against my leopard print comforter. She didn't seem to care if she left her fur behind. If it made her happy, I didn't mind much. I could clean the hair off.

My problem with sleeping was caused by a fashionably dressed ghost. Just as Charlotte hadn't wanted me to go to bed in the first place, she kept waking me up to ask if I was sleeping. I guessed that was the problem with being a ghost—she didn't need sleep. I, however, was still part of the living world and needed rest.

"Cookie, are you asleep?" she whispered in my ear for what must have been the hundredth time.

I groaned and pulled the pillow over my head.

"Stop moaning and talk to me," Charlotte said.

"Charlotte, if my eyes are closed, then I must be asleep." I lifted the pillow off my face.

She wore a red knee-length pencil skirt and a sleeveless, white and red polka-dot, silk blouse. Her red and white Christian Louboutin spectator pumps were like the cherry on top of the outfit. Her makeup looked just as flawless as the day before.

I had no idea how she did it, but I was almost afraid to ask. Being a spirit had at least one perk. It would be nice to have perfect makeup all the time.

She studied her elegantly manicured fingernails. "Well, you weren't snoring. How can I tell if you're sleeping when you're not snoring?"

"I do not snore. I just sleep."

She brushed imaginary lint from her skirt. "If you say so, but occasionally a little snort or two comes out." She wiggled her finger, pointing at my face.

I pulled the blanket over my head.

"You can't stay under there forever. You won't be able to breathe."

After thirty seconds I gave up and climbed out of bed. I was so tired that even my teeth hurt. I yawned and pulled on a pale yellow chenille bathrobe from the fifties, then shuffled to the kitchen with Wind Song and Charlotte following close behind me. The sun hadn't even woken up yet.

I set my coffeemaker to brew a cup of cinnamon mocha and popped a couple slices of bread into the toaster. From my refrigerator, I took out a jar of homemade peach preserves that Heather had given me. I avoided butter, but Heather's sweet preserves were impossible to resist. She made delicious apple butter, too. It made my mouth water just thinking of it. With my coffee and toast in hand, I sat at the breakfast nook and tried to read my *Lucky* magazine.

Charlotte sat across from me.

I felt her eyes on me. I placed the magazine down and met her stare. "What do you want to say?"

"Aren't you going to pour me a cup of coffee, too? I like it with cream and sugar."

What response could I give her? I hated to point out the obvious, but I did. "Charlotte, you can't drink coffee, anymore."

She propped her hand on her hip. "I know that, but I can smell it. Humor me, will you?"

I hopped up and filled a mug with steamy coffee, adding a bit of sugar and cream.

When I placed it on the table, she leaned down and inhaled. "Oh, the scent is divine."

"Glad you like it."

After another whiff of the hot liquid, she tapped her finger against the table. "Shouldn't you be doing something to find my killer?"

I pointed at my plate full of crumbs. "I have to eat breakfast."

"But you're finished, so let's get going."

I leaned back in my chair. "Okay. If you want me to do something, you need to make a list of your enemies, Charlotte. I can't just wander aimlessly around town asking people if they know who killed you."

She tapped her foot against the tile floor. "No way. That's the craziest idea I've ever heard. Where did you come up with that idea?"

"What else do you suggest? I've always heard that the killer is usually someone the victim knows." I sipped my coffee.

"I can't make a list of enemies. A true Southern belle doesn't have any. You should know that."

If that was true, I wouldn't have had to deal with Laura Sheldon making fun of my old-fashioned clothing back in high school. I was glad those days were far behind me.

I placed my dishes in the sink and rinsed them. "Fine, but I can't help if you won't give me information."

Instead of answering, she sniffed the jar of peach preserves as I closed the lid.

"Have it your way." I turned and headed for my bedroom.

"Are you just going to leave me in the kitchen?" Charlotte asked as she hurried up behind me.

Halfway across the hardwood floor, I paused. "Why did you stop your business relationship with Marie Vance?"

Charlotte stopped in her tracks. "That woman! She drives me crazy. Marie became increasingly irresponsible with money, so I felt it was best if we were no longer partners."

"What does irresponsible with money mean?" I asked.

One of her perfectly sculpted eyebrows tilted upward. "It means exactly what it sounds like."

"I mean, what did she do with the money?"

Wind Song sat in front of Charlotte and looked up as if she was waiting for an answer, too. She flicked her tail, looking alert and ready for action.

"She was not reporting all the money spent. Things were unaccounted for." Charlotte stepped over to the window and peered out. "I wonder what she was doing with all the money, because I never figured out where it was going."

I rubbed Wind Song's head and she purred in response.

"Did you ask her?"

Charlotte faced me again. "I did. She wouldn't answer, and that's when we stopped working together."

"Well, it makes sense that you would cut off ties with her. Do you think she was doing anything illegal? Or maybe she had a gambling problem."

"I doubt that. If anything, she had a shopping problem."

I turned toward my bedroom. "You better be thinking about that list while I change," I warned from over my shoulder.

"I told you, I don't have any enemies," Charlotte called out as I walked away.

I jumped in the shower, then stood in front of the closet to decide on my outfit for the day. With each new day, it was a treat to select an ensemble. Clothing was a way to express my personality. Every day held a surprise and a new combination based on my mood.

But what was my mood? Frustrated? Frustrated that I couldn't solve the murder and lose the constant chatter from Charlotte—although it wasn't so bad talking to her, I guessed. Sometimes it was fun to have someone to talk to.

I decided to invoke the feeling of the upcoming summer season. Maybe I should have worn black for all the deaths in Sugar Creek, but I hoped cheerful colors would help me forget, even for a moment, about the poor man who had been murdered and Charlotte's predicament. One minute, Edward Andersen had been walking down the street and the next . . . it was all over. Just like Charlotte. She'd been in her home, and suddenly, she was living in another dimension. It just proved that it was important to make the most of every day because one never knew when it would be the last.

"How do you decide what to wear?" Charlotte asked from over my shoulder.

I held a forties lime green and white pinstriped peplum blouse up to my chest and then placed it back in the closet "It's easy. I just try to have fun with it."

"How do you select which vintage item you want

to pair with another? I mean, if they're from different time periods. I know what I would do, but I guess you have your own method."

It was nice for someone to take an interest in the whole vintage clothing process. "Well, that part's not as easy as it looks. But you had immaculate taste in clothing, so you should know how it all works. Or did you forget when you . . . well, when you left this plane."

"Honey, I may be in the spirit realm now, but I still have my fashion sense." She placed her hand on her hip. "Everyone's method is different. I just wondered if you have a plan or do you just pick something out of the closet willy-nilly."

"No, I don't do it willy-nilly. I like to think I have an eye for it."

Charlotte looked me up and down. "You do okay."

I focused my attention on the contents in the closet again and decided on a gorgeous seventies sleeveless wrap-style dress in a divine shade of pink with tiny green pinstripes. It was the perfect summer dress. Long sashes wrapped around the waist to tie in a bow in the back and each side had a pocket on the hip. I paired the dress with a pair of straw-colored wedge heels and a watermelon-shaped green and red bag.

"You look like you should be lying on top of a checkered tablecloth at the park," Charlotte quipped.

"That's exactly the look I was going for," I said with a smirk.

"Well, it's a good thing because you succeeded."

I shoved the contents of the purse I'd carried

yesterday into the watermelon clutch and headed for the door. Wind Song hopped into the carrier as if she knew exactly what to do. I wondered if her previous owner had trained her to get into the carrier, or if she had some other reason to be so unfeline in her acceptance of it. Either way, she was proving to be a remarkable cat.

"Come on, Wind Song, let's go do the vintage clothing thing."

Chapter 11

Cookie's Savvy Vintage Fashion Shopping Tip

❧

*Start your vintage collection with a basic item
like a little black dress.*

I lowered the top on my car, turned on the golden oldies station, and pointed the Buick in the direction of It's Vintage, Y'all. My hair whipped in the wind as I cruised down the country lane. Bright green oak trees full of newly bloomed leaves lined the path and white fluffy clouds dotted the endless blue sky. It would have been a relaxing trip if not for Charlotte sitting next to me, tapping her fingers against the leather seat. Her anxiety oozed over to my side of the car.

When the last strains of Elvis singing "Love Me Tender" faded, I turned down the volume.

"What?" Charlotte asked.

I glanced down at her still-tapping fingers, although her movements had no sound.

"Oh, is this getting on your nerves?" She wiggled her fingers.

I grimaced. "Just a little."

She scowled but stopped the fidgeting.

"What are you so anxious about?" I asked.

"Oh, I don't know. How about the fact that my murderer is out there wandering around and I have no idea who it is?" She gestured toward the upcoming stop sign.

I braked at the intersection. "Fair enough. I can see how that would make you a wee-bit anxious."

"Thank-you."

I parked in my usual spot in front of the shop, where my car could be readily seen—part of my strategy for attracting customers' attention. Unlike many other shop owners, I had not been upset when the town fathers passed an ordinance limiting the size of business-related signage on Main Street. My red Buick announced "vintage" better than a neon sign could have.

After unlocking the door, I flipped the sign to OPEN and flicked on the lights. The excitement of each new business day never grew old. As soon as I lifted the lid of her case, Wind Song climbed out and stretched before making a tour of the store. She sniffed around as if patrolling her territory, before climbing into the front window and settling in the sunshine.

My work production had seriously diminished since Charlotte had come into the picture. I had no idea of when I would get around to the stack of clothing in the backroom that needed to be sorted. First, I had paperwork to process. I got that out of the way quickly so I could work with my passion, the clothing.

I started by tagging new items, like a black Escada pencil skirt with a gorgeous seam detail in the front and a Jean Varon purple and white maxi dress from the seventies. After I put them on display, I chose some items that had not moved after thirty days, marked them down, and placed them near the door on my sale rack. I loved every garment in my shop, but my practical side realized that I needed constant turnover to remain in business.

Wind Song was still lying in the sunshine that shone from the front window. In the short time since she'd appeared at my doorstep, she'd already found a favorite spot.

Charlotte was staring at me as I redressed one of the mannequins in a beautiful seventies beige silk dress. She sat on top of one of the tables with her legs dangling over the edge. "I think you should retrace my last steps in order to find a clue to my killer."

"I'm not sure that would be a good idea," I said.

Before she could answer, the bell above the door chimed. Marie Vance entered and headed straight toward me, a fake smile on her face.

Charlotte pointed at Marie. "That's my pants and blouse," she yelled.

Well, Charlotte's clothing had been sold, so more than likely Marie had purchased them at the sale. The silk pants were a lovely shade of taupe with wide legs and a high waist. The white blouse tapered around Marie's slim waist. Discreet pearl drops dotted her earlobes and a matching necklace finished off her accessories.

"Do you remember me?" she asked in a sweet voice.

"What is she doing here? Actin' all highfalutin

in my clothing." Charlotte jumped down from the table and moved toward Marie.

"Of course I remember you. How are you?" I matched her saccharine tone.

"Just fine," she said, looking around the shop.

"May I help you find something?" I ignored the faces that Charlotte was making.

"I can't believe she came in here," Charlotte said.

"I'll just get right to the point," Marie said as she touched the blouse on the mannequin beside her. "I want to buy the items that you acquired from the Charlotte Meadows estate sale."

"What?" Charlotte said. "That is crazy."

If she found Marie's request strange, I knew something was up. Charlotte loved her clothes. She'd even stuck around them in the afterlife. But why would Marie want them so badly? Even though I was in the business of selling clothing, I decided not to let Marie have any of Charlotte's things.

"I'm sorry, but the items aren't for sale yet. I haven't had time to price them, and I may not even sell all of them," I said with a smile.

Marie sifted through a few items on the sale rack. "They are beautiful items. I guess you can understand why I'd want them." She lifted a pair of eighties beige linen pants off the rack, then haphazardly shoved them back into the wrong spot.

"I don't understand totally. I'm sorry." I repositioned the linen pants neatly on the rack.

Marie pulled a tissue from her black handbag. "It's just that I miss her so much and I want something to remember her by."

"Oh, what a load of crap." Charlotte tapped her foot against the hardwood floor. Normally that would have made sound, but not in Charlotte's case.

I had to admit it did seem odd, but everyone had a different grieving process. Something about Marie's answer didn't seem honest, though, so I had to believe Charlotte.

"I'd be willing to pay more than you did for the items." Marie took a cobalt-colored silk blouse from the rack, studied it, then hung it back where she'd found it.

"Don't let her have them," Charlotte ordered.

Wind Song strolled over and plopped down beside Charlotte. The cat looked up at the ghost and meowed as if she was totally in agreement with her.

As Charlotte and Marie glared at me, I felt pulled in opposite directions. "I'm sorry, but they're just not for sale right now. If you'd like to check back later . . ."

Marie turned around and walked out the door. The bell above the door jingled in her wake.

"What do you think that was all about?" I asked.

Charlotte rested her hands on her hips. "She probably just wants to collect all my belongings so she can sell them at a profit."

Charlotte had a point. Maybe Marie did have a gambling problem or other financial motive that made her desperate for cash. I'd have to look into what was going on with her.

Charlotte and I marched over to the front window to spy on Marie as she stomped down the sidewalk toward her car. I was still trying to figure out why she had come into the shop. Something about her request just didn't make sense.

Without warning, she whipped around and stared back toward the window.

Charlotte and I ducked back. I hid behind a mannequin and Charlotte swooped over beside me.

"I don't think you have to worry that she'll see you," I said.

Charlotte grinned. "Oh yeah. I forgot."

I eased back to the window and peered out. Charlotte followed.

Marie climbed into her Mercedes and pulled away from the curb. She drove by slowly, her attention on me the entire time. If she wasn't careful, she'd smash into the car in front of her. The expression on her face sent a shiver down my spine. Apparently, she wasn't pleased when she didn't get her way.

She could flash scary stares my way all she wanted, but I wouldn't give in to her request to purchase the clothing.

Marie's wasn't the only car I recognized driving down Main Street. Soon after her car passed, I noticed that Detective Valentine was following her. At least, it appeared that he was following her. I got the impression that his presence wasn't a coincidence.

He noticed me at the window. He must have noticed that Marie was watching my store. Did he know that she'd been in my shop? Was he really targeting Marie? Or was I the object of his surveillance? Did that mean I was a suspect? I was probably putting too much thought into the incident. He just happened to be on his way back to the police station, right? "That was strange. Was it just a coincidence?"

Charlotte smoothed her hair off her forehead. "I don't know if anything is a coincidence, anymore."

I was beginning to wonder the same thing as both cars moved out of sight. After a few seconds, I asked Charlotte, "What are you thinking?"

She tapped her index finger against her chin. "You know, there's something on the edge of my memory and I can't figure out what. It has to do with Marie. I know that much. I just feel like there's something I should remember, but I don't know what."

"Maybe if you think really hard it will come back to you," I said as I turned my attention out the window again.

"I'm blank," Charlotte said.

"Well, I have no idea how the mind works once you're dead—why some of the memories are gone—but trust me, I forget things all the time. The thought usually comes back to me and I'm sure it will happen to you, too."

Charlotte frowned. "I suppose you're right. You'd think just seeing Marie's face would spark my mind and it would come back to me, though." Charlotte's voice sounded a little dejected.

I faced her again. "What can you tell me about Marie, Charlotte? I know that she was your partner and that she annoyed you a lot, but why did you become partners with her in the first place?"

Charlotte settled into the velvet settee. "Marie is a complicated person. I guess I've never really figured her out. She was really good with business and was great with other professionals. She really knows how to turn on the charm when she's talking to people."

"You're kidding. Marie doesn't seem very personable, although she does have that certain way of batting her eyelashes while flashing a sweet smile."

"Yes, exactly." Charlotte used her index finger as the exclamation point for the sentence. "I don't know how she does it. I guess it just comes naturally. Like the way you have a knack at finding vintage clothing."

I smiled, surprised that she had paid me a compliment.

Charlotte perked up. "Oh, there is one story that Marie never likes for me to share."

I quirked a brow. "What's that?"

"As I said, Marie is strange and more than a little stuffy, but she has a keen business sense. So when she asked to be my partner, I thought it would be a good idea. She's also absentminded. One time we were in a shoe store trying on these fabulous heels and she left the store wearing her black heel on the left foot and the bright red heel from the store on her right foot."

I frowned. "I think I know where this story is going."

"Well, needless to say she was embarrassed that she'd made such a fashion faux pas in public."

"Oh no."

"Marie had to go back into the place to get her shoe."

"Are you serious? I can imagine she wasn't happy with herself after that. What did you do?"

"I laughed, of course. That didn't make her happy, either."

Charlotte and I were still talking when Heather walked into the shop.

"Hey, guys. What's going on now?" Heather looked in the general direction where she thought Charlotte was standing. "Since you were talking to thin air I assume Charlotte is next to you?"

I tilted my head in Charlotte's direction. "She's here."

Where else would Charlotte be now that she'd attached herself to me? It was like having a shadow twenty-four hours a day, and it didn't look as if she was going anywhere anytime soon.

"We were just watching Marie as she drove past. She's not happy with me." I gestured toward the street.

Heather reached down and patted the cat's head. "Oh, you mean Marie Vance? She was in my shop earlier."

My eyes widened. "Really?"

"Yeah, it's weird. She wanted me to do a reading."

I exchanged a look with Charlotte. "Are you serious? Did you do it?"

"Well, yes, but . . . well, you know that I can't really give her a reading. I just gave her general information."

"What did you tell her?" I asked.

"Oh, just the usual stuff. Luck would be coming her way, blah, blah, blah. She asked me one curious question, though." Heather flashed a grin.

"Yeah? What's that?" I asked.

"She wanted to know if I believe in ghosts."

Chapter 12

Heather's Heartfelt Tip
for Getting Rid of an Unwanted Ghost

⬥

Ghosts sometimes have unfinished business
here on earth. That's why they hang around.
Help them write a letter or send an e-mail
and that should tie up any loose ends.

"Do you think Marie saw you?" I asked Charlotte.

Charlotte paced the length of the floor. "If she did she didn't let on. She probably is just curious about the paranormal."

A customer entered and interrupted our conversation. She removed her big black sunglasses, placed them on top of her head, and smiled. Her black sleeveless silk blouse had black beading around the scooped neckline, her black silk-blend pants flared at the leg.

"Welcome to It's Vintage, Y'all. May I help you find something?" I asked with a smile.

She pushed her auburn bangs out of her eyes. "I'm just looking. Thanks."

"I'll see you in a few," Heather whispered as she backed out of the shop.

Charlotte followed the customer around the shop as if she thought the woman would steal something. The woman kept glancing over her shoulder.

I guessed she must have sensed Charlotte's presence and I motioned for Charlotte to move along.

The woman glanced my way at that exact moment and placed the gold art deco necklace back on the table. "Is everything all right?"

I put on my best professional face, ignoring Charlotte as I walked past her. "Yes, um, yes, everything is fine. May I help you find something? Is there a specific piece you're looking for?"

Charlotte claimed that she wanted to help me attract more customers, but if she kept this up she would have the opposite effect.

The woman stared at me as if she was contemplating whether to actually allow me to help her or to run out of my shop.

I was thankful when she said, "I'm looking for a skirt."

"Great! Do you have a particular style in mind?"

"Tell her to get a mini skirt," Charlotte said with a smile.

I didn't dare look at her. I was afraid I'd answer her, and the customer would think I was talking to an imaginary friend.

"I'd like something just below the knee with a pattern. Oh, and muted colors, too," she added.

"Is this for a special occasion?" I asked.

The woman touched a navy blue dress on the

nearby display. "I just want something new . . . well, new for me."

"I think I have just the thing," I said as I hurried across the room.

Wind Song watched me, but she seemed bored.

I grouped the clothing by era, then divided into skirts, blouses, pants, dresses, and such. Organizing had always been one of my favorite things. I'd filed everything in my parents' house in alphabetical order, right down to my mother's herbs and spices. After taking a skirt from the sixties rack, I ran back over to my customer.

"That color won't look good on her," Charlotte said.

Obviously, she was wrong on that one. I knew the teal-colored A-line skirt with taupe and white flowers would be perfect for the woman. I held the skirt up for her to inspect.

"It's perfect," she said, grabbing it from my hands.

I pulled back the dressing room curtain and waited for her to enter. The space had a large mirror on the back wall and a white upholstered bench to the right. Plush white carpet cushioned my customers' bare feet as they tried on clothing.

The front door opened and a man with salt-and-pepper hair made eye contact. He wore brown slacks with a light beige button-up shirt. "Is that your Buick?" he asked with enthusiasm.

I stood a little straighter. "Yes, she's mine."

He peered out the window. "Is it all original?"

"Yes. It was my grandfather's car."

"How many ponies you got under the hood?"

"It's an eight cylinder straight-line," I said with

confidence. My grandfather had taught me all there was to know about the Buick. I loved talking about my vintage car. It captured the attention of a lot of men. It gave them something to admire while their wives shopped in my store.

"Mind if I take a closer look?" he asked.

"No, not at all." It would give his wife plenty of shopping time.

Charlotte paced outside the dressing room while the woman tried on the skirt.

I found a white blouse with a Peter Pan collar and handed it to the shopper. I refused to speak with Charlotte again until the woman was out of the store. It was just too risky—too risky that everyone would think I was bonkers.

Smiling, the customer emerged from the small room and carried the skirt and blouse to the counter. When she looked down to retrieve cash from her purse, I winked at Charlotte. Fortunately, the woman was clueless as to what was happening around her. She paid for her items and walked out with a bounce in her step.

I always loved to see how a vintage clothing purchase could lift a person's spirits. "See, a happy customer."

"You got lucky," Charlotte said.

Wind Song meowed as if in agreement.

What did they know?

Chapter 13

Don't be afraid to tailor a vintage item to fit you.
Ill-fitting clothing will take away beauty from the piece.

A couple hours passed while I checked my inventory for loose or missing buttons and did a few minor repairs. Around four o'clock I set my work aside and pulled out a pad of paper. Charlotte and Wind Song appeared to be dozing by the windows.

I took a seat and positioned the pen over the paper. I wasn't sure how to wake a ghost, so I just started talking. "Okay, Charlotte, I'm ready. Who is on your list of people who may have offed you? We have to get started if you want my help."

She sat up with a start. "I don't have anyone to put down on the list. Everyone loves me."

I pointed the pen at her. "I doubt that seriously. Everyone has someone who doesn't like them. It's inevitable . . . just human nature. That's just the way it works."

Charlotte paced a few steps before stopping next to me. "Fine. I'll give you a list, but I'm just making up things because I really don't think there's anyone."

"Okay. I guess it's a start."

Charlotte placed her hand on the counter, released a deep breath, and jabbed my paper with a pearly pink fingernail. "I guess the first person you can put down is Marie. She's as crazy as a sprayed cockroach. I wouldn't put it past her to have some grievances with me."

"But is she capable of murder?" I asked.

"No, I doubt it. She's all talk. She's not that crazy."

I scribbled a few notes. "Okay, who's next?"

Charlotte dipped her head. "I shouldn't say this, but write down Bud Butler. Although we hadn't dated that long, he seemed really nice and I thought he cared about me. He would never do something like that. He was never a violent person and he never had a harsh word for me."

"It sounds like you had a great relationship," I said.

"Well, he had his issues, but nobody can be perfect, right?"

I jotted more notes. "We're getting somewhere, I guess. Is there anyone else to put on your list?"

She marched back and forth in front of the counter. "This is crazy and I don't think we should continue."

"We have to go on, Charlotte. Come on, think hard. There has to be someone else to put on the list. If I can't talk to anyone, how will we get any idea of who may have done this to you? Just because they're on your list doesn't mean that they had anything to do with your death. It's just someone for me to talk to."

She leaned over and peeked at my list. "Well, that makes a little more sense. Why didn't you say that in the first place?"

"I thought it would be obvious."

"I guess Cindy Johnson wasn't happy with me. I mean, after all, I told her I would give money to her charity and then I pulled out at the last minute."

"Can you blame her for being mad?"

"More important, can you blame me for not giving the money? I had to know that it was going for the women and children who needed it, and not being used for something that it shouldn't be, right?"

I tapped the pen against the pad. "Of course. I understand your reasoning, but maybe she didn't."

"I didn't know Cindy well outside of business, but I don't think she is capable of murder," Charlotte said.

"Is there anyone else other than Cindy, Bud, and Marie? That's only three people." Leaving my pen and paper on the counter, I adjusted the curtains against the slanting rays of the late-afternoon sun.

"That's all that I'm aware of." Charlotte stood a little straighter, crossing her arms in front of her chest. "I just can't think of anyone else."

"Well, three is not enough. That's not going to work." I tried to show compassion for Charlotte's plight, but I had to ask questions of more than three people.

Wind Song batted her paw against the tiny gray and white mouse toy that I'd bought her.

"Isn't that the whole reason that we made a list anyway? So that you can talk to people? No matter if it's just one person, that's better than nothing," Charlotte said.

"Who was in your will?" I asked.

Charlotte stopped in her tracks. "Why do you ask?"

"I've seen things like this happen before. When someone thinks they're getting the money and then they don't, they get mad."

"Where did you see something like that before?"

"In the movies."

"Well, this isn't the movies," Charlotte said.

"Yeah, but you know life is stranger than fiction. It's happened before. Maybe that was the case this time. So tell me who you left everything to and we can narrow it down from there." I positioned the pen on the paper again.

Charlotte inched a little closer. "I left my belongings and other assets to various charities. I had no family, so I had no one else to leave them to. I didn't have any really close friends, after your grandmother passed on."

I tapped my pen on my bottom lip while I thought. "You know, maybe someone within the charities was mad that you didn't leave *all* the money to them. You split it up between the charities."

"So they're mad that I gave them money? How thoughtless of me."

"You know what I mean. They might have wanted

it all, so they got mad at you when you gave some to other people," I said.

She tapped the edge of the paper. "I guess that's possible. Go ahead and write down the various charities that I left everything to."

I wrote down the list as she rattled them off one by one.

Charlotte rounded the corner of the counter, distancing herself from the list. "Okay, I'm done. I can't think of anyone else. If you can't figure out something from that list, I don't know what to say."

The door jingled as Heather marched in with her Ouija board tucked under her arm. She smiled, trying to act casual.

"What are you doing with that thing?" I pointed.

Heather placed the Ouija board onto the counter. "Now just hear me out. This whole thing with Charlotte is huge. You've unleashed a psychic talent you didn't even know you had. I think you need to speak with other spirits." She positioned the planchette on top and pushed the Ouija board toward me.

I busied myself with straightening a shirt on a nearby rack of men's clothing from the Gatsby era. "I don't want anything to do with that thing."

Charlotte laughed from the corner of the room.

"I don't want to talk with the spirit hanging around now, much less another one," I said, brushing imaginary dust from the shirt's starched collar.

Wind Song meowed as she walked over, then jumped onto the counter. Her focus intent on the Ouija board, she acted as if she knew exactly what Heather was asking.

"Come on, Cookie. What's the worst that can happen?" Heather asked.

"I can have a whole room full of ghosts, that's what can happen." The words had barely slipped from my mouth when the cat sat down in front of the board, delicately wrapping her tail around herself. Wind Song placed a paw on the planchette and started moving the thing.

I glanced at Heather. Her eyes widened.

"The cat is trying to tell you something," Charlotte said from over my shoulder.

I didn't want to admit it. Something like that couldn't happen. It couldn't be real. Then again, I hadn't thought I'd be able to communicate with Charlotte either and that had happened.

The cat pushed the planchette across the wooden board and stopped on the letter *N*.

Heather looked at me in disbelief. We remained silent. I was in shock, as the cat guided the planchette with her paw again until it came to rest on the *O*.

"No? No, what?" Heather asked the cat as if Wind Song would look up and respond.

To my great relief, the cat didn't answer but moved the planchette around the board again, stopping on letters as if she did this type of thing all the time.

Heather grabbed my pen and pad and wrote down the message.

Was I dreaming, hallucinating, or was the cat really spelling? It had to be the latter, because I knew I was fully awake and Heather and Charlotte were witnessing the same thing.

"What does it spell?" I'd been unable to keep up with the cat's message because she had moved so quickly, and frankly, I hadn't been able to concentrate because of the sheer craziness of the whole scene.

"'No more cheap cat food.'" Heather read the words aloud, then burst out in laughter.

Charlotte soon joined Heather's laughter. I held back my laughter for as long as I could, and then joined them.

"This is crazy. I refuse to believe that the cat used the board to spell out words." I pointed toward the board. "I told you that thing was bad."

Heather's eyes remained the size of saucers.

"I can't say that I blame the cat." Charlotte shook her head. "I've seen the way that stuff looks when you dump it out of the can onto her dish. I wouldn't want to eat it either."

"It's cat food. You're not supposed to want to eat it," I said.

Charlotte stepped closer. "So the cat doesn't like the cheap cat food. I wonder what else she has to say."

I gestured for a timeout with my hands. "*She* doesn't have anything to say. Cats can't talk.

"Well, technically, she's not talking." Heather pointed at the board. "She's just using the board to relay her thoughts."

The cat was still sitting beside the board, her paw resting on the planchette. I was still trying to figure out what had happened. I couldn't allow myself to believe that the cat was communicating with us via a Ouija board.

"Ask her to tell us something else," Charlotte urged.

"I can't ask the cat to speak with us. I already look crazy for speaking with someone no one else can see," I said with a wave of my hand.

"Well, I'll ask Wind Song if she can speak to us," Heather said as she stepped closer to the cat.

My shoulders slumped. "This isn't going to work, is it?"

Heather leaned down with her face close to the cat. "Hello, Wind Song. Do you know that you are a very beautiful cat?"

"Oh good. Complimenting the cat so it will give us a message," Charlotte rubbed her temples.

I had to admit it was crazy. I wasn't sure sweet-talking would work. "Maybe we can give her a treat. Like bribery." I laughed.

Heather didn't respond; she was too focused on speaking with Wind Song. "Do you have anything else to tell us, Wind Song?"

The cat stopped licking her paws, seemed to collect herself, and pushed the planchette again.

How could this fluffy feline know how to move that thing?

She moved over the letters, pushing it to the *D* and then an *A*.

When she made it to the fifth letter, I knew that she was spelling a word. I swallowed the lump in my throat when I realized what that word was.

"She's spelling something again," Heather said with excitement.

Wind Song wasn't just pointing out a bunch of random letters. With this second performance, I knew that the first time hadn't been a coincidence. If Charlotte had blood to drain the color from her face, it would have. She stared like Heather and I did . . . in disbelief.

"The first word is *danger*. Is she telling you that you're in danger? Are we all in danger?" Heather's face reflected her worry.

I didn't answer. The cat was still moving the planchette. Again she spelled a word. It was *lurking*.

"Danger lurking," Heather said as she looked over her shoulder.

"Where is danger lurking?" I asked Wind Song. *Great*. I was communicating with a cat *and* a ghost.

As if on cue, the cat started spelling out another word. This time she spelled *nearby*.

She had actually answered my question.

"Ask her another question." Heather gestured toward the board. Her voice had reached an all-time high pitch.

Before I had a chance to ask Wind Song another question, she hopped down, took her place in the sunshine again, and turned to licking her paws as if this was no big deal.

"At least the cat is a good speller," Charlotte quipped.

"Yeah, I guess that helps," I said.

"What helps?" Heather asked.

"Charlotte likes the cat's spelling," I said so Heather would know what was being said.

Heather gave a half-hearted smile. I knew she was a little freaked out and so was I.

"You know we can't tell anyone about this, right?" I asked her.

She pushed hair out of her eyes. "No one would ever believe us."

"Exactly. I don't want to find out what people would do if we told them about this. They'd think we were crazy."

"You know I won't tell anyone," Charlotte said.

I had to find out what Wind Song meant when she said danger was lurking nearby. Was it related to Charlotte and the private eye's murders? The last thing I wanted was to be the next victim.

"Maybe you should get rid of this board," I said, picking up the thing, putting it back in its box, and handing it to Heather.

"Are you crazy? The cat is talking to you and you're getting rid of her only means of communication," Charlotte said.

"You can't get rid of her only way of speaking with you." Heather echoed Charlotte's sentiment.

"So you two are in agreement that I should keep the board." I placed my hands on my hips.

Heather scanned the area searching for Charlotte. "At least, we agree on something."

"I doubt that will happen often," Charlotte said.

I waved my hand through the air. "Fine, I'll keep the board, but if any other ghosts appear, it has to go." I cleared papers off the counter.

The cat glanced over at us, her green eyes sparkling under the light.

One thing was for sure. I had to find out where she came from. "Someone has to have seen her around town before she came to me. The cat wouldn't have just appeared at my store."

"I don't know where the cat came from, but I

agree someone has probably seen her before. If I were you, I wouldn't get too attached to her," Charlotte said with a frown. "Someone will probably claim her, eventually."

Charlotte was right, I shouldn't get too attached. But it may have been too late for that. I hated to think of going home alone to my little house. My feline friend had already found a spot in my heart. "I called the vet's office and the animal shelter this morning. They didn't know anything about the cat and no one has reported her missing," I said.

"She appeared when you needed her the most." Heather sat down on the stool beside me and traced her finger against the top of the counter. "It's good that you have her to talk to."

"I don't want to be the cat lady who ends up with twenty cats."

Heather chuckled. "I don't think you have anything to worry about."

"The vet's assistant said she'd let me know if someone comes in looking for Wind Song."

Heather's expression brightened. "Hey, I have an idea. Maybe we could make some flyers and put them around town."

"Yeah, I guess that would be a good idea. After all, if she belongs to someone, I definitely want to help them find her."

The cat meowed. I wasn't sure if that meant that she wanted to go back to where she came from, or if she wanted to stay with me. Maybe I needed to get her to use the Ouija board again. She could let me know if she was happy with me.

Heather glanced over at Wind Song. "She's certainly no trouble at all."

"Well, maybe the talking part. That could freak someone out. Her owners could have gotten rid of her just because of that."

Heather waved her finger. "That does make sense. I'll bet that's what happened. She spoke to them with the Ouija board so they just dumped her off."

"Yeah, but why here? Why did she find me?"

"We may never know," Heather said.

Did Wind Song have some other special talent that I didn't know about? As if using a Ouija board wasn't enough. It didn't bother me too much now that I'd kind of gotten used to the idea. I mean, it was kind of neat when I thought about it. Dr. Dolittle would have been delighted, so why shouldn't I? So far, she had communicated useful information, especially about her cat food issue. I thought cats loved all cat food. Now I knew that Wind Song had definite preferences.

Heather stood from the stool. "I'll ask around if anyone knows who she belongs to. If I find out anything, I'll let you know right away. We should ask as many questions as possible and try to get information from her, but don't worry about it in the meantime, okay?"

"I don't think the cat wants to be a novelty act. Plus, you know that cats have a stubborn streak. They do what they want, when they want, not what you want when you want," I said.

Heather and I watched Wind Song. She continued to stare as if she knew every word we'd spoken.

"Okay. I have to get back to work, but if anything happens, you call me immediately." Heather pointed at my pink cell phone, which lay on the counter.

I used my index finger to cross my heart. "I promise."

She stared at the cat the whole time she walked across the floor and then as she backed out the front door.

I waved to her, but she didn't even notice. She was too focused on Wind Song.

I glanced at Charlotte. "What am I supposed to do with a cat that uses a Ouija board?"

"See, this is even more reason why you need to help me find my killer," Charlotte said with a flick of her wrist.

"What does the cat talking have to do with me finding your killer?" I asked.

"The cat gave you a warning. I think you should listen," Charlotte said.

Her words echoed in my mind. She was right.

Chapter 14

*Heather's Heartfelt Tip
for Getting Rid of an Unwanted Ghost*

❈

*Call the ghost's loved ones. If they don't think you're
crazy and will actually speak with you, they may be able
to talk some sense into their deceased loved one.*

An idea struck as I mended a button on a sixties magenta-colored silk blouse. "Charlotte, we need to go back to the scene of the crime."

"I know I asked you to help, but do you think that's such a good idea? You might be bitin' off more than you can chew."

"It certainly can't hurt, right?" I pulled the needle from the fabric and cut off the thread.

"If you think it will help, okay."

After placing the needle and thread back into my sewing box, I set the blouse on the counter.

I grabbed the keys and said, "Maybe we can find clues that the police may have overlooked."

I locked up the shop, climbed into the Buick and I cranked the key and then merged out onto the road.

"I doubt there are any clues left since they sold

all my belongings." Melancholy filled Charlotte's voice.

The sun blanketed the air with warmth as we navigated the streets toward Charlotte's home. White fluffy clouds decorated the blue expanse of sky. I was thankful that at least it wasn't too humid yet.

"I used to love eating at Lonnie's," Charlotte said as we passed the restaurant, which was housed in a charming brick Victorian on Sycamore Street.

"My grandmother loved it, too," I said. "She couldn't resist their pecan pie."

"Are you sure we should visit the crime scene?" Charlotte asked. "I am sure the police scoured it for clues."

I turned on the car's signal and made a right. "Yes, but like I said, maybe they overlooked something."

"Well, that is possible. I'm not sure how much faith I have in their investigative abilities." Charlotte studied her perfectly manicured fingernails, which were a soft violet color . . . different from the previous pink.

"I'm sure they're doing everything they can," I said.

"And what about the private investigator? Are they searching for his killer?" Charlotte asked.

I didn't want to admit it, but his death had to be related to Charlotte's.

"Honestly, Charlotte, I will admit that I have my reservations about this." I stopped at a red light. "Heck, for all I know, a clue could bite me on the nose and I still wouldn't notice it."

Charlotte drummed her fingers against the

leather seat. "At first, I might have agreed with you, but now I think you should have more confidence in yourself. You don't know until you try it."

I pushed the gas pedal. "You're right. Let's give it a try."

With the top down on the Buick, I weaved in and out of traffic, soaking up the springtime sunshine.

Charlotte sat in the passenger seat, peering at the landscape. We'd moved into a less populated area with homes dotting the side of the road. "It will be strange to see my house again after everyone has been in there, all those people touching my things." She shook at the thought.

I wasn't sure what to say. It was a tough problem and I had no idea how I would handle it if I was in the same situation. "I'm sorry, Charlotte. You can stay in the car if you'd like and I'll go in and take a look around." I navigated around a curve.

She sat a little straighter. "No, I want to see what they've done with it. I thought when I drove off with you the other day that I'd never see the place again. Somehow that made it easier to leave . . . like ripping off a bandage. Plus, I was just glad to have someone to talk to."

I busied myself with the clutch, brake pedals, and turn signals as we veered onto Lee Street. I pulled into the driveway on the side of her beautiful mansion, put the car in neutral, set the emergency brake, and cut the engine. The robins chirped in the treetops and a spring breeze rustled the leaves, but other than that, it was eerily silent.

I hadn't thought of it as a crime scene before when I'd been there. I guess I'd been too excited about scoring the awesome clothing.

As I looked up at the house a thought crossed my mind. "Do you think the police have the place under surveillance?"

Charlotte scanned the area. "I sure hope not, but I don't think they'd have any reason to watch it. It's not like the killer is going to come back to the scene of the crime."

"You never know. Maybe he or she would come back. What excuse will I give the police if I get caught in your house? It wouldn't be easy to explain why I am here after I found the private eye murdered."

"That would be incriminating." Charlotte patted her hair into place.

"Plus, how am I going to get into the house? I'm sure they locked it when they left. Do you still have a key?" I looked down at her pants pocket.

"Oh, yeah, right. Where would I put a key? I'm a spirit."

"I'm sorry—I don't have a spirit-to-human conversion sheet."

"I hide my key under the statue in the garden." She pointed.

I looked in the direction she indicated. "Which statue? There's like twenty over there."

She gestured toward the area with a tilt of her head. "It's the small angel at the edge of the garden."

I opened the car door. "I'll be right back."

I scanned the area as I made my way across

the manicured lawn and into the garden. Weeds had popped up in what I assumed was once a well-groomed space. I lifted the little angel statue and sure enough, a key was underneath. I waved the gold key in the air as I made my way back to the car.

Charlotte eased out of the passenger seat and joined me at the front door. Checking over my shoulder to make sure no one was watching, I shoved the key into the door.

"Wait," Charlotte said. "The alarm system. You'll have thirty seconds to punch in the code or the alarm will go off."

I jumped back as if I had touched a live electric wire. "Are you serious?"

She leaned against the wall. "Well, if the code hasn't been changed. If it has, my code won't work. The alarm will go off and the police will arrive as soon as they can. Especially since I'm dead and no one should be in the house."

I stepped away from the wall. "That's it. I can't take that chance. I do not want to go to jail."

"You have to take that chance. We've come this far," Charlotte reached out and tried to push in the code. Of course her fingers never made contact.

"I'll say it again. I don't want to go to jail." My feet were frozen on the spot.

Charlotte reached for my arm, but her hand passed right through, sending a chill across my skin. "Look, if the alarm goes off, all you have to do is rush out and drive off. You'll be able to get out of here before the police arrive. It takes them at least three or four minutes."

"Oh, really? You make it sound so easy." My knees shook as I thought about the potential consequences. "Fine. I'll give it a shot, but I can't believe you've put me in this crazy situation."

"I'd do the same for you." She batted her eyelashes.

"Yeah, sure."

Chapter 15

Cookie's Savvy Vintage Fashion Shopping Tip

*Check the garment's fabric for fading,
pulling, or cracking.*

I opened the door and the alarm made a continuous beeping sound, matching my rapid heartbeat. "Where is the control panel?" I yelled over the noise.

"It's right over here by the door, under the portrait of Uncle Jubiliah." She moved toward the offending sound. "Try to remain calm."

"That's easy for you to say. You're invisible. No one can see you."

I rushed over to the wall where the canvas of the baldheaded portly man hung and flipped the cover down on the alarm. The keypad lit up, waiting for me to silence it. My hand shook as I raised my fingers to the pad. "What's the code?"

"It's either four-five-six-zero or four-six-five-zero," Charlotte said from over my shoulder.

"You don't remember the code? Are you kidding me?" My voice had reached an all-time high.

"Excuse me, but my memory is a little fuzzy now

that I'm dead. I'm sure you can understand." She placed her hands on her hips.

I punched in the first code that Charlotte had rattled off. The beeping noise continued.

"It didn't work, Charlotte," I said in a panic.

"Just stay calm. Take a deep breath." She displayed the palm of her hand in a stop sign motion. "Try five-six-four-zero."

I frantically punched the buttons, hoping that I'd get lucky. "I'm going to be joining you in the afterlife soon. The police will arrive and I'll have a heart attack." Still the beeping echoed.

"Okay, try four-zero-six-five," Charlotte said.

I clutched my chest. "I can't breathe."

"Just push in the code that I told you. You're wasting time," Charlotte demanded.

I pushed in 4-0-6-5 and the frantic beeping noise stopped. Finally, silence surrounded us. I released a deep breath and tried to steady my speeding heartbeat. In those frantic moments, my life had flashed before my eyes, but I didn't tell Charlotte. She might have found my comment a tad insensitive.

"I'm not sure what we're looking for." I looked around the massive foyer. The other day, I had been so preoccupied with the sale that I hadn't paid much attention to the space. Besides the circular staircase and marble floors, intricate wood trim adorned the pale blue colored walls. A large mahogany table with a marble top sat in the middle of the room.

"You don't plan things out much, do you?" Charlotte said.

"So I'm spontaneous. Some people find that

endearing." I eased across the foyer. The galumph
of my wedge heels echoed across the space.

"Well, I'm not one of them. We'll just go from
room to room until we make it through the whole
house."

"From the looks of the size of your house that
could take several days." I peered up at the grand
dark wood staircase. The banisters were intricately
carved with a scrolled pattern. Portraits of who I
assumed were Charlotte's ancestors decorated the
wall up the stairs.

"The house isn't as big as it seems." Charlotte's
heels made no sound against the marble floor.

"Didn't you get lonely in this big place?" I asked.

Her expression changed. The sassy spunk had
faded and was replaced with a melancholy frown.
"It wasn't too bad. Come on." She motioned over
her shoulder.

I sensed that she didn't want to talk about it, so
I didn't press the subject.

I followed her through the foyer and into the
enormous living room. Floor-to-ceiling windows
covered the far wall with heavy cream and navy
draperies flanking each window. Nothing seemed
out of place. However, the room looked like a
museum. Sheets covered the sofas and chairs,
making the finality of her death seem all too real.
Sunlight splashed across the massive crystal chandelier in the middle of the room, causing a prism
of colors to dance around the room. The racks of
clothing and other personal items from the estate
sale had been removed.

"I'll look around in those cabinet drawers." My voice echoed across the mostly empty room.

Charlotte paced across the hardwood floor while I opened drawers. It shouldn't have come as a surprise that the place was bare.

"There's nothing here," I said, running my hand through my hair.

Charlotte reached the end of the hallway within seconds. "We'll go in my bedroom."

I followed her down the hall. It felt strange being in this house with her and no other people around. I glanced over my shoulder several times, still expecting to see the police walking toward me with guns drawn. When we reached the end of the hall, she turned to the right.

She poked her head out the doorway. "In here."

Charlotte's bedroom was massive. Several floor-to-ceiling windows adorned each wall. Gold silk drapes decorated the windows. The only piece of furniture remaining in the room was an enormous mahogany bed.

A few boxes were stacked in the corner. "Apparently, most of my items have been boxed up or sold," Charlotte said with a click of her tongue.

I gave her a pitying smile.

She stood a little straighter and puffed out her chest. "Well, no matter. It is what it is. I have to suck it up. There's nothing to be done about it. It's not like I can come back to life."

Unfortunately, she was right.

I walked over to the boxes and looked in, hoping to find something good, but they were empty. "There's nothing inside," I said with a sigh.

Charlotte tossed her hands up. "This is useless. Let's go check the kitchen."

As I turned to leave, I looked back at the boxes one more time. On the floor beside them was a white handkerchief with tiny pink and green flowers on the trim. I walked over and reached down to pick it up. "Is this yours?" I asked, holding up the handkerchief.

Charlotte examined the item. "No, I've never seen it before. It's not mine. I have no idea where it came from."

"Maybe someone dropped it when they were packing up." After looking around to make sure I hadn't missed any other items, I shoved the handkerchief into my pocket and headed down the hallway.

We had just stepped into the kitchen when the front door clicked and then shut. We exchanged a terrified glance.

"Someone's in the house," Charlotte whispered.

I rushed around the island to the kitchen's entrance and peeked out. Detective Valentine was standing in the foyer, peering up at the staircase.

The breath was sucked out of me as if I'd been punched in the stomach. What would I do? I watched him for just a moment longer than I should have, but luckily, he hadn't seen me. I was convinced that he had a subtle aura that trapped people into stealing quick glances at him, so technically it wasn't my fault. I hurried back over to where Charlotte stood by the refrigerator. I had to get out of the house before he saw me.

Looking around the large kitchen, I spotted the back door and ran toward it. My shoes weren't helping my escape mission. The wedge heels were slowing down my pace and making a squeaky noise that the detective probably heard all the way in the foyer. It would be just a matter of time until he discovered me.

Once out the door, I eased it shut, then raced around the side of the house, weaving around the shrubbery and making a beeline for my car. The old Buick was like my lifeboat and I was swimming for my life. It was a good thing I'd parked the car at the side of the house, but what if he'd seen it? He'd come after me soon if he had. I'd have to come up with a good story for why I was in Charlotte Meadows' home.

I jumped into the car and after fumbling several times, shoved the key into the ignition. Charlotte was already in the passenger seat. Obviously a perk of being a ghost was the fast movements. I flinched as the car's engine roared to life. Why did it have to be so loud?

Pulling out of the driveway, I shifted into second gear and zoomed past the detective's car without looking over to see if he was watching. At the stop sign on the corner, I glanced back to see if flashing lights were informing me to pull over. After a couple minutes with no police in sight, I allowed my breathing to return to normal. I made it all the way back to town without the detective behind me. That was nothing short of a miracle.

"I can't believe we got out of there without Detective Valentine knowing you were there," Charlotte said.

"Well, we don't know for sure yet. He could still come after me," I said, glancing in the rearview mirror. "This is too stressful. I'm not sure I'm all that great at being a sleuth."

"Oh, what are you talking about? You're doing a great job. Well . . . you're doing as well as can be expected," Charlotte said.

I pulled up in front of the shop and jumped out. Heather had already closed her shop for the day. She would freak out when I told her about my near encounter with the detective.

Just as I knocked on the door, she peeked over the counter. After unlocking the door, she stepped to the side and motioned for me to come in. "What's wrong?" she asked as she almost shut the door on Charlotte.

Charlotte scowled as she stepped through the closed door.

"Charlotte's with me and you just shut the door in her face." I bit back laughter.

A sheepish grin curved Heather's lips. "Oops. Sorry about that."

Heather returned to behind the counter, where I could see she was in the midst of mixing her herbs for spells. Several candles flickered around the shop. The smell of patchouli and musk filled the air. I never knew quite what she did with all the spices. She'd shown me some spells, but they all seemed too complicated for me.

"What's up?" She poured some green leaves onto a small scale and adjusted the balance.

Leaning on the counter, I told her about my close call in Charlotte's house.

"Do you think he saw you?"

I picked up the bottle of herbs on the counter, studied it, and put it back down. "I don't know.

I hope not. Like I said, I took off while he was still in the house, but he could've looked out the window. Especially if he heard my car. You know, it's kind of loud."

Heather picked up the bottle I'd just touched and positioned it on the shelf behind her. "It's definitely loud."

"Yeah, well, the car's old and there's not much I can do about that. But anyway, I'm worried. What do you think I should do?"

Heather placed her elbows on the counter. "As long as you got away, I think you are fine."

We were interrupted by a comment from Charlotte. "While you two are yammering away, I thought you might like to know that the detective just pulled up in front of the store." Our ghostly sentinel stood in front of the large front window with her hands on her hips. She didn't even turn around to look at us as she spoke.

My stomach dropped. "What? You had better not be playing a joke on us."

"What's going on?" Heather's eyes were wider than ever.

"Charlotte said the detective just pulled up in front of your store."

Charlotte wiggled her index finger in my direction. "You are in trouble now."

"You're not helping," I said in a panic.

I'd made it halfway to the window when I spotted him walking toward the shop's entrance. Of course I freaked and froze.

"Well, don't just stand there. He'll see you." Charlotte motioned for me to get away.

"Twenty-three skidoo," I said as I ran toward the back of the store.

Heather ran beside me. "What are you doing?"

I pushed her toward the front. "Go talk to him. I'm hiding in the back room."

"What if he looks back there? I can't breathe," Heather said.

"We'll worry about that if it happens."

As I stood in the back room trying to steady my heavy breathing, I leaned over toward the open doorway and attempted to listen to the conversation. Charlotte had stayed near the windows.

"May I help you?" Heather asked with a squeaky voice when Detective Valentine entered her shop.

I hoped she didn't blow it and tell him I was eavesdropping in the back room.

"I'm just looking around," the detective said.

Oh, that wasn't good. I hoped he didn't look around all the way in the back.

"You have a lot of interesting things," he said.

I thought for sure that his voice was closer to me. When I realized I was holding my breath, I released it slowly, trying not to make a noise.

"Yes, I have books, jewelry, essential oils, and incense."

"You're friends with Cookie Chanel, right?" he asked.

Uh-oh. This was it.

"We're friends," Heather choked out.

"I thought I saw her come into your store just now."

Should I run out the back door? Maneuvering around a stack of boxes, I hurried over to the back door and pushed. It was locked. I was trapped.

With my hand on the door, I pushed again, but felt a hand grasp my shoulder. I gasped and spun around.

"He's gone. Were you trying to escape?" Heather asked.

I clutched my chest. "Yes, I was trying to escape. Wouldn't you?"

"That was too close," Heather said.

Relief washed over me. I'd avoided the detective, but how long would that last?

I sank to the floor, giggling uncontrollably.

Chapter 16

Heather's Heartfelt Tip
for Getting Rid of an Unwanted Ghost

If you have a particularly ornery ghost
don't be afraid to sprinkle the holy water around.

I went back to my shop and picked up the cat—again with no fuss. She was purring as I carried her to my car with Charlotte at my side. Did she know we were going home for the day? Maybe she was tired from her long day at "work"—which she mostly spent napping.

"You almost got me in trouble by dragging me into your house," I said to my ghostly sidekick.

She settled back onto the car's leather seat as if what I'd just said was no big deal. We drove home in silence, which was welcome to me. After parking, I retrieved Wind Song from the backseat and took her indoors. She meowed as I opened a can of Gourmet Kitty select tuna and herbs in simmered sauce. Watching her dig in, I hoped the pricey chow would satisfy her epicurean tastes.

After making a peanut butter and jelly sandwich, I settled onto the sofa with my snack and a glass of milk. Wind Song washed her face and paws, then stretched out to watch me from across the room. I had to admit it was a little strange. Had she really used the Ouija board to communicate? I'd often wondered if animals had the same thought process as humans. Now I couldn't deny it. I looked at my peanut butter and jelly sandwich. Did Wind Song approve of such humble fare?

After turning on my laptop, I pulled up my e-mail and scanned for any important messages. I hoped there would be good news. I was still waiting for a message from a movie director who was filming a Jazz Age drama in Georgia soon. My fingers were crossed that she would hire me as a wardrobe consultant.

Seeing a notification for a blog comment, I excitedly clicked on the link. I loved receiving feedback on my blog posts. Most of the time it was from another vintage clothing enthusiast.

When I read the message, I knew right away that this wasn't a fellow vintage fashion lover. Someone going by the username *killer* had left a threatening comment on my blog.

I'm watching you, too. Mind your own business or you'll be next.

The glass slipped from my hand and bounced once it hit the soft cushion of the rug. Luckily, I'd finished my milk and it was empty. The name surely indicated that this person was probably behind at least one of the recent murders in Sugar Creek.

Then again, someone could just be playing a

joke. I liked that scenario better. The anonymous poster had warned me to stop snooping around. How did this person know what I'd been up to unless they had been watching me? That thought sent a shiver down my spine.

"You look like you've seen a ghost." Charlotte chuckled.

I picked up the glass. "You're hilarious."

"Okay, I'll be serious. What's wrong?" She sat beside me on the sofa.

"Someone left a comment on my blog." I turned the screen so that she could read it.

She flashed a worried expression as she read the comment out loud. "You should definitely tell the police."

I stared at the message on the screen, wondering who could have sent it. "There's a problem with going to the police."

"What's that?" Charlotte asked.

"I can't let them see this message. They'll know I've been snooping around. And that would put an end to solving your murder. They'd probably put me in jail."

Charlotte laid a hand on my forearm. Even though I couldn't feel it, I appreciated the gesture of comfort. "But you may get hurt . . . or worse, the killer may come after you and do the same thing to you."

I closed the laptop. "I'll be careful, but I always finish what I start. I told you I'd help find the killer and I intend to stick to that."

Wind Song jumped up onto the arm of the sofa. She meowed and touched my arm with her paw.

Did she have another message for me?

I rubbed her head. "I'm sorry, Wind Song, I don't have a Ouija board. If you have any advice for me, you'll have to speak up." She answered with an emphatic "meow."

Not only was I talking to a ghost, but I was listening to a psychic cat.

Chapter 17

Cookie's Savvy Vintage Fashion Shopping Tip

*Take a tape measure when shopping
so you can get accurate measurements.*

The next day, Wind Song and Charlotte were back with me at It's Vintage, Y'all. I'd just finished my morning routine—checking the newspaper for ads about sales in other clothing shops while sipping a chicory coffee with molasses and cream from Billie Jean's Coffee and Such on the corner—when the bell on the door chimed. My stomach dropped when I looked up and saw the handsome Detective Dylan Valentine headed my way. He was wearing a tailored white shirt that emphasized his strong biceps and tapered trousers that showed his trim physique. His blue tie brought out the sky blue of his eyes. My granny would have called his looks recklessly handsome.

Apparently, my snooping around hadn't gone unnoticed after all. I should have expected his visit. After all, I knew he'd catch up to me eventually. He had a look of curiosity on his face that would have been noticeable from miles away.

Charlotte glided beside him and said to me, "Oh, you're in trouble now. This isn't good."

I didn't need to be reminded about my difficult predicament.

Since I wasn't cruisin' for a bruisin', I plastered the most realistic smile I could muster on my face. I'd pretend that everything was fine and maybe I'd get away with the act. "May I help you?" I asked, treating him like an ordinary customer.

"Something tells me he isn't here for a pair of vintage bloomers," Charlotte quipped.

"Good morning, Ms. Chanel," he said in a smooth voice.

He remembered my name? Who was I kidding? Of course he remembered my name. I'd discovered a dead man. That was a perfect reason to memorize someone's name. He probably knew everything about me, even that I liked to sing in the shower and eat peanut butter from the jar.

"Good morning, Detective Valentine. By the way, you can call me Cookie."

"All right, Cookie, you can call me Dylan."

The detective looked around my shop, taking in every inch. "This is a nice shop you have here." He picked up a handbag and looked at it then placed it back on the table.

I swallowed hard and hoped that I didn't let my nerves show through. I knew he wasn't there for clothing.

"Maybe he needs a new suit," Charlotte said, looking him up and down.

"Are you looking for anything in particular?" I asked.

He glanced over my shoulder toward the small

men's section. To be honest, he had an extremely awkward look on his face. I sensed that he wanted to be there but wasn't sure how to act. He shoved his hands in his pockets as if he didn't know what else to do with them. "I'm just browsing."

"I doubt he's here for clothing," Charlotte said as she walked around the detective.

She seemed to be right on. He looked like he had no idea what he was doing, but he kept looking at me as if he wanted to ask me a million questions.

"Make him try on some clothes. That will teach him to come in here and harass you."

Well, he hadn't harassed me yet, but it looked like he wanted something. Maybe she was right. I decided to have a little fun with him. "You must be looking for clothing. I bet you take a size large, am I right?" I stared at him.

He looked confused. Finally he said, "Yes."

"You're in luck. I have a great selection of men's clothing right here in the back. Let me pick out a couple things for you and you can try them on." I flashed him a wide grin.

"Thanks. That would be great." He seemed relieved to have some guidance.

I walked to the back and he followed a little too closely.

I pulled out a pair of dressy World War Two-era pants—a sharp pair of forties muted eggplant-colored rayon gabardine blend. The front had small pleats. No cuffs at the bottom. "I think these would be great for you." I held them up to his waist, just waiting for him to ask me about being at Charlotte's. I knew it was coming.

He held the pants and regarded them uncertainly as I turned around and searched for just the right shirt.

I pulled a subtle plaid shirt from the rack. "Here. This is a great shirt. Vintage forties."

He took the shirt from my outstretched hand. "It's in great shape to be that old."

"Yeah, it's a nice cotton blend. They're amazing and last forever if well-cared for."

He still looked a little lost.

"Now you need shoes." I looked down at his feet. "Size ten, right?"

He held the shirt up to his chest. "Yes. You're good."

"That's my job," I said with a voice full of pride.

I grabbed a pair of original forties Stacy Adams spectators in a warm brown and white. He'd be decked out in head-to-toe forties. All we needed was big band music. I'd switched the station to sixties per Charlotte's request.

"These are marked a size ten. I hope they fit. They're in excellent shape for their age. The leather is still quite supple, and the soles are barely worn." I handed him the shoes.

I was acutely aware of his nearness. A hot blush crept into my cheeks.

"Thank you," he said with a little wink.

"The dressing room is right here." I pulled the curtain back and waved him in.

As soon as he slipped into the dressing room, I collapsed onto an easy chair and blew an errant strand of hair out of my face. Charlotte sat across from me on an upholstered ottoman.

"He's on to you," she warned. "Why else would he be here?"

I scowled. "I know that," I whispered.

"You need to get him in some tight jeans," Charlotte whispered as if he could hear her. "Like the kind that Elvis wore."

"He isn't a Ken doll that I can dress up like I want."

She crossed her legs. "I know and that is such a shame. With his nice shoulders and narrow waist—"

"Will you stop talking." I put my hands over my ears.

"You can pretend all you want, but he's a smart one. Handsome, too. I could sop him up with a biscuit." Charlotte walked over and poked her head into the dressing room. She whistled and lifted her head out again. "Mercy me. He's got a big . . . smile." She looked at me innocently.

"Stop that right now," I demanded.

"Stop what?" Dylan asked from the dressing room. "Did I do something wrong?"

"I'm sorry . . . I was talking to the cat."

Dylan stepped out of the room, looking dapper in the trousers and shirt that I'd picked out.

I probably stared for just a little too long. "You look great."

Charlotte propped her chin in her hands and rested her elbows on the counter while looking at him dreamily. "He sure does."

Dylan looked down at his clothing. "I never thought I'd enjoy vintage."

"Would you like to wear the clothing now or should I bag it for you?" I asked, trying to sound businesslike.

He looked in the full-length mirror. "You can bag it. I'll save this outfit for a special occasion."

"I wonder what that special occasion is," Charlotte said.

After he changed back into his street clothing, I rang up the purchase and placed his items into a shopping bag. I was glad I had ordered white bags with my store name in small black letters so that a man or woman would feel equally comfortable in carrying one.

As he took the bag from my hand, he brought up the subject I'd hoped to avoid. "You know, I could have sworn I saw you at Charlotte Meadows' home yesterday. I thought I saw your car pulling out of her driveway." He looked me straight in the face. His blue eyes had small golden flecks in them.

I had a decision to make. Nerves danced in my stomach and I fought the urge to turn and bolt out of the store. Should I tell him that I was in her home or pretend that I had no idea what he was talking about? He would probably see right through my lie, so I had to admit that I was at least in the driveway. Why had he been there anyway?

"Don't tell him anything, Cookie. Not without a lawyer," Charlotte said.

When I glanced at her, I was sure my eyes widened. I didn't even want to think about needing a lawyer. She wouldn't be happy with me when I admitted to being in her driveway.

Gathering up my courage, I chuckled, trying to sound breezy and light. "I was actually in her driveway. I pulled in and saw a car so I turned around. Was that your car?"

He frowned, which made him look just as handsome as when he smiled. "Why were you there, Ms. Chanel?"

He was making me nervous calling me by my last name. It sounded so official. "Please call me Cookie." I busied myself straightening the collection of stick pins on my counter to avoid his stare.

Maybe I should have explained that Cookie wasn't my real name. But he probably already knew that, right? Had he done some kind of background check on me already?

His expression eased just a bit. "Okay. Cookie, why were you at Charlotte Meadows' home?"

"Like I said, I pulled in. I just wanted to have a look around." I tried to sound nonchalant.

"Why would you want to look around her home?"

Charlotte had moved around the counter and stood beside him. She leaned back and looked at his behind.

I couldn't believe she was checking him out. I glared at her as I spoke to the detective. "It's a beautiful house. I just thought I'd take a look."

"It seems kind of odd," he said as he leaned closer to the counter.

I wanted to step back, but I figured that would look awkward. I swallowed again. "What seems odd?" I managed to ask.

"It seems odd that you were talking to a man who was murdered, you discovered his body, and then you're at another murder victim's home. Yet you say you don't know either of the victims. I guess you can understand why I'm a little curious, right?" He didn't take his eyes off me.

A light sweat broke out on my brow.

"Don't answer any of his questions," Charlotte urged, moving over beside me. "He's got nothing on you."

Well, it was a good thing he had nothing on me because I'd done nothing wrong . . . other than being in a deceased woman's home for seemingly no reason.

"I understand that it seems strange." I moved over to a rack of clothing and straightened the blouses on the hangers. "But I can assure you that it was nothing more than coincidence."

He stood silent. Was he trying to make me uncomfortable?

Moving to the window, he peered out. After what seemed like an eternity, he turned his attention back to me.

"Now's your chance to ask him what he's doing to find my killer," Charlotte pushed. "As far as I can tell, he's not doing a darn thing."

I wasn't sure that asking him about his investigation was such a good idea. He already made me anxious. That feeling would only intensify if I started asking questions.

"It could be a long sleepless night for you if you don't ask him," she warned.

I couldn't bear the thought of further sleep deprivation. "Do you have any suspects in Charlotte Meadows' murder?" I asked, trying to sound casual.

"I can't discuss the investigation." His voice was tight, official-sounding. "Why do you want to know so much about her death?"

I feigned surprise. "I don't want to know about her death."

"You just asked about her murder," he pointed out.

"I was just curious. I mean, a man was murdered near my shop and that is a little concerning. What are the police doing to ensure that it doesn't happen again?" I asked, placing my hands on my hips.

"We're on top of it. In the meantime, can you tell me anything about your connection to the recent murder of Edward Andersen?"

"I told you everything I know."

"Did you know Charlotte Meadows or Edward Andersen?"

Charlotte shook her head. "Tell him no."

I lied about my connection with Charlotte. "I'm sorry that I don't know anything that would help you." Lying wasn't something that I enjoyed, but there was really no way around it. I'd have to be more careful or I might be accused of murder.

I walked past him and opened the door to usher him out. "Thank you for shopping at It's Vintage, Y'all. Enjoy your purchases."

He stopped in the doorway. "You'll tell me if there is anything strange going on?" he asked.

"Yes, of course," I lied.

Chapter 18

*Heather's Heartfelt Tip
for Getting Rid of an Unwanted Ghost*

*You can always hire a professional
to rid your home of the snarky spirit.
Just make sure they take the thing with them.
You want to get your money's worth.*

When I spotted Heather marching through the door with the Ouija board, I wasn't surprised. I'd known she wouldn't be able to resist trying to get Wind Song to talk with us again.

She placed the box down on the counter and smiled. "We have to know if the cat has anything else to say," she said before I'd even protested.

As much as the Ouija board scared me, I had to admit I was curious. Who wouldn't want to know what the cat had to say next? "Okay. But just one more time."

We didn't have to entice Wind Song to come over. She jumped up as soon as Heather opened the box.

Wind Song didn't waste a moment before she was gliding the planchette across the board with her little paw. Within seconds she'd spelled out an entire sentence. *Someone around you is bad.*

Heather held up her hands. "Well, don't look at me. I'm not the bad person."

We focused our attention on Charlotte. Well, I looked at her, and Heather turned in the same direction.

Charlotte folded her hands in her lap. "You can't be serious. I'm insulted that you would think such a thing. I'm dead, for heaven's sake."

I waved my hands. "Okay. Of course I wasn't blaming you. Besides, we shouldn't pay attention to what that cat says anyway."

Charlotte held her hand up. "Not so fast, Cookie. Maybe the cat is on to something. After all, what about the blog threats?"

"What is it? What did she say?" Heather asked, looking from me to the invisible Charlotte.

I'd avoided telling Heather, but I could no longer keep it in. "I wasn't going to tell you this, but I don't want to keep a secret."

"No more secrets from each other, remember?" Heather said with a smile.

I opened my laptop and pointed out the message.

Heather leaned down and read the screen. Her mouth opened in surprise. "What are you going to do?"

I massaged my temples. "I honestly don't know."

"There has to be a way to find out who left the comment." Heather studied the screen.

"I wouldn't know where to start," I said.

Heather looked up. "Maybe you could set a trap."

"I'm not smart enough for that."

"What if we engaged the person in conversation?"

I tapped my index finger against my chin. "That might work."

Charlotte braced herself against the counter. "They've threatened to kill you and you think you'll have a little chat?"

"Well, I'll have to think about it. I don't see you coming up with a better solution, Charlotte."

It had been a long day and collapsing in front of the TV was exactly what I needed. I fell asleep on the couch watching *I Love Lucy* and didn't wake until the next morning.

When I opened my eyes, I found Charlotte standing over me with a scowl on her face. One thing about being dead, she looked just as fabulous in the morning as she did in the evening. She never had a hair out of place or smudged mascara.

Sunlight streamed through the window behind her, making her look like an angel. She wore a white sundress with a delicate rose-colored floral pattern that hit just below her knees. Her fingernails were painted fuchsia.

She tapped her foot against the floor. "I thought you'd never wake up. I tried to be as noisy as possible. For a while, I thought you were dead."

I sat up and rubbed my eyes. "I guess I was just exhausted. It's been a long couple days."

Wind Song meowed. I didn't need a Ouija board to know that she was hungry. I stretched and pushed to my feet.

In the kitchen, I spooned Lively Lamb Shanks with Gravy into her dish. She sniffed it, then apparently satisfied, dug in.

"Now that you have a list of contacts, we need to start interviewing them," Charlotte said, pacing across the floor.

I made a parfait of yogurt, granola, and raspberries. "Okay. We'll go later today."

I knew it was useless to argue with her. I figured I needed to dress in my best business attire. I was more than a little nervous about talking to the people on her list. Just like Detective Valentine, they would probably wonder why I was interested in Charlotte's murder.

To bolster my self-confidence, I decided to wear one of my favorite outfits. I pulled on a pair of forties-era Claire McCardell beige high-waist trousers with three buttons running down each hip. My blouse was pale sage green with tiny white polka dots. It was nipped in at the waist and then flared out slightly at the bottom. A sweet little bow on the front accented the open collar and wide neckline. I finished the outfit with a pair of white and black spectator pumps and a white clutch purse. My hair had bouncy curls thanks to hot rollers. I placed a pale pink flower clip on the side. Some days when I had plenty of time, I styled my hair with victory rolls.

Pants had become part of women's wardrobes by the end of World War II and not quite as scandalous as they once had been. Some of my favorite styles were the tight-fitting cigarette pants and the pedal pushers. I loved dresses, but couldn't imagine wearing one every day.

"How's this?" I asked Charlotte as I gestured at my ensemble.

She marched toward the door. "Perfect. Now

come on. You're taking way too long." She motioned over her shoulder.

"But you didn't even look at me," I said as I opened the cat carrier for Wind Song to hop in. As usual, the feisty feline seemed to relish the chance to travel. I'd have to ask Heather if she thought Wind Song might be a reincarnation of Marco Polo.

I locked the front door and looked up and down the street before I stepped over to my car. Charlotte was already sitting in the front seat. She never wore a seat belt, but I guessed it didn't matter.

I placed Wind Song's carrier in the backseat and practically ran to the driver's side door. After the threatening blog post, I'd become more aware of my surroundings. Cotton clouds dotted the stunning blue sky. A whiff of gardenia from a nearby pot tickled my nose.

"Why are your heels on fire?" I asked, shoving the keys into the ignition.

"You'd be in a hurry, too, if you were dead and trying to find your killer," Charlotte said.

"I'm not sure what that has to do with anything," I said.

"Never mind. Just start the car and drive." She pointed toward the road.

Traffic was thin and we rode in silence for a couple minutes, but unfortunately that didn't last. In front of a house next to a red light, a woman saw her husband off to work with a light kiss on his cheek.

"Look at that. How sweet," Charlotte commented. "Why don't you have a boyfriend?"

"This town isn't exactly crawling with bachelors," I said, not wanting to talk about my break-up with Clark last year. His two-timing tomcat ways were still a sore subject. I couldn't believe I'd fallen for his glib line of excuses.

"So you don't have any family in Sugar Creek."

My hands gripped the steering wheel a little tighter. "Oh, I have plenty of family around. So many cousins that I've lost count. I was an only child, though. My parents moved to the beach."

Charlotte focused her attention on the road in front of us. "You and I are a lot alike."

The little voice in my head was screaming at me not to ask why, but so help me, I had to ask. "Why are we a lot alike? Am I that cranky?"

"We are strong independent women." Charlotte flashed a knowing grin.

Did she just pay me a compliment?

After we dropped Wind Song off at the shop, Charlotte gave me driving directions to the address that was first on our list. We were paying a visit to her former boyfriend, Bud Butler. As we drove through a well-kept residential neighborhood, the sun spilled brightness over the area, making the green on the trees and colors from the flowers pop.

We pulled up to the small charming ranch-style brick home. There were no flowers and not a lot of landscaping in front of the home, but the lawn looked like a putting green. I was surprised. I'd figured Charlotte would date someone who had a home equally as massive as hers. It was good to see that she wasn't dating Bud for his money. Not that she needed any, but I liked the idea of dating for love and not for the material possessions that the other person owned, although having a job or some kind of career goal was a must.

Parking along the street curb, I shifted the car into neutral and set the brake.

"I'm not sure what I will say to this man. It's going to be very awkward," I said, peering up at the house.

Charlotte touched her hair to make sure every strand was in place. "He's very friendly. I'm sure he will talk to you. How's my lipstick?" She puckered her lips. "Never mind. You don't have to answer that. I forgot it stays perfect. This is the first time I've seen him since . . . well, since I was murdered. I heard he was so upset that he couldn't even attend the funeral." She couldn't disguise the sadness in her voice.

"That's terrible, Charlotte. I'm very sorry. I hope he's feeling better."

"I don't. I want him to miss me."

"Charlotte, you want him to go on with his life, don't you?" I asked.

"Have you gone on with your life after the breakup with your ex? You should be dating."

My stomach sank. "Of course I have."

"Not completely and totally. You're not dating. And I bet you don't trust men," she said.

"I don't want to talk about it."

She continued to stare, so I said, "Everyone deals with breakups differently." I hopped out of the car, ready to change the subject.

"Now when we get inside, just ask the questions that I tell you," Charlotte said, matching my stride

"Is this my investigation or yours?" I asked.

She glided over to the path leading to the front door. "I know him and I know what to ask, so trust me with this, okay?"

"If you say so."

I'd agree with Charlotte, then do whatever I wanted when I got inside. After ringing the doorbell, I shifted from one foot to the other, trying to get rid of nervous energy. I had no idea what I was going to say to the man. *Oh, by the way, did you murder your girlfriend?* That wouldn't leave a great first impression with him.

The garage door was down, so I couldn't tell if his car was inside. "I don't think he's here," I said after a few seconds.

"Ring the bell again," she urged.

"Why don't you just go inside and see if he's there." I motioned toward the house with a tilt of my head. "He can't accuse you of breaking and entering, because he won't be able to see you."

Charlotte sat on the porch step. "No, I don't want to do that. After all, I am a Southern lady. I'll stay out here."

I scowled. "Oh, really? Were you a Southern lady when you peeked at Detective Valentine in the dressing room?"

"That was different. I didn't know him. Spying on a stranger is different from invading the privacy of a friend."

Her logic evaded me, but I didn't want to argue. "Whatever."

I did as I was told and rang the doorbell again. Just as I was about to insist on leaving, I heard the clicking of the lock from the other side of the door.

I looked at Charlotte in surprise. "I guess he's home after all."

She twisted her hands.

Why was she so nervous about seeing him again?

Bud was a tall, outdoorsy-looking man with a weathered face and pleasant laugh lines around his mouth and eyes. Gray hair sprinkled the temples of his dark hair. When he opened the door his eyebrows shot up. "Well, hello there. What can I do for you? It's not every day that a pretty lady shows up at my door." He smiled, flashing his intensely white teeth.

"I forgot to tell you that he is a huge flirt," Charlotte offered.

Now she told me. Bud Butler was exactly how I'd pictured him in my mind. His brown trousers had precise seams pressed down the front and the rolled-up sleeves of his white shirt exposed his tan forearms.

"Hello, my name is Cookie Chanel. I own the vintage clothing shop on Main Street. Maybe you've seen it—It's Vintage, Y'all?" He looked blank, so I hurried on. "I'm sorry for bothering you, but I'd like to talk to you about Charlotte Meadows. She was a friend of my grandmother's, and I was told that you were a friend of hers, as well. Could I talk to you about her?"

His expression faltered, but then he smiled again.

"See, I told you he was a nice guy," Charlotte said.

"Yes, I knew Charlotte well," Bud said. "She was a wonderful woman."

Charlotte let out a little giggle. "He has good taste."

"What do you need to know?" He looked me up and down, taking in every inch of my appearance. "You know, you dress a lot like Charlotte used to."

"I got my love of vintage clothing from my grandmother. She used to love to go shopping in Charleston with Charlotte. She always said Charlotte had the best eye for fashion."

Charlotte tapped her foot. "Come on, get to the point. Ask him if he's talked to the police."

Before I could say anything else, Bud opened the door wider and said, "Well, any friend of Charlotte's is a friend of mine. Same goes for any granddaughter of a friend of Charlotte's. Would you like to come inside for iced tea?"

I looked over my shoulder at Charlotte as she inched up behind me. Bud probably wondered what I was looking at.

"Yes, I'd like that. Thank you." I stepped inside the entrance to the foyer.

On the right was a small living room sparsely decorated in shades of blue and brown, but uncluttered and orderly. Knickknacks lined up like flea market trophies on the floor-to-ceiling bookshelves.

"He's a neat freak," Charlotte said.

Bud gestured toward the sofa and I sat on the edge.

"I'll get that tea and be right back," he said with a huge smile.

Charlotte followed him into the kitchen, leaving me alone in the living room. And she'd acted as if she wasn't even going into his house. I knew she wouldn't be able to resist once she saw him again.

I looked around at the photos on the side table. The images were all of Bud in various recreational activities—boating, skiing, and fishing. I assumed he had friends, so why were they not in the pictures with him? Why didn't he have a photo of Charlotte on the table?

I heard the refrigerator door open and close, the rattle of ice cubes tossed into glasses, and then he stepped back into the room. His eyebrows drew together in a frown and he spun around when Charlotte attempted to pinch him in the rear. Thank goodness she hadn't successfully made that move when I was near him. He would have thought I was making a pass at him.

He faced me again and chuckled. "I thought my pants caught on something."

Bud handed me an iced tea in a frosted beer mug. A nice manly touch, I thought. He'd even added a wedge of lemon on the edge of the glass. I took a sip and puckered my lips. It was so sweet that it must have contained a pound of sugar.

"So what do you want to ask me?" He sat on the sofa next to me, apparently feeling that his charm made him irresistible.

A chair was across from the sofa. Why did he have to sit so close?

I scooted away from him as far as I could. "I'm trying to make sense of what happened to Charlotte." She snorted, but I continued. "It's so upsetting. Who could do such a thing?"

"Oh, you were close? She never mentioned you." Bud patted my hand.

I moved my hand away from his touch. "Yes, we were friends. Um, she liked to stop by my vintage boutique in town."

I hoped Charlotte was listening. I wasn't happy that she'd never come into my shop.

"Well, that makes sense. I never really understood her fascination with clothing," he said.

Charlotte sat on the leather recliner in the corner, crossing her legs and placing her hands in her lap. "He never wanted me to dress him, either. I guess you can see why he needed my help."

I glanced over at his clothing. Actually, his casual attire seemed just fine to me.

"Do you like the photos of me?" Bud leaned over, stretching his body across mine, and picked up the photo of him on the beach.

I leaned back until he straightened up away from me.

"What do you think of my abs? Pretty good shape for an old guy, huh?" he said with a smile.

I looked at Charlotte, who had a scowl on her face. She muttered, "What does she care if you're in good shape?"

I was growing more uncomfortable by the moment. "Yes, you look very fit. Anyway, back to the topic. Do you know who would have done such a terrible thing to Charlotte?" I pressed.

He took a drink of his tea. "She had a lot of business affairs. I suspect it had something to do with that."

"Ask him about the police," Charlotte instructed.

"Have you talked with the police?" I asked, to appease her.

"Yes, I spoke with them. They had the nerve to

question me about where I'd been on the night of her murder."

"And what did you tell them?" I asked.

He avoided answering. "Did you see the photo of me doing my karate?" He reached toward another picture frame.

Before he could lean across me again, I jumped up from the sofa and placed the glass of tea on the table. "Well, thank you for the hospitality. I just remembered I have an appointment."

Bud stood and moved closer to me. He wiggled his eyebrows as he leaned down. "How about we grab something to eat? Do you like seafood? Bubba's has fresh oysters brought in every day." He had been a complete schmuck without even realizing it.

"I'm not hungry." Dashing across the room, I grabbed the doorknob.

"Well, don't leave mad. I didn't mean any offense. I was just trying to be nice," he said.

Charlotte shook her fist at him. "Bud Butler, I can't believe you."

I glanced back at him. When he wiggled his eyebrows again, I'd had enough. I yanked the door open and took off down the sidewalk toward my car. Halfway down the front path I stumbled on the uneven flagstones, but righted myself before I fell.

Out of the corner of my eye, I spotted Charlotte stomping along beside me. "I can't believe you dated this guy," I whispered.

"Obviously, good men are hard to find," she said in disgust.

Didn't I know it.

I jumped in the car, feeling bad for her. She'd obviously liked the guy. "I'm sorry, Charlotte."

"I can't believe that jerk. Why did I ever date such a snake? And why couldn't I realize what a skirt-chaser he was?"

"Don't blame yourself," I offered as I turned the ignition. "It's not your fault he's a rat."

Bud was standing at the front door with his arms up like he was shocked that I'd taken off.

I was glad that I had a full day of work ahead to make me forget about talking with that polecat. Could he be the killer? He didn't seem too concerned about what had happened to Charlotte. All he'd wanted to talk about was himself.

"Bud was always talking and joking with other women." Tension tightened Charlotte's face. "I always thought he was just outgoing. I thought it was innocent. Now I know the truth." She looked at me from the passenger seat. "Do you think he could have killed me?" Her expression grew bleak.

As I pulled out onto the street, I said, "I don't know, Charlotte. I'd like to think it wasn't possible, but I just don't know."

Chapter 19

Cookie's Savvy Vintage Fashion Shopping Tip

*Don't forget to check with family members
when looking for clothing.
A great aunt or grandmother could have beautiful
garments just sitting in a closet waiting for you.*

Two hours had passed since the last customer
had exited the shop without buying anything. I
was sitting behind the counter watching Wind
Song as she slept in the sunshine. Her tail wagged
even though her eyes were shut. I had a feeling
she knew that I was watching her. The cat had an
uncanny ability to understand what was going on
around her.

Charlotte popped up beside me. After the visit
to Bud, she'd been quiet all day. I couldn't say that
I blamed her.

"I promised that I'd help you with marketing, so
how about we get started?" Even though she was
upset, she was keeping her promise of helping me
write up an ad for the shop. She could have easily
put it off, but she was forging ahead.

I folded a Jimi Hendrix T-shirt. "I suppose that would be good." I kept a stock of vintage rock star tees to attract younger customers to the shop.

If Charlotte had been alive she would have worn a path in the floor in front of the counter. "You definitely need to start online sales, too. We can find a simple website that allows you to add the BUY feature to your site and helps you accept payments, too." She eased down on the settee. "Plus, we need to work on the design of your website."

I looked at the computer screen. My website was simple—white with a logo of a pink fifties dress at the top. I'd figured the clean layout would be a breeze for customers to navigate. "What's wrong with my site?"

She shook her head. "It's not flashy enough."

I adjusted the computer screen for a better look then placed my hands on my hips and glared at her.

"Don't just stand there with your mouth open. Grab a pen and paper and write this stuff down. I'll expect you to do what I tell you to." She pushed to her feet. "I'll harass you in the middle of the night if you don't."

I knew she would, so I grabbed the pen and paper.

Charlotte stood beside me. "We'll do the ad first. Write this down. Find timeless fashion at It's Vintage Y'all. Styles from the twenties through the nineties. One of a kind, just like you."

After telling me what to write on the newspaper

ad, she gave me the name of sites where I could set up a better page for the shop.

I didn't know how I'd missed the bell on the door jingle, but apparently I had. When I looked up, Detective Valentine was standing in front of me with the strangest look on his face.

I couldn't tell how long he'd been standing there listening to me talk with Charlotte.

Since she was invisible and inaudible to everyone but me, he must have figured I was insane. Not only would he think I was involved in her murder, but that I was nuts, too. On top of that, it was hard to ignore how handsome he looked in his black pants and white dress shirt.

He looked around to see who I was talking to. Unfortunately, I had no one to save me. But then I remembered Wind Song. Thank goodness for my fabulous feline friend.

I chuckled. "I guess you're wondering who I was talking to."

He attempted a smile and held up his hands. "Hey, it's none of my business."

"I was talking to the cat."

As if on cue, Wind Song leaped onto the counter and rubbed her head against my hand. It was as if she'd come to my rescue. She'd definitely get an extra treat for that.

A smile spread across Dylan's face. "What a beautiful cat." He reached out and rubbed her head.

Wind Song stretched out on the counter, closed her eyes, and purred. Her tail moved slowly back and forth as her satisfaction grew.

"I think she likes you," I said.

He smiled and for a moment his tough exterior broke. It was as if I'd gotten a glimpse of the man inside. But why was he in the shop again? My heart sped up. Had he somehow found out that I'd been to talk with Bud Butler?

"What can I do for you, Detective?" I asked, trying to sound casual.

"He's just poking around again, that's all. He suspects you of something. I think it's funny that he can't figure it out." Charlotte walked a complete circle around him.

He looked as if he'd felt her presence, but he didn't mention it. "I just stopped in as a follow-up. Don't worry. It's just routine."

"Why would I worry?" I tried to sound nonchalant.

"Yes, well, I just wanted to know if you'd remembered anything about the other day when you discovered the body. Sometimes a couple days pass and a person's memory is sparked."

I shut my laptop. "I wish I could help you, but I don't have any other details."

He stepped aside uncomfortably.

I saw that Charlotte was touching his arm and scowled.

He noticed my expression, probably thinking again that I was slightly kooky. "Well, thank-you for everything. You know how to find me if you think of anything."

I threw my hand up in a wave. "I'll make sure to call you if I think of anything."

The bell above the door jingled as he left.

"He thinks I'm kooky," I said when he'd walked out the door.

"Don't worry about what he thinks. All guys are jerks, anyway." Charlotte had soured on the male species since watching her boyfriend flirt with me. But why did Dylan keep coming around?

Chapter 20

Heather's Heartfelt Tip
for Getting Rid of an Unwanted Ghost

Become an annoying roommate.
A ghost probably won't hang around if you crank up
the speakers and sing along as loud as you can.

After closing the shop, I pointed the car in the direction of Cindy Johnson's house.

Since Cindy had talked with the private investigator at the meeting the night before he died and had acted as if she knew him quite well, I decided to ask her what she knew about him.

"Are you going to tell me what your falling out with Cindy was about? It can't just be because of the charity." As I navigated the car down the road. I pulled down the visors against the glare of the bright, late-afternoon sun.

My ghostly passenger stared straight ahead. "Oh, I guess it's not important."

"Not important? How can you say that? She was talking with the private eye who was asking about

you. You added her to your list, you know. I think
sharing the story is a little pertinent."

She shifted in the seat. We were leaving the
downtown area, approaching the gracious old
neighborhood of Shady Elms. Streets were wide
and tree-lined, and multi-story homes set back on
spacious lots.

"Marie told me that Cindy was being accused of
stealing money from the charity, so I poked around
and found proof," Charlotte said.

"How did you find the proof?" I asked.

"Let's just say I was in her house."

I was completely intrigued.

We pulled up in front of Cindy's house and I
hopped out. The white two-story Georgian was
surrounded by a white picket fence. Flowers spilled
out from the window boxes and daffodils lined
the front path. Cindy had gotten the house in the
divorce. I'd heard she'd tossed her ex-husband's
belongings out onto the street. Cindy and her ex
had a daughter in college. I wondered how often
the girl came home for a visit. I rang the doorbell
and waited.

Luckily, within a few seconds, Cindy opened the
door. "Oh, hello." Her eyes opened wide. "I wasn't
expecting you. Is everything okay?"

I'd never been to Cindy's home before, so I
could understand why she was surprised to see me.

She wore a casual pair of beige linen trousers
and a lovely aqua-colored silk blouse. The color
brought out the blue in her eyes. I'd seen the
blouse in the window of the clothing boutique
down the street from mine.

"I hope I didn't come at a bad time." I smiled.

"Um, no, I guess not. Would you like to come in?" she asked hesitantly. She tucked a strand of her blond hair behind her ear.

"She's acting suspicious already," Charlotte said from behind me.

Cindy was acting a bit strange, but I wasn't ready to call her the killer just yet. As I stepped into the room, she picked up pages from the newspaper strewn around the coffee table and gestured for me to have a seat. I eased down onto a yellow plaid chesterfield sofa, hoping that this visit went better than the one with Bud.

She twirled a large topaz ring around her finger but didn't say anything. Apparently, she was waiting for me to speak first.

I cleared my throat and asked, "I guess you're wondering why I'm here."

She eased down onto the yellow upholstered chair beside the sofa. "The thought had crossed my mind. Does it have something to do with the committee?"

I leaned forward on the sofa. "No, I want to ask you about Charlotte Meadows. You knew her, right? She was the Sugar Creek woman who was murdered recently."

Cindy straightened in her seat and her expression stiffened. "Yes, I knew her. Why do you ask?"

I had to think of something quickly.

"Tell her we were friends. She won't know the difference," Charlotte said.

After a pause, I said, "We were friends."

Cindy had a surprised expression. "Oh. Well, what did you want to ask me?"

"I saw you talking with the private investigator. You do know that he was murdered, too, right?" I searched her face for a reaction.

Her expression turned bleak. "Yes, I'm aware of that." She shifted in her seat as if the mere mention of what had happened made her want to get up and run away.

"I saw you speaking with him at the meeting. What did he want?"

Cindy frowned. "He was just asking me about Charlotte's murder."

"What did he ask?" I pressed.

Her expression turned more frustrated. She looked as if she was searching for just the right words. I knew by her reaction that no matter what she said, I wouldn't believe her.

"He asked me if I knew her. That's all." She twisted a strand of hair around her index finger.

"What did you tell him?"

"I told him that I knew her from the charity, and nothing more." She spoke with a quiet certainty.

"Why do you think he was looking for information about Charlotte?" I asked.

"She's being awfully hostile," Charlotte's expression was shadowed with suspicion. "But then again, that's nothing new for Cindy."

"How should I know? Charlotte Meadows was probably into some shady business and now someone wants to collect money from her estate." Cindy's full lips thinned in frustration.

"Why, if I wasn't a ghost I would snatch her

hair out. Let me at her." Charlotte stepped over to Cindy and swung a punch, then another. Fortunately, she was a ghost and nothing was making contact.

Every time Charlotte punched, Cindy frowned and looked around. I was sure she was sensing something.

Charlotte stopped swinging punches through the air long enough to say, "Cookie, get over here and punch this woman right now."

My patience was fading. I couldn't tell Charlotte that she needed to calm down, so my expressions would have to do.

"Do you feel something strange in the air?" Cindy rubbed her arms as if fending off a cold chill.

"No, I don't feel anything. Are you okay?" I wondered if she sensed my uneasiness.

Cindy tried to smile, but it fell flat. "I guess the air conditioner is set at the wrong temperature. I felt a chill."

"It seems a little hot in here to me."

Charlotte flashed a smug smile. At least she'd calmed down for the time being.

Cindy turned and looked in the general direction where Charlotte stood. I couldn't tell if she was looking at Charlotte or if she was looking out the big front window.

Cindy jumped up. "I forgot something in the kitchen." She hurried out of the room.

Charlotte sat on the arm of the sofa. "What did I tell you? That woman is wacky."

I leaned over and tried to peek into the kitchen

to see what she was up to. "I don't see her," I whispered.

Several minutes passed and Cindy hadn't returned. I looked around the room. Her bookcases were full of historical fiction. I spotted a tattered old volume of *Gone With the Wind* and opened it. To my surprise, it was from the first printing—a real collectible. "What is she doing?" Charlotte asked.

"I don't know," I whispered. "But I'm going to find her." I stepped through the small hallway, through the dining room, and into the kitchen. It was silent except for the faint ticking of a clock hanging next to the bay window.

Charlotte walked right behind me as I looked around. The space was immaculately clean. It didn't look as if Cindy had forgotten anything on the stove, but the back door was open a little. "I think she left." I looked at Charlotte.

"I don't see hide nor hair of her," Charlotte agreed.

"Do you think she saw you?" I asked.

Charlotte leaned down and studied a framed photo of Cindy wearing a hoop skirt at last year's Spring Fling. "I think she's just crazy."

I knew Cindy wasn't in another area of the house because she had to pass through the living room to get to any of the other rooms. Maybe she had just stepped outside for some fresh air, but why hadn't she said so? Why leave me alone in her house? I stepped over to the back door and looked out. Cindy's car, a white Toyota Avalon, was gone. It had been in the driveway when I parked mine.

What kind of mess had I gotten myself into? Just when I thought things couldn't get any stranger, a car door slammed at the front of the house. Charlotte and I moved forward at the same time.

"Maybe it's Cindy," I said.

We hurried across the kitchen floor, made our way through the dining room, and to the window in the living room. A man was walking up the sidewalk, all businesslike.

I didn't recognize him. "Someone's coming,"

Charlotte peeked out. "He's coming to the door."

A black sedan was parked along the curb, and I knew we were in trouble.

The tall, lanky man wearing a brown suit seemed intent on carrying out his mission—whatever that was. He pounded on the door and rattled the knob as if he was trying to break the door down.

Charlotte and I exchanged another panicked look. I wasn't sure why she was worried—she was already dead. I was the one who had to worry about being harmed or even murdered.

"Let's get out of here." I raced toward the kitchen so I could slip out the back.

I'd almost reached the door when another man popped up. He had dark hair and wore a suit like his companion, but he was stocky. Thank goodness he didn't see me. I had to stop myself from letting out a loud scream. I ran back toward the living room, but the first man was still pounding on the door.

"Go in the bedroom and hide," Charlotte ordered.

I ran down the hallway and turned into the first bedroom on the right. As quietly as I could,

I shut the door and wove around the cherry bed to the closet. How would I explain to Cindy if she found me hiding in her closet? But she had a lot of explaining to do—like why she'd taken off and left me in her home, and who were the men trying to break in.

I tried to slow my breathing as I stood in the pitch-black closet. Hangers and what I hoped was a fur coat hung in my face.

"I can't believe the size of this closet. It's so small," Charlotte whispered.

I clutched my chest. "Don't do that to me."

A loud crash rang out and I knew that meant only one thing—the men had entered the home.

Chapter 21

Cookie's Savvy Vintage Fashion Shopping Tip

❧❦❧

Don't be afraid to try fashion from different eras.
You might be surprised which ones are your favorites.

My heart raced. I tried not to move an inch so that I wouldn't make a noise. If they heard me and discovered I was hiding in the closet, I'd be toast.

The men's voices carried down the hall, but I couldn't make out what they were saying.

Their footsteps echoed around the house and I heard a lot of crashing noises. They were definitely looking for something.

When I heard footsteps enter the bedroom, I held my breath. Of course, that only lasted a few minutes before I had to exhale. Could they hear my breathing?

It sounded as if they were pulling out drawers, and I realized that they would most likely open the closet door, too. Would I be able to get past them and run away? I wasn't sure I was willing to give that plan a shot. I'd have to come up with something else.

I moved to my left and hid behind some clothing.

Footsteps sounded in front of the closet and then stopped. I held my breath and waited for the door to open, but it never happened. A few more seconds passed and the footsteps sounded as if the men were walking down the hallway. Had they really left? I'd seen that trick in the past. Just as I thought they'd left, I'd open the door only to discover that they were still standing right in front of me. But what other option did I have? I couldn't stay in the closet all day.

I moved to my right and fumbled in the dark for the doorknob. After finding my way, I twisted the knob and eased the door open. I peeked out and looked around. No one was in the room. I couldn't understand why the intruders hadn't opened the closet door. I didn't want to have a false sense of security as I eased out of the small closet, wondering if the men would grab me as soon as I stepped out of the room. Where was Charlotte? She didn't follow me out of the closet. I tiptoed across the room.

With my heart hammering, I slowly opened the bedroom door. I poked my head out, but didn't see her. Thank goodness the men were nowhere in sight. Mustering as much courage as I could find, I moved down the hall. At any moment, the men could pop up in front of me. I didn't know what I would do if that happened.

Turning the corner, I saw Charlotte standing in the living room. "Where have you been?"

"I wanted to see what the men were doing," she said.

"What did you find out?"

"Unfortunately, not much. They seemed to be looking for something."

"Do you think they were looking for me?" I was almost afraid to think about what would have happened if they'd found me.

"Why would they be looking for you in Cindy's house?" Charlotte asked.

"Maybe they saw me," I said.

She peered around the corner into the kitchen. "I think they were looking for Cindy or something that Cindy has."

My eyes widened. "Do you think so?"

She nodded. "They were opening drawers and stuff, so that tells me they were looking for something."

"Well, at least they weren't looking for me. Let's get out of here before they come back." Had the men seen my Buick parked in front of Cindy's house? I was ready to get out of there when something registered in my mind.

"What?" Charlotte asked when she noticed that I had stopped moving.

"Cindy's computer was on in the sitting room off the bedroom," I said.

Charlotte quirked an eyebrow. "You're not thinking about checking her computer, are you? We don't have time."

"Well, the men are gone now." I peeked out the window again. The dark sedan was nowhere to be seen.

"What if they come back?" Charlotte asked.

"They think Cindy isn't here, so they probably won't come right back. We can hurry in, check out the computer, and get out before anyone comes back. If Cindy comes back, well, I'll just sit in here. She'll think I never left." I smiled.

"Well then, let's do it." Charlotte winked as if giving me permission to proceed.

I tiptoed across the room as if someone would actually hear me. I looked to my left and right for any sign of the men. I was scared, of course, but if I wanted to figure out any clues it was something I had to do. We made it back down the hallway and stepped into the bedroom.

"Okay. Just do this." Charlotte pointed toward the computer that sat on a desk in the corner of the room.

The screensaver was frozen, but I tapped the keyboard, and the screen lit up. A little box popped up wanting the password.

"Okay. Let's go." Charlotte motioned.

"No, no. Wait. Maybe I can figure out the password," I said.

"How will you ever do that?" she asked.

"Maybe Cindy used a word that I can guess."

Charlotte scoffed. "Yeah, fat chance of that happening."

I typed in a couple words, but nothing happened. Charlotte tapped her foot impatiently.

"What is her cat's name?" I pointed at the photo on the desk of Cindy holding a cat in her arms.

Charlotte tapped her finger against her chin. "Let me see. What was the name of her cat? Buttons." She shook her head. "No. Boots? No, that's not it. I got it. The name was Marmalade."

"That's a far cry from Buttons or Boots, Charlotte," I said.

She drummed her fingers on the desk. "Just enter it in and see what happens."

I typed in the word and hit enter. The screen changed.

"Bingo. People really shouldn't use their pet's names as passwords." Before I had a chance to look at anything on the computer, a screen for a video chat popped up. This wasn't good.

"Quick, turn it off." Charlotte waved her hands. "Before something else happens."

I reached down to click it off, but I hit the wrong button. I was experienced with computers, so why was I having such a hard time? I guessed my nerves were making me clumsy. Sweat had broken out on my forehead and it felt as if I'd stuffed a bag of cotton into my mouth.

"It's dialing someone," I whispered. "What do I do now?" My voice was in a panic.

"I said shut it off." Charlotte pushed at the computer's power button, but of course nothing happened.

I reached over and started to shut the computer off completely, but a woman's face popped up on the screen. She looked familiar. Her gray hair was piled high on top of her head and she had bright blue eyes.

She scowled as she stared at us. "Who are you?"

I should recognize that scowl, but I couldn't place it. I was frozen as I stared at her. My mouth wouldn't work. No words came out.

"I asked who you are and why are you on my daughter's computer?" she repeated.

Oh no. We had contacted Cindy's mother. She would for sure tell Cindy about what we had done.

How would I get out of this mess? My mind was blank. I needed to think of something quickly before she called the police and reported that we'd done something to Cindy. Well, that *I* had done something since she couldn't see Charlotte.

"I'm a friend of Cindy's," I managed to say.

Her scowl deepened, and I finally recognized it. Cindy had that same scowl.

"Why are you using her computer?"

I couldn't blame her for that reaction. I would have felt the same way if a stranger had contacted me out of the blue.

"Cindy said I could use her computer," I said in my sweetest Southern drawl.

"Can you put Cindy on, please?"

"She just stepped out," I said. "I'm sure she'll be back soon."

"What is your name?" It was more of a demand than a question.

No way was I was providing her with my name. I decided to turn off the chat session. "My name is—" I clicked the button on the screen and her face disappeared.

Charlotte laughed. "You'd better hope that she never finds you."

"I hope she never does," I agreed as I jumped up from the chair and ran to the front door. I had to abandon my plan of snooping on the computer. After all that had happened, I was exhausted.

"We can't leave just yet," Charlotte huffed.

I stopped with my hand on the doorknob. "What are you talking about? If you want me to wait around for Cindy, that's not going to happen."

Charlotte peered out the living room window.

"No, I don't want you to wait for her. I need you to get something."

"What? You want me to steal something from Cindy's house?" I asked.

"You aren't stealing anything. This item was mine. Follow me." Charlotte glided off down the hallway until she reached the bedroom door. She gestured for me to join her. "Hurry up. The faster you do this, the quicker we can get out of here."

"I don't know what you're up to, but it can't be a good idea." I hurried down the hallway.

When I stepped into the room, Charlotte was beside the closet door. She touched the doorknob. "Open the door. I want to show you something."

"Is this some kind of trick? Are you going to lock me in the closet?"

She smoothed down the skirt of her dress. "You should know me better than that by now. Of course not."

I marched over to the door. "Okay, I'll do this, but if you lock me in there, I swear I'll find a way to get out and come after you with holy water or something."

"Oh, so now you think I'm a demon?" She clutched her chest. "I'm hurt."

"I'll know you're a demon if you lock me in that closet." I yanked the door open and backed away. "Okay, the door is open. Can we get out of here?"

Charlotte pointed at the back of the door. "See that scarf right there?"

I saw a green, blue, and white silk scarf draped over a hook. "Yes, I see it."

"That's my scarf."

"Okay. So what?"

"It shouldn't be here. I was wearing it the day that I was murdered." She reached toward the scarf.

I felt the color drain from my face. "Are you sure, Charlotte? If so, this is significant."

"I know. Grab the scarf and let's get out of here."

I didn't have time to think about it. I had to get out before Cindy came back and caught me in her bedroom. I grabbed the scarf and dashed out of the room.

Charlotte was already standing by the front door when I rounded the corner.

"How do you do that?" I asked breathlessly as I opened the door.

I didn't give her time to answer before I burst out onto the porch, not even bothering to close the door behind me. Heck, Cindy had left the back door open when she took off, so apparently she didn't care if her doors were locked. The sparrows chirping in the trees seemed to be mocking me as I jumped over the daffodils and sprinted across the front lawn.

How had Cindy gotten Charlotte's scarf unless she'd been in Charlotte's home?

"Cindy has to be my killer, right?" Charlotte asked as we peeled away from the curb.

I glanced in my rearview mirror, but there was no sign of the black sedan. "Not so fast," I warned. "We have no way to prove it."

"You have to tell the police." Charlotte's brows were arched in worry.

"I can't go to the police with this info. Detective Valentine is already suspicious of me."

"To think she took the scarf off my dead body." Charlotte shivered.

It was a disturbing thought. And I'd been in the woman's home. But who were the men who had obviously been searching for something?

Silence filled the car. Charlotte was upset by what had happened and the feeling was mutual. Wind whipped my hair as we cruised the highway with the top down. Strangely, Charlotte's hair didn't budge.

"What was it like when you—you know." I downshifted to slow for a slight curve.

"When I died?" Charlotte's voice didn't waver.

"Well, then and now. I mean, did you see some bright light?" I asked.

"To be honest, I don't know. I don't remember anything after it happened. I didn't see my attacker and the next thing I knew I was dead." The corners of Charlotte's mouth tugged downward.

"How did you know you were dead?"

An unexpected vulnerability sounded in her voice. "I just knew. I don't know how I knew."

"Was it hard getting used to it?"

"You should have seen me the first time I tried to touch something and my hand went right through." She looked at her hand as if surprised that she could see through its misty shape. "You could have knocked me over with a feather."

"I bet that was a strange feeling."

Charlotte patted my hand. "I want to thank you for your help. I know I can be demanding, but I really do appreciate it. You're just like your grandmother, you know—a real friend."

I figured this was as close as I'd ever get to witnessing the softer side of Charlotte. But I knew she was being sincere.

"I feel like we haven't made much progress, but I won't give up," I assured her. "I know there has to be a connection between your murder and the private investigator's death. Right now, we need to pick up Wind Song at the shop, then go home. I need some sleep. In the morning, I'll figure out what to do next."

Chapter 22

*Heather's Heartfelt Tip
for Getting Rid of an Unwanted Ghost*

*If being a bad roommate doesn't work,
try to befriend the ghost.
A friendly ghost is better than a hostile one.*

The sun shone across my eyes. I blinked, opening my lids and looking around the room. Charlotte stood in front of my bed. Wind Song was sitting on the floor, licking her paws.

"Well, it's about time you woke up. Hop up and get dressed. Let's get a move on." Charlotte motioned.

I sat up in bed. "Whoa, not so fast. I have an estate sale this morning."

When I glanced at the clock I saw that I'd overslept. *Great.* All the bargains would be gone. I jumped out of bed in a panic and fed Wind Song. She graciously accepted the Seared Polynesian Sardines in Lobster Sauce that I'd found in the gourmet aisle of Pets Please.

I dressed quickly. The temperature was supposed to be hotter than usual, so I decided on a pair of fifties Roberta Di Camerino leopard print pedal pushers, a white halter that appeared to be hand-made, and black wedge heels. I grabbed my black Cartier clutch I'd gotten at an estate sale for next to nothing that was one of my better finds.

I headed out the door and down the front steps. As usual, Charlotte was waiting for me in the car. I didn't have time to put the top down or to drop off Wind Song, so I'd have to come back for her after the sale. Watching us from the living room window sill, she didn't look pleased about being left behind.

The sale was all the way across town. Preoccupied with my thoughts, I had no idea what Charlotte was chatting about for the entire ride.

The next thing I knew, we'd pulled up in front of the two-story brick home. A modest-sized house compared to Charlotte's, it was still big as far as I was concerned. I climbed out from behind the wheel and hurried up the driveway, speeding past several people.

"It doesn't look like they have much here. You should just give up before wasting any time. We can get back to my case," Charlotte said as she followed me toward the house.

I talked out of the side of my mouth in case anyone was watching. "I can't talk to you while I'm in this house. People will think I'm crazy. I don't need that kind of rumor going on around town. And I have to go to work after this. Remember that store that I have all my money invested in? If my shop doesn't produce an income, I will be starving and homeless, and so will Wind Song. Plus, I heard there were some great bargains to be found here."

"If you say so," Charlotte said.

Little had I known when I'd gone to the last estate sale that I'd suddenly find myself with an otherworldly companion and a psychic cat. And that *that ghost* would be following me around at the next sale.

I made my way around the first floor, looking through the clothing and odds and ends. After a little searching, I picked up a super-cute vintage eighties strapless black party dress with white polka dots. It had a gathered bodice and peplum ruffle-tiered skirt. Pairing it with the right current-style shoes would give it a modern twist. It might go for a small fortune in my shop. Getting it for a good price would make the whole trip worthwhile.

Since I had been born in the eighties, it was hard to label anything from that era as vintage, but sadly, it was already in that classification.

Holding the party dress, I moved on to another rack of clothing. Charlotte followed closely, offering her advice. I tuned her out, wanting the fun of making my own fashion choices.

On that rack, I found a pink cocktail dress. I wandered a little and picked up a Gucci wallet and a pair of green spike-heeled Jimmy Choo sandals. All great finds.

My next discovery practically made me swoon. It was a fifties swimsuit by Catalina. I picked up the navy-colored suit and realized that it still had the tags. After all these years, no one had worn it. I couldn't believe my luck. The suit was in amazing condition and made of a cotton blend. It had a pique fold-over cuff. The sweetheart neckline was trimmed with tiny white bows. "Look what I found," I whispered, unable to hide my excitement.

"Wow. Cookie, that is an amazing find. Can we go now?" Charlotte checked the delicate watch on her wrist.

Way to rain on my vintage clothing parade. I gathered up the items I'd chosen and headed for the cash register. "Fine, we'll go."

When I reached the door, I spotted the woman who had been collecting money at Charlotte's sale. Her snow white hair was styled close to her head like a little helmet. She was petite, even shorter than me at probably about five foot. She wore a gray T-shirt with cats on the front and a pair of denim pedal pushers. I recognized her right away, but would she recognize me?

Probably not, since she saw a lot of people at these events.

She told me the cost of my items, and I handed her the cash. "You were at the other sale that I went to recently."

She studied my face.

"It was for Charlotte Meadows," I reminded her.

Her eyes widened. "Oh yes, I remember seeing you."

I smiled. "This sale isn't as crowded as the last one."

"Yes, well, Ms. Meadows had a lot of lovely things."

"Of course I had a lot of nice things. I had great taste," Charlotte said with a smile.

The woman counted out the money I gave her and handed me my change. "My name is Ednah

White, by the way. What happened with that crazy woman?"

I frowned. Did she mean Charlotte?

"She'd better not be talking about me." Charlotte tapped her foot against the floor.

"What crazy woman?" I asked.

"The woman who bumped into you. Remember? You were on your way out the door and she wanted to buy the clothing from you," Ednah said.

"Wow, she heard the whole conversation," Charlotte said.

And I had thought she hadn't been paying attention.

"She's something else, huh?" the woman continued. "Why, she went around to everyone that day trying to figure out what they'd bought, wanting to purchase their items, too. I thought I was going to have to call the police. Some people may have called them for all I know. It wouldn't have surprised me in the least."

"What do you mean? She was following people around?" I asked.

"You heard what the woman said," Charlotte said. "Marie has finally lost it."

Ednah pulled out a piece of candy from her purse and popped it into her mouth. "Yes, she was angry. I think she was looking for specific items. Apparently, she thought you'd purchased whatever she had been looking for. She got worse after you left. I heard her complaining."

This woman liked to eavesdrop.

"What did she think I'd bought?" I asked.

Ednah twisted the candy around in her mouth. "That I don't know."

With all the eavesdropping she'd done, I thought she would have found out that detail.

"Just look out for her. I think she's crazy," Ednah warned.

"Yeah, thanks." I turned to leave. Clutching my new acquisitions under my arm, I hurried toward the car with Charlotte gliding beside me, as usual.

As I drove away down the quiet tree-lined street, I noticed that I wasn't the only one heading back downtown. A black sedan drove along behind me, and I knew right away that it was following me. Another black car was back there, too.

I strained to look into the rearview mirror and not wreck. "Can you see that car back there?"

Charlotte peeked in the mirror. "The black one?"

"Yes, the one that is following dangerously close." My hands grasped the steering wheel tighter.

"Yes, I see it. What do they want?" Charlotte asked.

"That's what I want to know."

Chapter 23

Cookie's Savvy Vintage Fashion Shopping Tip

You can easily mix the old with the new.
Vintage items look great when paired with new clothing.

"Can you see who is driving the car?"

Charlotte turned around in the seat and peered toward the road behind us. "Maybe I'm wrong and I hope I am, but it looks a lot like one of the men who broke in to Cindy's home yesterday. I think the other man is in the car, too."

My stomach dropped. "This is not good. What about the car behind that? Doesn't that look like Detective Valentine's car?" I asked, gesturing behind us.

Charlotte peered behind us again. "Uh-huh. It is him."

"Why is he following me, or is he following the men behind me? Maybe he's following all of us," I said in a bit of a panic. "What do I do now?"

"How should I know? I've never had a car follow me before," Charlotte said.

I glanced in the rearview mirror every couple seconds. "Okay. Since the detective is also behind me, I'll just act like nothing is wrong. I'll drive to the store and act as if it's no big deal that a car with two strange men is following me."

Charlotte straightened in the seat. "Good idea."

When I reached the stop sign at Greenbriar Avenue, I had second thoughts. I'd made it to downtown Sugar Creek, and knew that I had to do something different. The Piggy Wiggly came into view. It was closer than my shop, so I decided to pull in. The dark sedan with the two men turned in behind me.

"They're still following you," Charlotte said. "Wait until they see the policeman. Then they'll have a change of heart."

I clutched the steering wheel tighter. "Maybe they're the police just like Dylan."

"That's a good thing, right?"

"Not if I'm in trouble. Do you think he suspects me? Maybe he found out that I was really in your house."

"Try to remain calm." Charlotte touched my arm.

"Easy for you to say." I drove across the parking lot.

"Okay. Let's talk about something else. It'll help your nerves."

"What do you want to talk about?" I asked.

"Well, how about finding my killer?"

"That's not a huge variation from the last topic." I steered to the left.

"I'm telling you there has to be a way to find my

killer. Someone had to have seen something."
Charlotte looked out the window.

"I wouldn't be so sure about that. After all, you
didn't see your murderer." I clutched the steering
wheel.

"Touché," Charlotte said.

The parking lot of the Piggly Wiggly was packed.
After circling twice, I whipped into a spot several
aisles away from the entrance. "With any luck, they
won't follow us into the store. They can't arrest me
in a store, right?"

"Wrong," Charlotte said matter-of-factly.

As I hurried across the parking lot, Charlotte
warned me. "They're parking in the back row."

I reached the store's entrance. As far as everyone was concerned, I was alone on my shopping
trip, but of course, Charlotte went in with me. What
would they say if they knew I was with a ghost?

Instrumental music played over the speakers.
The steady beep from the cash registers flowed
across the store. As usual, an arctic blast of air
made me wish I'd worn a winter coat.

"Did the men come into the store?" Charlotte
asked.

"I don't know. What will we do if they did?" I
peered around a potato chip display to check left
and right.

"I guess we'll have to fight them off if they attack,"
Charlotte said.

"*We'll* have to fight them off? How will you be
part of that?" I motioned from me to her. "It'll
be two against one—me."

Charlotte stood beside the tower of mayonnaise
jars on display at the end of the aisle. "You are just

being dramatic. They probably won't even come in here. I bet they're halfway across town by now. They probably weren't even following you in the first place."

"Yeah, right," I said. "Then why were they parking at the Piggly Wiggly? To pick up some Goo Goo Clusters?"

Heading past an end cap full of granola bars, I tilted my head to the side and noticed that the professional-looking men were checking me out from the produce section. How had they gotten inside so quickly? With their suits and ties they looked as if they were on official business.

When the men spotted me looking at them, they turned away.

"You should go over there and ask them what they want," Charlotte said.

"No way." I backed away on tiptoes. "They're like giant spiders. As long as they leave me alone, I'll leave them alone."

"That's just it. They're not leaving you alone, so you need to squish them." Charlotte smashed her hands together.

"I know one way to get rid of them."

"How's that?" Charlotte asked.

I motioned for her to follow me with a tilt of my head. "I'll lose them in the feminine products area."

Charlotte chuckled. "Good thinking."

"No way will they step into that aisle. Men freeze when they get near that section. It's as if some kind of invisible force shield is wrapped around it."

I glanced up at the signs above each aisle until I found the correct one. I glanced over my shoulder. The men weren't behind me.

Charlotte and I walked the length of the aisle, but the men weren't at the other end. Had I really lost them? Had it really been that easy?

"Do you think they're gone?" I whispered.

Charlotte didn't answer.

I stepped out from the aisle expecting to see them waiting for me right around the corner, but they weren't in sight. Thank goodness for small favors. "I think we lost them."

Would they be waiting for me when I went outside? I didn't think they'd do anything too crazy out in public. That was probably why they hadn't confronted me in the grocery store.

"I think you are safe now," Charlotte said. "Let's get on with this."

I still wasn't totally convinced that I was safe and hung out for just a few more minutes in the store to make sure.

Charlotte and I walked up and down the aisles, on the lookout for the strange men or Detective Valentine. We reached the pet section. I found the gourmet cat food and paused. "I'll buy some cat food so that we don't look so suspicious."

"You know you already look suspicious, right?" Charlotte replied.

She had a point. After all, I was technically talking to myself in the middle of the Piggly Wiggly.

The selection of fancy cat foods was bewildering. I pulled a few cans from the shelf, choosing the ones that sounded most like people food. They seemed to be the ones that Wind Song preferred.

Charlotte pointed toward the end of the aisle where a gray-haired woman wearing a mint green cotton dress was selecting a bag of cat food from the shelf. "Look, it's Bernice Roby. We were shopping together once and she tried to pretend the Depends in her cart weren't for her, but were mine. We all know they were hers."

I glanced at Bernice's shopping cart. She had Depends and cat litter.

"Will you stop gossiping," I whispered. "I do not know that the Depends are hers. She could be buying them for someone else—or to donate to the senior center. We'll all need them eventually, so who cares."

Bernice turned around and glared at me.

When she turned down another aisle, I said, "You're going to get me into trouble. Her shopping items are her business."

Charlotte surveyed the contents of my shopping cart. Once again she warned me. "You know, those diet drinks won't matter if you continue buying those potato chips."

And once again, I told her, "I like potato chips," I said.

Charlotte gestured toward me. And yet again, she had the last word. "It's your hips."

I ignored her comment and scanned the area. The coast seemed to be clear, so I rushed to the first open register and placed my items on the conveyor belt. Charlotte walked to the front door and waited for me to finish.

Once outside, I scanned the area and much to my relief, I didn't see the black sedan.

We walked toward the Buick. When I thought no one was looking, I said, "I think you should just let the police handle this case. I'm sure they're doing all that they can to find your killer.

I'm clearly not cut out for this. Strange men are following me now."

She snorted. "Oh, please. The police have other things to worry about other than finding my killer." Irritation filled her voice.

"Like what?" I asked.

"I told you before—eating doughnuts." She smirked.

"You shouldn't say such things." I took the bags from my cart.

"I said it once and I'll say it again. I'm not happy with them at the moment. Speaking of which, Detective Valentine is watching you from across the parking lot. He's not very good at his job if you ask me." She pointed across the parking lot.

"Are you sure he's watching me?" I asked.

"Oh yeah. I'm positive."

My curiosity won and I looked toward where Charlotte said the detective's car was parked.

Dressed in a red T-shirt and jeans, he unintentionally showed off his well-muscled arms as he leaned against the hood of his black car.

I stared, surprised to see him dressed so casually.

He looked over at me and quirked his eyebrow.

My stomach took a dive and my heart rate sped up. Why was I nervous? So what if the detective was looking at me? He couldn't possibly know I was talking to Charlotte or that I'd been to her house, right? She was a ghost. He couldn't see her. No one could but me.

After shoving the bags into the trunk, I climbed behind the wheel and took off. Not too fast, though. I didn't want to get a speeding ticket. I glanced in the rearview mirror and noticed that the detective was still watching as I pulled out of the parking lot.

"Why was he watching me?" I asked.

"Maybe because you acted as if you'd killed someone," Charlotte offered.

"Oh, that's preposterous," I said, trying to sound confident.

Chapter 24

Heather's Heartfelt Tip
for Getting Rid of an Unwanted Ghost

◆

If the ghost won't be your friend, you can try to ignore it.
I know I hate the silent treatment.
If someone gives me the cold shoulder, I won't stick around.

I pulled up in front of It's Vintage Y'all and turned off the ignition. I looked in the mirror, and much to my chagrin, the detective had pulled his Crown Vic right up behind my Buick. *Darn.*

"I told you that he wouldn't just let you drive off." Charlotte's voice was full of certainty.

I checked myself in the mirror. Hair a bit wild, but lipstick still intact. Okay, time to roll down the window. Sometimes I could almost wish for power windows. I cranked down the handle.

Detective Valentine leaned on the open window. "Good morning, Ms. Chanel. You're out early this morning."

Charlotte slipped out of the car. "I'm waiting inside the shop. I don't want to watch this train wreck."

She was abandoning me in my time of need.

I gave the detective my most wide-eyed, innocent look. "I could say the same about you. I couldn't help but notice that you were following me. Did I do something wrong? Was I speeding?"

He studied the interior of my car. "I think you know why I followed you."

My heart rate increased. "I have no idea what you're talking about."

I looked toward the shop, wishing that I could escape. Charlotte stood outside the car. I guess her curiosity got the best of her.

"I can help you if you'll just tell me the truth," he said.

How would I explain being inside Charlotte's house? My story sounded completely crazy. How could I look at him with his sexy blue eyes and tell him that I talked to a ghost? If I told him about the men who had followed me, I would have to explain *everything*.

"Were you at the estate sale today?" he asked. "I thought I saw you there."

"Of course I was at the sale. It's my job. So you were following me." I clutched the steering wheel.

His blue eyes seemed bright even in the sunlight. "I happened to be in the area. It just seems like something is off. I guess it's my instinct that tells me you aren't being completely honest with me."

It must have been his detective instincts.

"Did you see the car that was following me?" I asked.

He quirked a brow. "No, I didn't notice."

So much for his detective instincts. The car behind me seemed strange to say the least. I couldn't tell him that I'd seen the men in Cindy's house.

I needed to contact Cindy again and find out what had happened to her and why she'd taken off. Did she know those men?

"What was wrong with the car?" he asked.

"I think I saw the men before and . . . well, it was nothing." I brushed off the thought.

The detective was growing more doubtful by the minute.

I rattled on. "Oh, like I said, I was just being suspicious. I mean, after all, there have been two murders in Sugar Creek. I'm sure all residents are a little on edge."

He continued to lean down with his strong arms resting on the door. I knew that he didn't believe my story, but what could he do? I wasn't about to admit to anything.

"So you'd tell me if you were involved in something," he said.

"What could I possibly be involved in?" I tried to sound natural, but I didn't think it was working.

He opened my door and extended his hand to me. "Would you like to go for a walk?"

Was he sincere? Was he luring me away so he could arrest me? No, if that was the case he'd just go ahead and do it.

"Sure."

He stepped back as I swung my legs to the side—knees together, just as my grandmother had taught me—and got out, remembering to lock the door. He placed his hand on the small of my back and guided me to the sidewalk.

Acutely aware of his touch, I glanced back at Charlotte. She smiled.

I decided to find out more about Detective Valentine. "Are you new in Sugar Creek?"

He gave me a sideways glance. "Yes, I am new to this great town."

Was that it? He wasn't going to explain where he'd come from? This would be harder than I thought. Was there some reason why he didn't want to share any details about himself?

"Where are you from?" I asked.

"I'm from Atlanta. I worked there for a couple years." He steered me around a crevice in the sidewalk. "How about if we go into Billie Jean's Coffee and Such, down the street?"

Did he want to take me for coffee so he could ask more questions about the murder investigation?

"I've had my quota of caffeine for this morning." Noting the look of disappointment on his face, I went on. "But I guess I could go for a cup of herbal tea for a change." I'd barely agreed to go when his phone rang.

He held up his finger. "If you'll excuse me."

"Of course." I pretended to study the geraniums in front of the medical office where we were standing. They needed watering.

Dylan looked over at me as he hung up his phone. "I'm sorry that I can't get that coffee now. They need me at the station. Can I get a rain check?"

I wasn't sure if I was relieved or let down. "Sure. No problem."

He put a hand on my forearm. "You have my number if you need to talk, right?"

I smiled. "Yes, I'll call you."

Detective Valentine walked away. Reaching the car, he turned around and saw me watching him. I hurried back toward my shop.

Unable to resist, I peeked over my shoulder. Our eyes met for a moment, and he smiled as he drove off. I had to admit, I hoped we could talk about more than the investigation.

Chapter 25

Cookie's Savvy Vintage Fashion Shopping Tip

*If you're not ready to wear vintage clothing yet,
you could start with accessories like a scarf, hat, or jewelry.*

After racing back home to pick up Wind Song, I stepped into my shop, hoping that I hadn't missed any customers. She climbed out of her carrier, stretched, then made her way to her favorite spot in the sunshine.

"Why aren't you saying anything else?" I asked her as I looked over at the Ouija board.

Having that thing in the shop still made me nervous. I'd heard too many stories about evil spirits coming through. I wondered if that was really true but wasn't willing to find out.

After checking the paper for more estate sales, I turned on my computer to check my e-mail. Much to my chagrin, there was another comment on my blog waiting for me. Normally, I would have been excited to read it, but I was anxious. I clicked on the link and waited for it to pop up. My stomach dropped when I read the comment.

"What does it say?" Charlotte asked over my shoulder.

I moved to the side. "You can read it for yourself."

Charlotte read aloud, "I warned you to mind your own business. Now I'll have to stop you."

This was not good. I had to tell the detective what was happening. My life could be in jeopardy if I didn't.

Charlotte's brow creased with worry. "I'm so sorry, Cookie. I don't want you to be in harm's way, but you can see that I didn't have any other options. You were my only hope."

I could see that now. But why me? Why was I the only one who could see Charlotte? I closed the computer in a hurry. "I have to call the detective."

Charlotte tried to block me from grabbing the phone by stepping in front of me. "I don't think that is really necessary, is it?"

"I know you don't want to involve him, but I think this is over my head. After all, I'm just a boutique owner. I can't fend off a criminal. This could be a serial killer!"

Wind Song meowed and jumped up on the counter. She looked as if she wanted to be part of the conversation. As I was rubbing her head, the bell on the door jangled. I jumped and clutched my chest.

Heather walked through the door wearing an oversized tie-dyed T-shirt and black leggings. Her hair was braided in the back. "Hi, Cookie. Hi, Wind Song."

"What's buzzin' cuzzin'?" I asked.

Heather looked around. "Is Charlotte here, too?"

"She sure is. Right next to the windows, where she can spy on people."

"Well then, hi Charlotte, too." Heather flopped onto a stool. "Is everything okay?"

"What makes you think that everything isn't okay?" I asked with a forced smile.

She sorted through my new arrivals in jewelry that I'd placed on the counter. "I could tell by the look on your face."

I picked up a shiny necklace and showed it to her, hoping to distract her from what I was about to say. "I got another threatening message on my blog." I didn't tell her the full gravity of the message.

"You have to tell the police about this," she said, handing the necklace back.

I placed the silver pendant back on the display rack. "I plan on it."

I pulled out Detective Valentine's card and studied it. He'd said to call him if I thought of anything. What would he say when I told him about the messages?

Heather rubbed the cat's head and whispered, "Has she said anything else?"

I shook my head. "I don't think it's necessary to whisper."

Heather placed a deck of cards on the counter and tapped them with her electric blue polished fingertip. The top card featured a cat wearing a royal costume.

"What is that?" I asked.

"They're tarot cards. A deck of cat-themed tarot cards, to be specific."

"Heavens to Betsy. This should be interesting," Charlotte said.

"What are you doing with those?" My voice rose.

"Well, I'm hoping that the cat will respond to them as she did to the Ouija board." Heather looked over at Wind Song.

"You actually think the cat will use tarot cards?" I asked.

"She used the Ouija board, so I figured this was the next step," Heather said.

"So the cat is going to read our fortune?" I asked.

Charlotte said, "Oh my stars. If this don't beat all."

Heather stacked the cards on the counter. "Yes, that's what I'm saying."

"Well, I've got to see this." Charlotte sat on the chair next to the counter and crossed her legs.

Right on cue, Wind Song launched herself onto the counter and sat next to the deck of cards. Her big green eyes seemed full of fire.

"See. She already wants to use them." Heather pushed the cards in front of the cat and we waited. Wind Song inched her paw toward the deck, then pushed the cards until they fell to the floor.

Charlotte burst out in laughter as Wind Song jumped down.

"Charlotte is laughing," I said.

"That doesn't surprise me," Heather said.

Charlotte leaned down next to the cat. "You gave it your best shot, Wind Song."

Wind Song sat next to the spilled deck. With her

front paw, she reached forward, touching one of the cards. She pulled it away from the others, then placed her paw on two more and dragged them away from the deck. With remarkable agility, she then scratched an ear with her hind foot.

"I think she's done," Heather said.

"Done with what?" I asked.

"She picked out the cards. Now all I have to do is read them." Heather picked up the cards and spread them out on the counter.

Charlotte moved closer. "I have got to see this."

Wind Song commenced to lick her delicate paws. Her toes were pale pink, to match her nose. She didn't seem concerned with what we were doing—her job was already done. Heather turned the cards face up and studied them. Each card showed a cat dressed in an elaborate costume with gold and jewels.

"I can't believe you brought cat-themed tarot cards," I said.

"I thought they were fitting," Heather said with a smile.

"So what do the cards say?" I asked.

Heather tapped the first card. "Wind Song pulled out the Fool. That means she is trying to warn you of recklessness and risk-taking."

She studied the next card. "This is the Magician. It means that you should tap into your latent talents."

Wind Song moved from grooming her front paws to the back paws.

"Well butter my butt and call me a biscuit," Charlotte said.

Heather picked up the third card and placed it

in front of me. "This card is the lovers." She wiggled her eyebrows. "Maybe you'll meet someone soon."

"I certainly hope so," Charlotte said.

My cheeks turned red. "The cat is incredible! It's as if she knew exactly which cards were relevant to the situation."

The three of us stood next to Wind Song, unsure of what else to say. I knew one thing. I hadn't bought any of that cheap cat food since the Ouija board warning.

Chapter 26

*Heather's Heartfelt Tip
for Getting Rid of an Unwanted Ghost*

━◆━

*Burn white candles to surround yourself
with positive energy.
Again, don't forget the fire extinguisher.*

The next morning, I was busy dressing one of the mannequins in a lovely apple green colored Dior pantsuit when Detective Valentine entered the shop. It wouldn't have been a problem if he hadn't caught me talking to Charlotte again. Wind Song was nowhere in sight. How would I blame the cat?

He looked around the shop. "Talking to the cat again?"

I chuckled. "Yes, but it looks as if she disappeared without telling me."

I'd left the detective a message to call me as soon as possible, but I hadn't thought he would stop in the shop. I'd assumed he would just return my call.

It was time to tell him the truth. Well, maybe

I wouldn't tell him the part about talking to ghosts and cats.

He leaned against a rack of pillbox hats from a millinery shop that had gone out of business. "I just picked up your message this morning. It sounded like something was wrong." His blue eyes sparkled under the lights.

I finished fitting the jacket onto the mannequin and faced him. "Yes, there is something I need to tell you."

Charlotte piped up from my side, "You can always back out now. Don't tell him anything."

I ignored her. I knew telling him was something I had to do. "You asked why I was so concerned about Charlotte's death. Well, I was at Cindy Johnson's home the other day and I found something." I rushed my words.

He straightened. "What did you find?"

I walked over to the counter and reached underneath, retrieving the silk square scarf from my purse. I held it up. "I found this."

"And?" he asked.

"Charlotte was wearing this scarf the day she was murdered." I swirled it through the air for dramatic effect.

"I love that scarf. The deep emerald color with the gold diamond pattern is stunning." Charlotte's low voice carried memories from when she'd worn that scarf during happier times.

He stepped closer and took the item from my outstretched hand. "How do you know that she was wearing the scarf?"

Hmm. I hadn't thought this part through well enough. "Oh," I ad libbed, "because I saw her wearing it that day?" I hadn't meant for it to come out as a question.

"That was lame," Charlotte offered.

His strong jaw tensed. "You saw the victim on the day of her murder."

"Hey, I am not just a victim. I have a name," Charlotte said.

I didn't like lying, but what other option did I have? "Yes, that's right."

"Where did you see her?" he asked.

"Um, right here in my shop."

"Okay. Let's say she was wearing this scarf. What does that have to do with anything?" he asked.

I took the scarf from his hand. "I believe it was used to kill Charlotte."

He ran his hand through his thick dark hair as if that would make clear what I'd just told him.

"Uh-oh. I think you're in trouble now," Charlotte warned. "See, you should have kept this info to yourself."

She was probably right, but it was too late.

"And why do you think this was used to kill her?" He pointed at the scarf.

"Well, I happened to see it at Cindy's. How else would it have been there if not for the fact that it had been used to kill Charlotte?"

Unfortunately, now that I thought about it other possibilities came to mind. Cindy could have borrowed it from Charlotte. Or even stolen it. Or Charlotte could have lost it and Cindy picked it up to give back to her next time they saw each other. But Charlotte had never mentioned those possibilities—only I couldn't tell the detective that.

"I don't think he believes you," Charlotte said.

Why should he believe me? I'd made up this story and I knew it didn't sound right.

"Are you accusing Cindy Johnson of murdering Charlotte?" he asked. "That's a pretty strong accusation."

"Well, how else would she have gotten the scarf?" I asked.

He chuckled. "Did you ever think that maybe she had a scarf just like the one Charlotte Meadows was wearing?"

"It was a rare scarf. It was highly unlikely that Cindy Johnson would have one, too."

"You got him," Charlotte said.

He couldn't argue with that. If there was one thing I understood, it was clothing and he knew that. He might be the professional when it came to solving crimes, but I knew fashion, and those two things had crossed paths.

But I couldn't tell him why. Then he'd know I had been snooping around Cindy's home.

"I have to tell you, Ms. Chanel, this is a bit of a stretch. I can't accuse someone of murder just because you found a scarf. You did find the scarf, correct?" He touched the silk fabric one more time.

"Of course?" Once again my answer came out more as a question than an answer and I certainly didn't sound convinced.

"I don't think Detective Valentine is buying your story," Charlotte said.

Yeah, she didn't have to point that out.

"I appreciate you telling me all of this, but I think it's better if you leave the investigation to the police." His pushed the scarf across the counter toward me.

I was in too far to get out now, but I wouldn't tell him that. "You asked me to tell you the truth." Well, I'd almost told him the truth, but that was neither here nor there.

"Yes, and I appreciate that. If you think of anything else, don't hesitate to let me know."

Charlotte scoffed. "Yeah, right. So he can act like you are crazy."

"Are you sure there isn't something else you want to tell me?" he asked.

I glanced over at Charlotte. Could he see her, too? No, he wouldn't be able to keep that quiet.

"There was one other thing," I said.

His eyes widened. "Yes? I'm listening."

"There were strange men at Cindy's home."

"Don't tell him you were hiding in the closet," Charlotte said.

"I'm confused. Who were these people?" he asked.

"Cindy was acting weird, too. She took off when I was at her home and then the men showed up. I think they were looking for her. And I saw them behind me yesterday."

He pondered what I'd just told him. "Did you speak with the men?"

"No, I didn't want to get involved." I folded the scarf so that I could keep my fidgeting hands busy.

The cat weaved around Dylan's legs, purring as she made the loop.

"Don't you think it's a little late for that?"

"What? I'm not involved." I wanted to bat my

eyelashes and play innocent, but didn't think he would fall for that.

"I'll speak with Ms. Johnson. I'm sure if you saw those men again, it was purely a coincidence."

I absentmindedly picked at the edge of a paper sitting on the counter. "Yeah, you're probably right."

"Well, we won't wait for him to look into it. We'll track those men down ourselves," Charlotte huffed.

I didn't know how to break it to her, but I had no desire to track down those dark-suited strangers who'd felt the need to break in to Cindy Johnson's home.

"There was something else," I said hesitantly.

He flashed that sexy look at me again. "Yes?"

"Someone-has-left-threatening-messages-for-me-on-my-blog." I rushed the words.

He moved a few steps closer. "Show me."

I opened my laptop and waited for the e-mails to pop up. He leaned in close and the smell of woodsy spice surrounded me. I ignored his closeness and concentrated on the task at hand.

"There. Read that." I pointed to the screen.

His expression changed from curious to worried as he read. "You don't know who left the messages?"

I closed my laptop. "No, I've never had anything like that happen, not until I discovered the dead man. The second one came after I found the scarf."

Dylan studied my face. "Do you have an alarm system in your home? What about mace? Make sure to carry your cell phone with you at all times."

"I'll look into getting an alarm and mace." My voice didn't sound quite as confident as before.

"I'll look into this and see what I can find out.

Do you mind if I have the password for your blog for our tech team?"

I jotted down the password and handed it to him.

"You'll call me right away if this happens again?" He put the paper in his pocket.

"Yes, right away."

"I'll be in touch."

As he walked out of the shop, I wondered if I'd done the right thing. What would happen now?

"You shouldn't let his good looks get in the way of this investigation," Charlotte said.

I scoffed. "I hardly think that's a concern. And this isn't an investigation. I own a clothing boutique. I'm not one of Charlie's Angels."

"Well, that's evident," she said.

I lifted the mannequin and placed it in the window display. Wind Song watched from her favorite spot in the sunshine.

"Cookie, I just remembered something," Charlotte said as she marched toward me. "Why didn't I think of it earlier?"

I placed the mannequin's arms in position, then looked at her. "What?"

"My no-good boyfriend had me cosign for a loan." Anger dripped from her words.

"And? What about it?" I asked, stepping away from the window.

"Well, I was suspicious of the papers because they had some odd clauses in them. She fidgeted from foot to foot.

"Then why did you sign?"

Charlotte pasted a polite smile on her face. "I wanted to trust him."

The expression on her face made me feel bad

for her. I understood what it was like to be let down by someone you thought you could trust.

The bell jingled as Heather opened the door and stepped through the doorway. She wore designer jeans and a loose white silk blouse. Her gladiator sandals slapped the floor. "How's it going? Has Wind Song said anything else?" She whispered as if she didn't want Wind Song to know we were talking about her.

I straightened the sale sign above the rack on my way past. "No, she's been quiet."

"Tell her about what happened." Charlotte nudged with her elbow.

"I told Detective Valentine about finding the scarf and about the threats on my blog."

Heather pulled a treat from her pocket and handed it to the cat, who batted it across the floor before pouncing on it and eating it. "What did he say?"

"He basically told me to stay out of the investigation." I slumped my shoulders.

"That's not good," she said.

"No, it's not, but it's too late for me to stay out of it now, right?" I asked.

A strand of blond hair fell across Heather's forehead and she brushed it back. "Maybe if you drop it, the person making the threats will leave you alone."

"Don't listen to her," Charlotte said with panic in her voice.

Wind Song jumped up on the counter, stretching out in front of me.

I stroked the cat from her head all the way down

her back to her fluffy tail. "I promised Charlotte I would help her."

Charlotte's expression softened. "Thank-you."

"I understand, but I don't want to see you get hurt . . . or worse." Heather touched my arm.

"I promise I'll be careful," I said.

"So what are you going to do next?" Heather asked.

"Well, Charlotte was just telling me that she'd cosigned for a loan for her boyfriend. I figure maybe I should go back and ask him about it." I picked at the edge of my shirt.

Heather picked up a pink cotton blouse with a white Peter Pan collar from the stack of clothing on the counter. "After the way he acted?"

I handed her a hanger. "I know, but what other option do I have?"

"Well, I can't let you go there by yourself. He won't act that way with two of us." She straightened the blouse on the hanger and placed it on the rack of clothing that I had been preparing to take out to the sales floor.

"Three of us." I smiled and gestured toward Charlotte.

Heather grinned. "Yeah, the three of us."

Chapter 27

Cookie's Savvy Vintage Fashion Shopping Tip

⧫

Be early for estate and yard sales.
The early bird gets the worm. Or the de la Renta.

I jumped into my Buick. An awkward moment later, Heather and Charlotte tried to sit in the front passenger seat at the same time.

"Heather, watch out. You just sat on Charlotte's lap."

Heather leaped back to the sidewalk. "Oh, I'm sorry! I didn't know!"

Charlotte drifted to the rear seat. "See how nice I am? I'm letting her have the front seat."

I looked at Heather. "Get back in. She moved to the back." When my passengers were settled, I shifted into gear and headed to Bud's house.

"What's it like having a ghost around all the time?" Heather glanced over her shoulders.

"It's absolutely divine," was Charlotte's answer.

"It's not that great," was mine as I glanced in the rearview mirror.

"I'll get you for that later," Charlotte warned.

As we pulled up to Bud's house, I noticed there

was no car in the driveway and the garage door was open. "That's odd."

Charlotte scoffed. "Oh, it's nothing. He's so ditzy that he forgets and drives off with the door open all the time."

I inched the Buick forward a little more and then stopped. "So you're saying he's not home?"

"Probably not," Charlotte said.

"Even better," Heather said, climbing out of the car when I shoved it into neutral and set the parking brake.

I took the keys from the ignition, then joined Heather on the sidewalk. Charlotte was already on the porch motioning for us to hurry up.

"What are we going to do if he's not at home?" Heather asked as we made our way up the driveway toward the front door.

I hadn't thought about that. "I'll just ring the doorbell to make sure. If he's not, we'll have to come back later."

"Ring the bell and if he doesn't answer, I'll find another way for y'all to get in," Charlotte said.

My eyes widened. "I can't go into his house if he's not home. The police would frown on that." I'd already entered Charlotte's home and didn't want a repeat of that fiasco. And I'd been in Cindy's house after she left.

"We won't tell the police, now will we?" Charlotte winked.

"She wants us to break in to his house," I said to Heather.

"I didn't say *break in*. I just said we'll *find another way in*," Charlotte said.

"What's the difference?" I asked.

"You know, I don't think that's a bad idea," Heather said.

"I'm beginning to like this girl." Charlotte wiggled her finger with a smile.

Stepping up to the door, I pushed the bell. A loud drawn-out chime sounded through the house. I wasn't holding out much hope that Bud was home. I rang the bell again just to make sure.

"I told you he wasn't home," Charlotte said. "Go around to the door inside the garage. He usually leaves it unlocked. Like I said, he's not the smartest guy."

"Then why did you go out with him?" I asked.

"He was nice to me. When he was around me, no one else was in his world. He made me feel like a queen," she said wistfully.

We hurried around the house to the garage. I was hesitant to go inside. "I don't think we should be doing this," I said to Heather.

"Well, I guess if the door is open . . . it wouldn't be like we'd broken in or anything," she said as much to herself as to me.

I released a deep breath. "Yeah, I guess not." I eased over to the garage entrance.

We weaved around the lawn mower and other various pieces of garden equipment on our way through the garage. I knocked on the side door.

Charlotte glided in front of me. "I told you he's not here. Why are you knocking?"

"To be polite," I said.

"Just open the door," she urged.

I shook my head. "I can't just open the door."

"She's a pushy ghost, huh?" Heather said.

"Well, you'd be pushy, too, if you had been murdered," Charlotte said.

I reached out and twisted the knob. Sure enough, the door was unlocked. I looked back at Heather. She motioned for me to go forward. I lifted my shoulders, stuck out my chest, and marched forward. Okay, it was more like I inched into the kitchen, but I digress.

A clock ticked in the background and water dripped slowly from the faucet. The counters were clean. No dirty dishes or leftover food were visible.

"This is so wrong on so many levels," I whispered.

"Oh, stop being a chicken." Determination flashed in Charlotte's eyes.

My anxiety increased and I figured a panic attack was near. "I don't even know why we're here. What are we looking for?"

"I want you to find the papers I signed for the loan." Charlotte surveyed the kitchen.

"Don't you have a copy?" I asked.

"I doubt they're still at my house. I'm sure the beneficiaries got rid of them. They couldn't wait to get rid of my belongings." Charlotte couldn't hold back the anger in her voice.

She did have a point. Only a few pieces of furniture had been left at her house. It had all been eliminated as if she'd never been there in the first place. Her lawyer had wasted little time taking care of that little detail.

"What did she say?" Heather asked.

"She wants us to look for some loan papers she signed for Bud," I said.

"Where do we start?" Heather took in the small kitchen.

"His office is at the back of the house. That's where he keeps all his papers." Charlotte started across the room.

Heather and I followed.

"I hope you're right and he's not here," I whispered to Charlotte.

The silence was nerve-wracking as the three of us made our way through Bud's house. Only the sound of our footsteps and breathing could be heard. We were like a bunch of bumbling burglars. We weren't very good at breaking and entering, but that was okay with me. I didn't want to be good at it.

When we reached the dining room, Heather stopped. She picked up some magazines from the table and waved them through the air. "Hey, look what he reads. It's the *Enquirer* and *People* magazine. Apparently, he likes to keep up with the celebrities."

"Will you put those down, please? We can't touch anything," I said.

Heather tossed down the magazines and we continued on to the living room—the scene of the earlier offense when Bud had been so obnoxious.

I hoped he didn't show up and catch us. I wouldn't be able to handle that again. I'd have to say something a little harsher. I figured Charlotte wouldn't put up with it either. She'd do something worse than pinch him on the butt. I glanced over at her. She was scowling. I assumed she was thinking about Bud, too.

Much to my chagrin, Heather stepped into the living room.

I went after her, grabbing her arm. "We shouldn't be in here. We need to find what we came for."

As we weaved around the tall DVD tower, Heather stumbled and fell right into it. The thing crashed to the floor with a bang and all of the DVDs went with it.

I took Heather's arm and helped her up. "Are you okay?"

She pushed her hair out of her eyes. "Yeah, I'm fine."

We peered down at the mess on the floor. It was not good . . . at all.

Charlotte tapped her foot. "You know that all of those were in alphabetical order, right?"

I blew hair out of my eyes "You're kidding me."

"No, I'm not kidding. You have to pick them up and put them back just the way they were. If you don't, he will know that someone was in his house."

I motioned for Heather to help me. "Okay, we have to pick the movies up and alphabetize them." I explained why.

Heather and I sat on the rug, grabbed DVDs, and sorted them into piles.

"Which ones do you have?" I asked.

Heather flashed the copies of *Ferris Bueller's Day Off* and *Sixteen Candles*. She crammed the movies onto the shelves.

"No, no, no," I said, taking one from her. "*Goonies* goes before *Weekend At Bernie's*."

"What's with this guy's fascination with all the eighties movies?" Heather asked.

"The eighties was his favorite decade," Charlotte said.

"I gathered that much," I said.

"Y'all are terrible at this." She gave a wave with her hand.

"I can't help it. I'm in a panic. I can't think straight right now. How am I supposed to organize all of these when I'm worried about being caught?" I picked up a couple cases.

"It's making me nervous, too." Heather gathered an armful of DVDs.

"N is after M," Charlotte pointed out.

I released a deep breath. Okay, I had to calm down if I was going to finish. The more panicked I felt, the longer it would take to clean up our mess.

Finally, all of the DVDs—at least one hundred or more—were back in the tower, A to Z. I hadn't bothered to count, but there were a lot. I stepped back and perused our work, scanning them to make sure that they were in order. As far as I could tell, we'd gotten it right. I took a deep breath. I never wanted to see that place again.

We had barely stepped out of the room when a loud bang sounded. We froze on the spot.

"I wonder what that was?" I asked, looking from Heather to Charlotte.

Heather scanned the room. "I don't know."

Charlotte glided across the room. "I don't know, either."

"We should check it out, I guess." I was already thinking up excuses in case Bud had come home. He would probably think I'd come back to his house for a date.

Ignoring my desire to avoid the living room, Heather and I rushed over to the living room window, Charlotte right behind us. I eased back the curtain, peeking outside. I wasn't sure that I would be able to see if Bud had pulled his car into the garage, but I didn't want to go back through the house and open the door leading to the garage. Maybe we should have just hidden in a closet, but with my luck, he would have come home and I would have to stay in the closet all night until he left the next day.

"I don't see anything," Heather whispered.

"Me either," I said. "I guess it was nothing. If it was Bud, he would've been in the house by now, so I guess we're safe."

Charlotte leaned against the wall. "You two looked like a couple of scared cats."

Yeah, like the noise hadn't startled her as well.

"Look, that watering can fell off the porch. It must have been the wind," Heather said.

"Come on. Let's finish what we came here for." Charlotte signaled for us to follow her.

When we reached Bud's office, I paused. The door was closed.

"You'd better hurry before he returns." Charlotte tapped on the door.

"You didn't tell me he would be home soon." I didn't hide the apprehension in my voice.

"Well, I have no idea where he went. I'm a ghost, not a psychic. That's your friend's job." Charlotte smirked.

"What did she say?" Heather asked.

I decided not to relay the message. "She doesn't

know where Bud went. He could be home at any time."

Heather peeked in the bathroom across the hall. "Let's just look around really quick and then get out of here."

I opened the office door and hurried into the room, scanning the space. It was sparsely decorated with a desk, a chair, and a bookshelf that held more photos of Bud. He looked especially happy, posing with Mickey Mouse at Disney World.

"I didn't know they had adult size mouse ears." I leaned in for a closer look.

"Bud's a big Disney fan," Charlotte said.

"Where do I start?" I asked.

"Start with the desk and have Heather look in the file cabinet," Charlotte ordered.

"I'll look here," I said, pointing to the desk. "You look over there."

We searched in silence. Well, except for Charlotte. Every time I picked up a paper that wasn't what she was looking for she said, "No." I picked up another paper. "No," Charlotte said again.

I dumped papers onto the desk, causing one to fly out of the stack.

"What's that?" Charlotte slipped to the right.

"Which one? This receipt for men's hair cream?"

"No, that one." Charlotte directed again.

I grabbed the next paper and studied it. Heather abandoned the file cabinet and joined me.

"It looks like an insurance policy." I tapped the paper with my index finger.

Charlotte stepped closer. "What does it say?"

I showed her the paper. "It's in your name, and he's the beneficiary."

She was already dead and her color was pale, but I swear her face drained of the little color it had. Heather's eyes widened. I couldn't believe that we'd discovered an insurance policy that Charlotte hadn't known about.

"He must have tricked me into signing it. My signature is right there on the policy at the bottom. I never would have signed that." She crossed the room to the windows and peered out.

"When do you think this happened?" I asked.

"*How* did it happen?" Heather asked.

"The only papers I signed were for the loan. Considering we can't find those papers, I'm guessing that I was really signing for an insurance policy." Charlotte faced us again.

It was a good thing she was a ghost. Otherwise she would have worn a path in the rug.

"Take that paper with you." She closed the distance between us.

Following her order, I stuffed the paper under my arm. "Let's get out of here. This is making me nervous."

As I passed the desk, I noticed something sticking out from a drawer. Its cotton fabric looked familiar. I opened the drawer, reached down, and picked up the white fabric. It had tiny pink embroidered flowers on the corners.

"What did you find?" Heather asked.

I held up the handkerchief and Charlotte gasped.

"It's a handkerchief just like the one we found on the floor at Charlotte's house," I said breathlessly.

"Do you think Bud left it at Charlotte's house? Maybe it's the same one," Heather said.

"No way," Charlotte said. "He never used handkerchiefs."

It finally hit me. "I know where this came from. It's sold in packages of three in the shop down the street from me, Hortensia's Haberdashery."

"Are you sure?" Heather asked.

I folded the handkerchief. "When it comes to fabric, I have a photographic memory."

"Hey, maybe if we can find out who bought the handkerchiefs, we'll find the killer," Charlotte said. "I know Hortensia's. I shopped there a lot."

"Thanks for going there instead of shopping at my place." I closed the desk drawer.

Charlotte reached the office door. "Really? You are worried about business at a time like this? Besides, I told you I didn't want to be seen in clothing that used to belong to someone from town."

"I'll have you know that vintage and thrift shopping is very trendy," I said.

Charlotte huffed. "That doesn't matter right now. We have to focus on the task at hand."

I clutched the white handkerchief in my hand and headed for the door. We couldn't get out of the house fast enough for my taste.

Outside, I looked around the neighborhood as I walked down the sidewalk. Luckily, I didn't see anyone. My fingers were crossed that no one had seen us.

"I can't believe we went into his home when he wasn't there," I said as I climbed behind the wheel of the Buick. Its smooth leather seat had never felt more comforting.

Heather reached in her purse and pulled out black wayfarer sunglasses. "Just think of it as if we thought he was home and wanted to say hi so we walked on in."

"Well, bless his Disney lovin' heart, he left the door open. If he didn't want anyone in his house, he shouldn't have done that," Charlotte said.

We'd only made it a short distance from Bud's house when I noticed a familiar dark sedan following me. "I don't want to panic y'all, but that car with the men from Cindy's house is behind me again."

"That's not a coincidence." Heather whipped around and looked at the car. "What do you think they want?"

"I bet it has something to do with Cindy taking that money. They probably saw your car and think you are involved with her scheme," Charlotte said from the backseat.

"I don't want them to catch up to me and ask. I'd rather not talk with them at all. Do you think they are the ones leaving the messages on my blog?" I glanced over at Heather.

She lowered her sunglasses to the tip of her nose. "I don't know how they would possibly know about your blog."

I glanced back at the black car. "Yeah, that doesn't make sense. How can I get rid of them?"

Heather shifted in the seat. "I don't know."

"Oh, y'all are ridiculous," Charlotte said. "If you make enough turns, you will lose them. Didn't you notice the New York license plate on their car?

They aren't from around here. You should take the long way back to Main. They won't know their way around these roads."

"Well, that's a good point, Charlotte, but why didn't you tell me that you noticed their license plate?" I said.

She leaned forward from the backseat. "You didn't ask."

"Apparently, their license plate says they're from New York, so the plan is to take them around the back roads," I explained to Heather.

Heather changed the radio's channel to eighties rock. "Good plan."

"Why thank you," Charlotte said, then smiled.

I turned the big steering wheel on the Buick and navigated several turns. I sped up and cut the wheel, making a sharp left-hand turn, then immediately turned to the right. The little subdivision was like the Bermuda Triangle. I used to take piano lessons from a lady who lived in the neighborhood. It had taken me years to figure out how to get out of there.

"You know, I kind of feel bad for them. They may never get out of here." I chuckled.

"It serves them right for following us," Charlotte said.

My fingers were wrapped around the steering wheel so tightly that I thought I might not ever get them off. I had to tell Detective Valentine about the new discoveries. But since he'd told me to stay out of the investigation, I wasn't sure how he would react. Breaking into a man's home wasn't exactly staying out of it. I'd have to find out what the insurance policy meant and who the men were before I laid out my findings to the gorgeous detective.

We made it back to the shop without the men in sight. I'd managed to lose them before making it to the Sugar Creek. But try as I might, I couldn't shake my worries about what would happen next.

Chapter 28

Heather's Heartfelt Tip
for Getting Rid of an Unwanted Ghost

❖

Use garlic. It's not just for vampires any more.
It repels all kinds of nasty spirits.

As soon as I climbed out from behind the wheel, Charlotte said, "We have to go to the boutique down the street." She pointed at Hortensia's Haberdashery. Its turquoise awning irritated me, as usual.

I locked the Buick's door. "Why? It's my competition," I said with a frown.

"She sells *new* clothes." Charlotte waited for me on the sidewalk by the pot of petunias.

I shoved my keys in my handbag. "Yeah, but it's still clothing. More people need to wear vintage as far as I'm concerned."

"Right now, I don't care if everyone runs around naked. We need to talk with her.

I joined Charlotte on the sidewalk. "Okay. Don't get all tangled up. We'll walk down there, but I doubt she'll have anything to share with us."

"Where are you going?" Heather asked as she got out of the car.

"Charlotte wants to go to Hortensia's Haberdashery."

"I'd love to go with you, but I need to open the shop. You'll call me if you need anything?" Heather asked.

I reached out and hugged her. "Thanks for everything."

"What? I didn't do anything." She grinned.

"You were there for moral support. You stuck your neck out for me and I appreciate that."

She smiled. "What are friends for? Besides, I know you'll do the same for me someday." She headed down the sidewalk toward her shop.

"I hope that neither one of us ever has to do that again," I called out in her wake.

Charlotte and I headed down the sidewalk toward Hortensia's. I'd only been to the shop a couple times. To be honest, it was a nice place. Its owner Winona Sam—there was no actual Hortensia; Winona just liked the name—had a lot of beautiful items. I bought new things sometimes. I wasn't against a modern purchase. But for me, wearing clothing that had been through so much history made it feel special.

Sparrows and robins chirped in the trees, purple and white petunias stood at attention in the pots lining the sidewalk, and the sun shone down. It was a lovely day, but a lovely day for a murder investigation? No day was good for that.

We reached the door, which had a glass panel with the store name etched on it among a floral motif. The sign above the door read OPEN.

I looked around before entering. I wondered if anyone would spot me and think I was talking to myself. "I'll talk to her, but try not to say too much in my ear, okay? It's distracting," I said to Charlotte.

"I was never known for my subtlety," Charlotte warned.

I was learning that.

I stepped into the shop and looked around at all the new items. It was hard to believe that someday these pieces of clothing would be considered vintage. Her shop was decorated in shades of turquoise and cream. It was very shabby chic with paint chipped furniture and white rose arrangements around the room.

I didn't know Winona well, but we'd talked a few times since we both owned businesses in Sugar Creek. I was nervous about asking her about the handkerchiefs. It had to sound suspicious that I would be asking. I mean, what business was it of mine, anyway? I rehearsed what I was going to say in my mind.

A couple women were in the shop and Winona was helping them. They looked to be a mother and a college-age daughter who was holding up a cute lavender-colored strapless sundress. I hoped the women would soon find their way to my shop, too.

Winona's ash-blond hair was styled in a shoulder-length bob. Her outfit consisted of a silver sequin-covered tank top paired with white capri pants. Rhinestones adorned the tops of her white sandals. She hadn't noticed that I'd slipped in. I picked up a size four midnight blue dress with a full skirt and cap sleeves and help it up to my waist.

"You should try it on," Charlotte said. "It's a nice color on you."

"You think?" I asked.

"Absolutely." She motioned for me to move to the dressing rooms.

Winona still hadn't noticed that I was there. Either that, or she was ignoring me, but I didn't think that was the case. She was kind of quiet, but she'd never been rude to me.

I headed to a dressing room, hurried out of my clothing, and slipped on the dress. It felt a little weird to wear new clothing. Most of the new clothing I owned was pajamas, pants, or workout gear. The exercise clothing didn't get nearly as much use as it should have, though.

"How's it going in here?" Charlotte asked, sticking her head through the curtain and not bothering to let me know before she entered.

"I don't know," I whispered. "It's hard to tell in this little room."

I stepped out of the confined space and faced the mirror that lined the outside of the dressing room wall. As I studied my reflection, I caught movement out of the corner of my eye. Detective Valentine was walking down the sidewalk in front of the store.

"The detective just walked past," I whispered.

"I'll go see what he's doing." Charlotte floated away.

I peered across the store, waiting to see the detective again, but he didn't show up.

Charlotte popped up beside me. "I didn't see him."

"Maybe I just thought I saw him."

"You're too stressed." Charlotte stepped over to the display case. "You should take your mind off this mess for a couple minutes—just for a couple minutes—and then you can think of it again. Look at this bracelet. That will distract you. I had one just like it," she said, tapping the glass front of a display unit.

"Charlotte Meadows had a bracelet with peach-colored roses? I didn't think you liked peach," I said.

"How did you know Charlotte had that bracelet?"

I whipped around. Winona was right behind me. Suddenly, I was very aware that I was still wearing the blue dress. It was beyond awkward.

"How did you know? Are you spying on me?" Winona frowned.

"What? No way. I wouldn't do anything like that." Why was she even asking me such a question?

"Tell her you saw it at the estate sale," Charlotte said.

"I saw it at the estate sale," I muttered. It sounded like a plausible explanation, other than the fact that I'd blurted it out and looked as if I was talking to myself. "I'll just change out of this dress." I gestured over my shoulder toward the dressing room and hurried inside.

Winona stared at me, probably at a loss for words.

"Well, congratulations," Charlotte said. "You left her speechless."

Yeah, thanks to Charlotte I'd made the woman wonder about my sanity.

I slipped out of the dress and back into my clothing faster than ever. After what had happened

I had no choice but to purchase the dress. It was a good thing that I liked it. I closed my eyes and took the price tags in my hands. I quickly opened them and looked at the price, then released a breath of relief. At least I had the money to pay for it. As much as I wanted to hide in that room for the rest of the day, I knew I had to go out.

I placed the dress on the counter and waited for Winona to ring up my purchase.

"Would you like the bracelet, too?" She pointed. "It's the only one like it, other than the one that Charlotte had."

"I told you that I like unique things," Charlotte said.

I regarded Charlotte with a scowl before realizing that Winona would think I was making the face at her. I needed to stop doing that. "No, thank-you. The dress will be all."

She wrapped the dress in tissue paper, slipped it into a bag, and handed it to me. Thank goodness she didn't ask any questions. I noted with satisfaction that her generic white store sacks were nothing compared to my elegantly designed bags.

"Don't forget to ask her about the handkerchief. You can't leave without asking her," Charlotte urged.

It looked as if I had put it off as long as I could.

Winona said, "Is there something else you need?"

Just then the door opened and two women I recognized from the library entered. Their names slipped my mind, but I knew the brunette was the children's librarian and the gray-haired woman was the library director.

Charlotte stood by the door as if she was keeping

count of how many people entered. "Well, I'll be a monkey's uncle. This woman's store is too busy. Too bad you don't have this many customers."

Okay. That comment was totally uncalled for. I would have to hang around until they left or wait and come back at another time. I knew Charlotte wouldn't be happy with the last option.

She closed the distance between us. "This is taking forever. I'll get rid of them."

Oh no. What was she going to do?

While Winona helped the children's librarian, Charlotte walked over to the library director and shoved the blouse out of the woman's hand. The customer gasped, but didn't run away. She picked up the blouse from the floor, and Charlotte again knocked it from her hands. Charlotte was learning to use energy to touch items and this was her way of practicing.

That did it. The woman had had enough and marched right out the door. Her friend glanced up and hurried after her. Winona glanced over at me as if to ask what had happened. I shrugged innocently.

Winona came back over to the counter. "You still here, Cookie? Did you need something else?"

I smiled. "Oh yes, I'm fine. Everything's fine." Once I'd made sure there weren't any other customers, I added, "I have one thing I wanted to ask you."

She set the blouse she'd been holding down and focused on my face. "Yes?" she asked with a raised eyebrow.

I knew I'd piqued her interest. "I'm looking for a specific item and I think you sell it here."

She moved the blouse to the side of the counter. "What is it? I'll try to help."

"I'm looking for a handkerchief like this." I pulled the white square of fabric I'd found at Charlotte's house out of my purse. "Do you sell them? I was told you had them in your shop."

She glanced at the object. "I believe we carried them, yes."

"Ask her if she remembers who she sold them to," Charlotte pushed.

I knew it was a long shot, but I had to try. "Do you remember who purchased the handkerchiefs?"

Winona shuffled through a stack of receipts. "I've sold so many items that I can't possibly remember who bought them."

I wouldn't leave it at that. I pulled out the scarf. "Do you recognize this?"

She held the scarf and then handed it back to me. "Yes, it's lovely. I sold them here."

"Do you remember selling one to Charlotte Meadows?" I asked.

She set the receipts aside. "I guess I do remember selling one to her. I only had two of that kind."

Why hadn't she said that in the first place? She had acted as if she had lots of scarves and wouldn't possibly be able to tell me who bought it.

"You say there were only two?" I asked.

"Yes, they are limited edition. One was sold to Charlotte and the other to Cindy Johnson."

Another twist.

"So Cindy had a scarf just like mine?" Charlotte asked.

Winona tapped her fingers against the counter. "You know, that's strange. I remember seeing

Marie Vance wearing the same kind of scarf one day while she was here in the shop."

"Does she come in here often?" I asked.

Winona replied, "No, not often."

Was the scarf somehow connected to the murder?

"I don't care what she says, even if Cindy had one like mine, " Charlotte said.

Winona said she had only two, and one went to Cindy and the other to Charlotte. So how did Marie have one, too?

"Thank you for your help," I said and headed for the door.

"Enjoy the dress," she called after me. "Come again."

Chapter 29

Cookie's Savvy Vintage Fashion Shopping Tip

Remember vintage items are one of a kind.
So if you see something you like, buy it.

Later that day, I was back in my shop trying to focus on work. Charlotte was standing on the sidewalk outside the store. I guess she was contemplating all that had happened.

When I was anxious or needed to think things through, I always worked with the clothing. I was rearranging the store window again, changing it to all white. I dressed one of the mannequins into a darling cotton white cut-out front flare dress from the eighties. It had a flattering empire waistline, a zipper at the back, and the skirt hit just above the knees. It was in practically new condition. I changed the next mannequin into white linen pants and a white silk blouse and accessorized each with white clutch purses and flat white sandals.

Wind Song lay beside me watching and wagging her tail.

"Don't you have anything else to say?" I asked her. She looked at me, then closed her eyes.

"I take that as no comment," I said as I stepped away from the window.

The bell over the door chimed and I looked back. Heather had a sheepish smile on her face. She gave a peek of the deck of tarot cards she had hidden in her burlap tote bag and approached the counter. "I couldn't handle it any longer. I have to know if she'll pick more cards."

"If it's more bad news, I don't want to know." I turned back to the window and inserted a couple straight pins to make the white dress look slimmer.

Heather placed the cards on the counter. Before I had a chance to object, Wind Song jumped up and sat beside them.

"See. She is ready. She knows what she's doing. I think she likes it." Heather turned to the cat. "You like it, don't you, Wind Song?"

The cat yawned as if she was bored and just wanted to get on with the task.

I gathered the items I'd been using for my window display and walked to the counter. "Okay. Let's see what she has to say."

Heather spread the cards across the counter. Wind Song stretched her paw forward and placed it down on one of the cards. Slowly, she moved her paw back, taking the card with it.

We waited for her to pick another card, but she jumped down and went back to her favorite spot in the sun. She stretched out and closed her eyes, signaling that she was done with our game.

"What is the card?" I asked.

Heather turned it over. "It's the Death card,"

she said in a small voice, holding it up for me to examine. The cat was dressed in black and was surrounded by black roses. It was an ominous sign.

"What?" My voice came out a lot more panicked than I'd intended.

Heather grabbed my arms. "Don't panic. This card just means that mourning is natural. It doesn't mean that you're going to die today."

I was in full freak-out mode. Who could blame me? There had been two murders in Sugar Creek and I was smack dab in the middle of both of them.

Heather grabbed the cards from the counter and stacked them neatly into a pile. "Cookie, you need to learn to deal with death before you can accept anything new." She rubber-banded the pack. "I don't think this card has anything to do with the murders. I think the cat was trying to tell you something else."

"How did she know?"

"That I can't answer," Heather said.

I rubbed my temples. "I understand, but it's kind of hard to take advice from a cat."

Heather tucked the deck of cards into her tote bag. "Maybe she knows more than we do about this stuff."

I looked at Wind Song still lying in the sunshine with her eyes closed and tail swaying slowly. "I think she knows we're talking about her."

Heather draped the tote bag on her shoulder. "Listen, I have to get back to work. Call me if you need anything, okay?"

I tucked a strand of hair behind my ear. "Yeah, I think it's time to go home for the evening and collapse into bed."

"I'll see you tomorrow."

Wind Song opened her eyes briefly as Heather walked past, but then closed them again and went back to her nap.

As I posted on my blog that evening about what to look for when shopping at estate sales, I kept checking the comments. I'd deleted the threatening ones, but still had the e-mails with the messages. After clicking POST, I wondered if another message would soon show up or if the killer would take the bait and leave a message. I didn't want another threat, but another message might be one more clue that would point me in the right direction.

Charlotte was lying next to me in the bed, staring up at the ceiling. As always, her hair was styled to perfection, her sunshine yellow sundress was immaculate, and she wore the perfect gold jewelry for her outfit. I considered chiding her for putting her shoes on my bedspread, then realized it didn't matter.

"What are you doing?" I asked, not ready to wake up fully yet.

"Just thinking about our next move."

I groaned. "Oh great. I'd hoped that when I woke this all would have been a dream."

Charlotte sat on the foot of the bed. "No dream."

"Well, while you think about the next move, I'm going to shower and have breakfast." I slid out of bed, but coffee was calling to me first. I slipped into my robe and left Charlotte contemplating her strategy.

I started the coffee, showered, and then went to my closet. I picked out a sleeveless navy blue dress with a red and white leaf pattern. It had a beautiful V-neck fold-down collar detail at the front and side zip. White buttons lined down the front to the waist, and a white braid trim on the shoulders and flared skirt ultimately finished with a red braided belt. Red and white spectator pumps and a red leather bag completed the outfit. After dressing and finishing my coffee, I tiptoed through the foyer, stealthily moving toward the door with Wind Song in her case.

Charlotte met me just as I thought I was going to slip out of the house without her.

"Where do you think you're going?" She stood in front of the door. Technically, I could have walked through her, but I was too squeamish.

I set Wind Song's carrier on the floor. "I was just putting Wind Song in the car," I said innocently.

Thinking I had forgotten to lock the back door, I walked toward the kitchen.

"You were going to leave without me, weren't you?" Charlotte followed me.

"Of course not. What makes you say that?" I smiled.

"You skipped breakfast just because you thought I was in there waiting for you." Charlotte walked beside me as I crossed the living room back toward the front door.

I grabbed my keys. "Oh, don't be ridiculous."

She stood in front of me. "You need red lipstick." She pointed at my lips. "You're too pale without it. You need to add some color to your face."

I picked up the cat's carrier and opened the door. "I'll put it on when I get to the store."

"You never know who you might see. You should put it on now."

"What does that mean? Is there something I'm forgetting?" I checked my purse.

The doorbell rang. I looked at Charlotte.

She shrugged. "I tried to warn you."

I peeked out the window and saw Detective Valentine standing on my front porch dressed in khaki pants and a navy blue polo shirt. He removed his sunglasses while he waited for me to answer the door. I could see his gorgeous blue eyes. His athletic body made me wonder how often he worked out.

"How did you know he was coming?" I asked.

She held her hands up. "I saw his car pull up when I walked past the window a second ago."

Oh, how I wished I'd followed her advice and put on the lipstick. Charlotte had an *I-told-you-so* look on her face.

I straightened my dress, stood a little taller, and opened the door. "Detective Valentine. This is a surprise. What are you doing here?"

A little smile spread across his face. "Wow. You're gorgeous."

Heat rushed to my cheeks. "Thank-you." I willed my heart to be still, then asked, "What can I do for you?"

"I just wanted you to know that we are investigating the messages left on your blog." He shoved his hands in his pockets.

"He came all the way to your house to tell you that? He couldn't have called?" Charlotte asked.

His attention was locked on my face. "I was in the area and thought I would let you know."

"I appreciate that."

"You are being careful, right?" he asked. "Did you get the alarm system set up? And do you have your container of mace in your purse?"

Wind Song meowed as if she was trying to rat me out.

"Of course." I indicated the blinking green light on the alarm indicator on the wall. "Well, okay, I'd better go."

"I'll call you as soon as I find out anything." The sides of his mouth curved into a soft smile.

"Thank-you." I watched as he stepped off the porch.

Charlotte studied her fingernails. "Yeah, sure, he'll stop by and see you if he finds out anything. Heck, I think he'll just stop by even if he doesn't find out anything."

I shushed her.

Dylan turned around. "Did you say something?"

"No, it must have been the wind," I said.

He looked up at the still tree, then climbed into his car and drove away.

"You get me in trouble every time I'm around him," I said to Charlotte as I walked down the sidewalk toward my car.

"Since we are early and you didn't eat breakfast, this is the perfect time for you to stop in and say hello to Dixie Bryant. We went to high school together, you know? That was many years ago," Charlotte said.

I looked over at my companion, who was sitting in the passenger seat. "Why did I know you were going to have an assignment for me this morning?"

"That's why you were trying to sneak out of the house." Disapproval was splashed all over her face.

"For the last time, I wasn't trying to sneak out."

Okay, I was, but I couldn't admit to it. The fact was, I had wanted to see Dixie. It had been too long since we'd had a chat and I needed someone to steer me in the right direction. Dixie had been like a second mother to me when I was young. Now, she felt like an older, much wiser sister. I thought Dixie liked thinking of herself that way, too.

Chapter 30

Heather's Heartfelt Tip
for Getting Rid of an Unwanted Ghost

❦

A Ghostbusters backpack or a magic wand
will not get rid of an unwanted ghost.
You have to use your heart to wish them away.

I pointed the car in the direction of It's Vintage, Y'all, dropped off Wind Song, and headed to Glorious Grits.

"I'm glad that you didn't put up a fight about going to Dixie's. I'd hate to have to wake you with my singing again." Charlotte watched the scenery of oak trees and blue sky.

"Yeah, like I have a choice." I parked and we entered the restaurant, jingling the cowbell above the door.

Patrons stopped what they were doing and looked up. Almost every time, they knew who'd walked through the door and today was no exception. I was greeted warmly as I made my way across the room, tossing my hand up at a few of the regulars.

Red and white checkered tablecloths covered

the tables and every inch of space on the walls was adorned with a picture or a sign with some cutesy saying like *Country Cookin' Makes You Good-lookin'*. Booths lined the walls and tables were in the middle of the room. The smell of apple pie lingered in the air. Dixie made the best apple pie for miles around . . . other than the pie my grandmother used to make, of course.

I'd tried Granny's recipe many times, but mine never came out quite as good. Dixie had homemade ice cream to top off the pie, too.

I snagged an empty booth.

Dixie hurried over with a pot of coffee and a menu. "Hey, here's my favorite fashion diva." She wore a red and white checkered apron over her white T-shirt and jeans. Of course, she had on her signature big-rimmed white eyeglasses.

I didn't need the menu, having eaten there so often over the years, but I gave my best attempt at a smile. It was hard to say what my favorite thing on the menu was. Dixie claimed her specialty was fried green tomatoes. She wouldn't reveal the secret ingredient, although I'd asked many times. She'd probably take that info to the grave.

Charlotte sat across from me. "Now make sure to tell her everything. I know she will help you figure out how to solve this case. Dixie always had a level head and knows what's best."

I scanned the crowd, pretending to watch Dixie rush around the diner like a hummingbird. Luckily, no one seemed to pay any more attention to me. I was paranoid that someone would catch me talking to Charlotte.

Dixie placed a mug on the table and sat across from me.

Charlotte scooted aside, out of the way. "Don't forget to eat breakfast. And set that coffee over here where I can smell it. Mmm, Dixie uses just the right amount of chicory in it."

"I'm glad you finally came in. I thought I was going to have to come and get you," Dixie said.

"Well, I've been awfully busy."

"You're never too busy to see me," she said.

I chuckled. "No, you're right. I'm never too busy to see you." I dumped sugar into my coffee and stirred, then took a sip and looked at her over the top of the mug.

Dixie said, "You look worried. Tell me what's going on."

I set the mug down. "What makes you think anything is wrong?"

"Oh, for heaven's sake. She's not stupid. You got that droopy look on your face and anyone can tell you are down in the dumps. Now come clean with her so we can get this moving. I have places to go," Charlotte said.

Yeah, like she had anywhere else to go.

Dixie looked at me funny when she saw me scowling at nothing beside her.

"Okay, I guess there is something bothering me."

"Well, that's what I'm here for. Talk to me." Dixie smiled.

I traced the edge of my mug with my finger. "It's just everything that's happened. You know, the murders in town and the fact that I discovered a dead man in the alley."

She folded her hands together. "I figured that

was what was wrong, but I didn't want to mention anything. I didn't want to bring it up if you didn't want to discuss it. I knew you would when you were ready."

"What do you think happened?" I asked.

She leaned back against the booth. "I think bad things can happen even in small towns. You shouldn't let these things worry you. They are out of your control."

I played with my napkin. "Yeah, but it is bothering me. Do you think the killer is still around town?"

The delicate features on her face tensed. "I think it's possible, but I certainly hope not. It's scary to think that a dangerous person could come into the diner or walk past us on the street."

I took a sip and then said, "Yeah, I think about that often."

"Is there something else you want to say?" She touched my hand.

"Here's your chance to tell her," Charlotte pushed.

I looked around to see who might be listening to us. "Well, I guess that isn't all that's on my mind."

Dixie smiled. "I'm listening."

"I know this will sound crazy, but I have to tell someone. Well, Heather knows, but that's because she is . . . well, she just knows. Anyway . . . do you believe in ghosts?" I studied Dixie's face.

Dixie pondered the question, then said, "Yes, I do."

I patted her hand. "That was the answer I was hoping for."

"What makes you ask?" She arched a brow behind her big glasses.

I scanned the diner again.

"Oh, no one can hear you. Just go ahead and tell her," Charlotte said.

I cleared my throat. "There's a ghost sitting next to you right now."

Dixie glanced beside her, then she looked at me again. "You're serious, aren't you?"

"I'm afraid so," I said.

She scooted away from Charlotte. "Who is the ghost?"

"Well, here is the tricky part. It's the ghost of Charlotte Meadows." I watched Dixie's face for her reaction.

Dixie lowered her voice. "Charlotte Meadows is sitting next to me?"

I drew my attention to where Charlotte sat.

"Tell her that I used to come in and order the pancakes with no butter and extra syrup."

I relayed the message to Dixie.

Dixie's mouth dropped. "How did you know that? Did someone tell you?"

"Who would have told me?" I asked.

She pushed a chestnut-colored curl off her forehead. "I don't know."

"Dixie, you said you believe in ghosts," I said.

She waved her hand. "Yes, I do. It's just that I didn't know they could really talk to people. I just thought they haunted houses. Is she here all the time?"

I slumped my shoulders. "Unfortunately not. She is *with me* all the time."

Charlotte wiggled her eyebrows. "You know you love me."

"Why is she around you all the time?" Dixie asked.

"She wants me to help solve her murder," I said matter-of-factly.

Dixie swallowed hard. "Are you serious?"

I wrapped my hands around my mug. "Yes. She's been pushing me in full detective mode."

"What have you discovered?" Dixie asked.

Charlotte leaned back in the booth. "Not a heck of a lot of anything."

"Hey, I'm trying my best," I snapped without thinking.

Dixie adjusted her eyeglasses. "What did she say?"

"Oh, she's complaining because I haven't solved the murder yet. She fails to realize that I'm not a trained detective."

"Speaking of detectives," Dixie said, motioning toward the door. "Here comes Dylan Valentine. Did I see you talking to him the other day?"

"Yeah. He probably thinks I had something to do with the murder of that private eye."

"How could you? You didn't know him, right?" Dixie asked.

I leaned in closer. "Of course not, but the private eye was asking me about Charlotte Meadows the night of the committee meeting."

"I bet he was trying to find out who murdered Charlotte." Dixie looked over at her.

"Tell her hello for me, okay?" Charlotte asked.

"Charlotte wants me to tell you hello," I whispered.

Dixie smiled. "Hello."

"She's right, you know. The private eye was looking into my death," Charlotte added.

"Yes, I agree he was probably trying to get answers about her death, but why?" I asked. "Who hired him?"

"I hope the police are looking into that," Dixie said.

"Well, they're not doing it fast enough for her liking." I pointed my spoon toward Charlotte.

"You'd feel that way too if you were in my Jimmy Choos," Charlotte said.

Detective Valentine took a seat at the counter.

"He's been asking me a lot of questions," I said.

Dixie soaked in his appearance. "Well, there are certainly worse people to be questioned by."

He was getting a to-go order. Fortunately, he hadn't noticed me. And for that, I was grateful.

"I'd rather he not ask *any* questions," I said.

Dixie peeked over her shoulder. "Well, he is just doing his job."

"Not fast enough if you ask me," Charlotte said.

It would never be fast enough for her.

"Back to the private eye. Why do you think he was killed?" I asked.

Dixie waved at someone who'd entered the diner, then said, "Maybe someone felt he was getting too close."

"That's what I'm afraid of. Maybe someone will think I'm getting too close to finding the killer, too."

Charlotte drummed her fingers against the table. "At the rate you're going, they don't have to worry about you finding the killer."

"Charlotte, be patient." I stirred my coffee again.

Dixie chuckled. "Charlotte is being Charlotte again, huh?"

I took a drink of coffee and then said, "Yeah, her usual sweet self."

"I take offense to that comment." Charlotte's neatly plucked eyebrows drew together.

I glanced in Dylan's direction again. Apparently, he still hadn't noticed that I was in the diner. The thought had barely left my mind when he turned around and looked directly at me. He smiled and walked straight toward the table.

"Speak of the devil," Dixie said.

"Hello, Cookie. How are you?" A wide smile covered his face.

"I'm doing okay." There was an awkward pause "Are you having lunch?"

"Yes, at the best place in town." He looked at Dixie and winked.

"How are you, Detective Valentine? Glad to see you stopped in today. Did you get what you needed?" Dixie asked.

He answered, "I'm doing great now."

"Oh, he likes you," Charlotte said.

I had to ignore her.

Dixie noticed that we were staring at each other in an awkward silence, so she broke up the quiet. "So Detective Valentine, I guess the things going on around town have kept you busy."

I wanted to poke Dixie under the table. The last thing I wanted her to bring up was the murders. Now I had no choice but to talk about what had happened.

"It's been busy, but we're dealing with it as best

as we can." His expression seemed torn, as if he didn't want to reveal too much about the case.

Thank goodness he didn't say anything else. Maybe it was because I didn't give him time before I asked, "What are you eating, Detective?"

Charlotte placed her head in her hands. "That's a lame question."

He seemed distracted by something at the front of the diner. Finally, he looked at me again. "Um, yeah, I'm just having a burger."

He looked toward the front of the diner again. Dixie and Charlotte were looking, too.

I turned around and saw Cindy Johnson's car parked at the curb. She was getting out of it. Was she headed into the diner? Would she speak to Dixie with me sitting in the same booth? Why was Dylan watching her? Maybe he had information about her in regards to the murder. I'd love to know what he'd discovered.

The next thing I knew, Charlotte was standing by the door. Her face was practically smashed up against the glass. What was she doing? I knew she wouldn't be able to leave the diner. Much to my chagrin, Charlotte couldn't go very far from me. I hadn't figured out why this was the case, but I guess the unanswered question was what made the paranormal so mysterious. Was she just trying to get a better look at Cindy? She was making me nervous. I'd rather she just come back over and sit down with us.

Dylan still focused his attention on Cindy, as if he had forgotten we were even sitting there.

She moved away from her car and down the

sidewalk, out of our view. Dylan still watched the door.

Charlotte motioned down the sidewalk. I didn't know what she was trying to tell me, but then Cindy came back into view and I realized that she was trying to warn me that Cindy was returning. I didn't want her in the diner with us.

Dylan turned to me and said, "It was great seeing you, Cookie. Dixie, thanks for the wonderful food. I have to run. I have an appointment. Thanks so much again." He dashed for the door and I knew he was going to follow Cindy.

"What do you think that was about?" Dixie asked.

I didn't want to tell her that Cindy was on Charlotte's suspects list. How would I explain that? I mean, it was one thing to have Charlotte around as a ghost, but it was another for me to have an actual list of people that she had given to me. I wasn't going to touch that subject. "I don't know. I guess he had an appointment."

I was still surprised that Dixie had believed that Charlotte's ghost was haunting me. I'd thought for sure she'd think I'd lost my marbles. "I have to be honest and say that I am surprised you believe me about Charlotte."

"If there was one person who would come back to haunt, it would be Charlotte." Dixie laughed.

Charlotte's mouth twisted at the corners as if she was proud of that accomplishment.

"How did you get her?" Dixie whispered as someone walked by.

"Let's just say she was attached to her clothing."

Dixie laughed again. "That sounds exactly like Charlotte."

"Can I help it if I love my clothing?" Charlotte grinned.

Dixie leaned in close. "You know, I overheard something earlier this morning." She looked around and over her shoulder.

I perked up. "What did you hear?"

Charlotte scooted over in the booth. "Do tell."

"I heard that the private eye was stabbed." Dixie shivered.

"That's terrible." I remembered seeing the blood under his body.

Dixie snapped her fingers against the table. "You know, now that I think about that morning, I recall taking the trash out and seeing Marie Vance leaving the alleyway. That was where the man was discovered, right? I would think that she would have discovered him before you."

"Really?" I said to Dixie.

"That is interesting," Dixie said.

I pushed to my feet. "Thanks for everything, Dixie."

She hugged me and I could smell her rosewater scent—in addition to that of fried onions. "Don't wait so long to talk to me next time, okay?"

"I'll be back soon." I made my way out of the diner with Charlotte matching my pace.

"So now what are we doing?" she asked eagerly.

"Let's just take a stroll," I said. "I need to think."

The diner was two blocks from my shop on the opposite side of the street.

When I neared Hortensia's Haberdashery, I stopped. The CLOSED sign hung in the window.

"What are you looking at?" Charlotte asked.

I shrugged. "Just thinking, that's all."

The spring air carried the scent of freshly bloomed honeysuckle. Cotton white clouds filled the blue sky. The weather was beautiful, but I felt a storm brewing.

At first, I didn't want anyone to see me standing in front of the shop. I thought it might look as if I was lingering there a little too long. Then I supposed there was nothing wrong with window-shopping and stepped up closer and peered in. "So this is where you bought the scarf, huh?"

Charlotte stood next to me. "Yep, this is the place."

I turned around, I'd seen enough. I looked both ways, then crossed the street. Out of the corner of my eye, I noticed movement in the alley next to me. I peered closely and saw a man and woman talking. "Doesn't that look like Cindy Johnson?"

Charlotte studied the couple. "It does. And that looks like one of the men who was at her house."

I stepped back so that I would be hidden from view and peeked around the corner of a building. At least I hoped I was hidden.

Footsteps sounded from behind me and I whirled around. If only I could have been invisible like Charlotte.

Detective Valentine regarded me solemnly. "Are you spying on someone?"

"It does look that way, doesn't it?"

"Yes, it does," he said.

I wasn't sure how to explain this one. I mean, I'd discovered a dead man in one alley, and now I was lurking around another. The only option was to be completely honest with him.

"Tell him you lost your cat," Charlotte said. "Whatever you do, don't tell him the truth."

I motioned over my shoulder. "I thought I saw Cindy Johnson talking to a man."

Charlotte groaned. "Why don't you listen to a word I say?"

"And you were watching her talk to a man because?" the detective asked.

"That was one of the men who was following me."

"Okay, now you just sound paranoid, Cookie. I beg you to shut your mouth now."

Charlotte was probably right. The more I talked the worse it sounded.

"I just wanted to make sure she was safe. You never know who to trust, right?" I gave a half-hearted smile.

"Yes, you're right about that." He stepped around the building and looked down the alley. "Wait right here."

He walked down the alley halfway, turned around, and joined me again on the sidewalk. "There's no one there now. Was there some reason why you thought she wouldn't be safe?"

"No. I guess I was just spooked," I said.

"Where are you headed now?" he asked.

"Back to my car. It's in the diner parking lot."

"Okay, how about I walk you there?" An air of confidence swirled around him.

I adjusted the purse strap on my shoulder. "Sure."

Charlotte smiled. "An escort by the handsome detective. I don't know if it's because he wants you to be safe or he thinks you're off your rocker."

I wanted to remind her that the only reason he would think I was off my rocker was *because of her*.

"Well, don't just walk. Talk to him," Charlotte pushed.

He shoved his hands in his pockets as we walked. "You know, that shirt I bought from your shop really is comfortable. I wish I could buy another one like it."

I smiled. "Yeah, that's the only downside. With vintage, you usually can't buy extra, but at least you know it's one of a kind."

We'd just reached my car when I spotted a stocky man with short dark hair nearby. When he spotted us, he took off around the side of the building. I wasn't the only living person who saw him.

"Wait here," Dylan said. He ran after the man.

"Thank goodness he saw him this time," I said to Charlotte.

"What do you think he was doing here?" she asked.

"I assume he was talking with Cindy, but why he was around my car, I don't know. He may have been looking for me."

"I hope you're not right," Charlotte said.

After a couple minutes, Dylan appeared from around the corner.

"Did you find him?" I asked.

"No. I'm sorry to say I think you're right— someone may have been following you. Why don't you let me follow you back to your shop?"

I clutched my purse close to my chest as if that would offer some kind of safety. "I wasn't going to the shop now. I'm sure I'll be fine."

He opened the Buick's door. "I'll find out who that guy is."

"Thank you, Detective—Dylan."

I climbed in the car and cranked the engine. When I pulled out, I glanced in the rearview mirror. Dylan was still watching me.

"Are you going home? Wind Song is still at the shop," Charlotte asked with a smile.

"You're right. I've got work to do. But when I go home, I'm going to eat a pound of chocolate after what just happened."

"A moment on the lips, forever on the hips," she warned.

"It's a chance I'm willing to take," I retorted.

I pulled up in front of the shop and checked the rearview mirror. So far no one had followed me.

"You should try yoga to relax." Charlotte slipped out of the car.

I climbed out and locked the door. "I should try not talking to ghosts to relax."

Chapter 31

After a full day at the shop, I loaded up Wind Song and pointed the Buick in the direction of home. I'd sold the pink prom dress from the estate sale, turning a nice profit, just as I had hoped.

Inside the house, I pushed the buttons on the security device that would avoid alerting the police of a break-in, then reset the alarm. I let Wind Song out of the carrier, made myself a PB&J, and poured a glass of chocolate milk. Going to the living room, I plopped down on the sofa with my laptop. Maybe blogging would take my mind off things for a while. I opened my e-mail and froze. Another comment had been left on my blog. I clicked it open.

Charlotte saw the look on my face. "What does this one say?"

I swallowed hard. "It says, 'Curiosity killed the cat and I will kill yours if you keep snooping. Stay out of other people's business or watch your pretty shop go up in flames.'"

It was the scariest one yet. I knew that whoever was leaving the messages was serious about their threat. They'd killed before and I knew they wouldn't hesitate to take me out. Apparently, that was what had happened to the private eye.

I picked up the phone to call Dylan, but after punching in half the number, I hung up.

"Not calling him is probably for the best," Charlotte said with confidence.

I'd already told him once. He had enough on his plate. I'd just have to be extra careful. Be more secretive about snooping around. Watch my surroundings. If the killer was after me, I wouldn't let him have the chance to get to me.

My PB&J tasted like sand, even washed down with chocolate milk. After cleaning around the house, I pulled out my laptop and spent a couple hours working on the blog. I closed the computer and headed off for bed. Before reaching my bedroom, I double-checked the locks on the doors, just in case.

It took me forever to fall asleep. When I finally drifted off, I dreamed of the murdered private eye wearing a vintage dress and that emerald and gold diamond patterned scarf.

Charlotte wasn't in my room pacing when I woke up, which was unusual. Wind Song was on the edge of the bed sleeping . . . or pretending to sleep. I wasn't sure which.

I slid into my pink fuzzy slippers. As well as

pajamas, vintage slippers were hard to find, so I'd
settled on a new pair from Target and the matching striped pink and white cotton pajama set that
went with them. Actually, since they were so cute
I'd purchased every color the store had in stock. I
was a real connoisseur of pajamas.

I stepped out into the hallway, and looked
around for Charlotte. Had she left? Maybe I'd
gotten rid of her. Oh, I couldn't get that lucky.
But to be honest, I was beginning to enjoy her
company.

I sat at the kitchen table and pulled out my computer. After logging on, I was relieved to see that
there wasn't a new message.

I brewed toasted hazelnut coffee and poured
myself a bit of orange juice then put a couple pieces
of whole grain bread into the toaster. When it
popped, I spread apricot preserves on top, grabbed
the coffee, and headed for my bedroom, only to
spill the coffee and drop my breakfast when I
found Charlotte standing in front of me. "What the
heck are you doing?"

"While you were sleeping, I went out."

I grabbed the toast from the floor where Wind
Song was sniffing it. "What? You mean you can go
places without me?"

"Well, I couldn't get farther than the front
porch, but I had time to think and I am more mo-
tivated than ever. Get dressed so we can get this day
started."

Since Charlotte was making me nervous, I didn't
have a lot of time to select an outfit. I decided to go
with a navy blue and white mod polka-dot mini
dress from the nineties. It had a raw scissored hem,

open sleeves, and an exaggerated nautical sailor collar.

I slid into white leather sandals and grabbed a red leather purse from the closet. After stuffing my belongings into the bag, I ate the slice of the toast that hadn't fallen on the floor and grabbed my coffee cup. I refilled my cup, turned off the coffeepot, and headed out the door with Charlotte behind me and Wind Song in her carrier. It was becoming routine.

Charlotte and I piled into the Buick and headed downtown. I turned up the music—the Andrews sisters singing "Boogie Woogie Bugle Boy"—so that Charlotte wouldn't feel the need to constantly talk. Sometimes it was just nice to be lost in my own thoughts, although lately, my mind had been consumed with helping my ghostly friend. I needed this investigation to be over so that I could go back to finding clothing for the shop and writing my blog without worrying about threatening messages. I also needed to follow up with the movie people about the wardrobe consultant possibility.

At the shop, I busied myself with rearranging clothing that customers had put back in the wrong locations. The bell over the door jangled and I looked up to see Heather. Her outfit stood out right away. Not her tie-dyed T-shirt, not her love beads, and not her stone-washed denim jeans. It was the scarf around her neck—the exact same one that Charlotte and Cindy had.

"Where did you get that?" I asked.

Charlotte turned around to see who I was talking to. Her eyes widened when she saw Heather. "She is wearing my scarf."

Heather touched the scarf. "It was on the street in front of the yellow house on Sycamore Street."

"That's my scarf. I know it's my scarf," Charlotte repeated again.

Since I had the one that we'd found at Cindy's, it really could have been Charlotte's. Actually, Winona had said that she'd had only two, so the one Heather was wearing *had* to be Charlotte's scarf, right?

"Charlotte says that's her scarf," I said.

Heather looked like she was ready to rip it off and stuff it in the trash can. "Actually, I found this scarf and a handkerchief at the same time." She shrugged. "I figured they were meant to go in the garbage since it was next to the trash can, so I picked them up. Don't judge me," she said with indignation. "So what if I like to Dumpster dive?"

"Hey, I would be the last one to judge. I would totally climb in the Dumpster if it meant finding a great vintage piece," I said. I walked to the counter and sat down on a stool.

"How did this happen?" Heather asked. "It wasn't the scarf Charlotte was buried in, was it?"

"I don't know. You say you found it on Sycamore Street? Was that the house with the black shutters and the red door?" I asked.

"Yeah, that's the one."

I turned to address Charlotte. "Will you stop pacing? You're making me nervous."

Heather took the scarf from her neck and placed it on the counter. "Well, I'm not wearing it anymore." She plopped down on the stool beside mine.

I picked up the scarf and examined it. It was

exactly like Cindy's. A memory floated back to my mind. I remembered seeing Marie come out of that house.

I asked Charlotte, "What connection does Marie have to the house on Sycamore? I saw her come out of it one day."

Charlotte leaned against the counter. "Simple. That's her home."

"What does the handkerchief look like?" I asked Heather.

She described it and I knew it was probably the third from the set that Winona had sold. Finding the items in the trash in front of that house meant they had to have been Marie's, right?

I grabbed my purse. "We have to go to Marie's home right now."

Charlotte and Heather followed me to the door.

"What are you going to say to her?" Heather asked.

"I don't know. I guess I'll figure that out when I get there."

Chapter 32

*Heather's Heartfelt Tip
for Getting Rid of an Unwanted Ghost*

❧

*Never use a Ouija board unless you have the help
of a professional . . . or a psychic cat.*

While Charlotte and I headed out to confront
Marie about the scarf and handkerchief, Heather
watched the store for me. I had a feeling she would
try to get Wind Song to use the tarot cards or
Ouija board while I was gone. If it was bad news,
I wasn't sure I wanted to know. Heather and I
watched each other's store on occasion. Usually,
I'd put a sign in the window indicating for customers to go next door for assistance. Since it was
Saturday, I knew it would get busy, so I'd have to
hurry back.

I wasn't going to deny that I was nervous. What
would I say to Marie? After all, she had been
really strange about Charlotte's clothing since
the estate sale.

We pulled up to the curb and I cut the engine.
The yellow plank house was trimmed in white.
Pink flowers burst from the white window boxes on

the two front windows. It was a small but lovely, well cared-for home. A breeze rustled the leaves of the magnolia tree in the small front yard. A green box-wood wreath hung on the red front door. Small hedges and daffodils filled the flower beds.

"Don't worry, Cookie. We'll just go up to the door and ask her about the scarf," Charlotte said.

"*We'll* ask her?" I said, glancing over at Charlotte. "Don't you mean *I'll* ask her? She can't see you, remember?"

"Don't get technical about it." Charlotte floated out of the car. "You can do it," she urged.

I got out, locked the door behind me, and made the trek up the brick path to the front door. My heart rate increased when I pressed the doorbell. It was too late to turn back.

"Don't forget to breathe," Charlotte said.

Footsteps sounded from the other side of the door and the door opened.

Marie looked shocked when she saw me standing on her porch. Her white and black striped maxi dress was layered with a white short-sleeved blazer. She wore a chunky gold bracelet and wedge heels. Her makeup and hair were perfect as if she'd just left the salon.

"Cookie, I'm surprised to see you here. How did you know where I live?" A smile may have crossed her face, but there was suspicion in her eyes.

I couldn't tell her that Charlotte was standing right beside me and had told me where she lived, so I said, "I happened to be driving by the other day and saw you walk in your front door. I thought I'd take a chance and see if you really do live here.

It looks like I was right." I looked over her shoulder to see the inside of her house.

She stepped in front of me to block my view. "So you just wanted to say hello?" An idea struck her. "Did you decide to sell Charlotte's clothing to me?"

"Tell her you'll make a deal with her. Maybe that will get her to talk with you about the scarf," Charlotte said.

"Yes, that is exactly why I came by." I smiled.

Marie's eyes shone with delight. "Oh, that is fantastic news. Won't you come inside?" She moved out of the way and motioned for me to enter.

"Thank-you." I stepped inside the room and looked around. It was stylishly decorated with matching furniture. A fireplace and bookshelves lined the far wall. The room was painted almost the exact shade of pale yellow as the exterior of the house.

"Why don't you have a seat on the sofa? Would you like something to drink? Iced tea?" she offered.

"Yes, iced tea would be nice. Thank-you." I eased down on the gray sofa.

"I'll be back in a jiffy." Marie bounced out of the room.

"She seems awfully excited now that she knows she's getting the clothing. If I didn't know better, I'd say she's lost a few marbles," Charlotte said.

"You might be right about that," I whispered.

I spotted a handkerchief on the table across the room. Maybe my eyes were deceiving me, but I thought the pattern was like the ones at Bud's house and Charlotte's place, except this one had purple flowers. "Aren't those the same handkerchiefs?" I whispered to Charlotte.

I pointed to the table. "I think that's the third handkerchief in the set," I whispered. "What do you think?"

Charlotte floated over to the table to take a look and nodded. "Yep. Same design. Looks like the third hanky in the pack."

Marie sashayed back in the room with two tall glasses of iced tea and handed me one.

I took it and said, "Thank-you."

"I'm so glad you decided to sell me the clothing. You know, I really wanted something to remember Charlotte by." She stood opposite me, one hand on a damask-covered club chair. "It's such a tragedy what happened."

Charlotte stepped up nose-to-nose with her. "Yeah, you seem really broken up about it."

"That will be nice," I said, then took a sip of my tea.

Maybe it was Marie or maybe it was just the dimly lit house, but something was making me antsy.

Marie's phone rang. "Oh, will you excuse me please? I need to get that."

"Sure," I said.

Charlotte and I watched her walk out of the room.

"I wonder who is calling her?" Charlotte asked. "I bet it's real estate business that I should be handling, but instead I am dead. This isn't fair. I was good at what I did."

Too bad I couldn't give Charlotte a hug. "I'm sure you were, Charlotte."

"You're darn tootin' I was. Now I have to walk

around with you for the rest of your life. And then what happens?"

I didn't like where this was going.

"No offense," she said.

"Yeah, none taken, I guess."

Charlotte motioned for me to get up. "You should take this opportunity to snoop around."

I set my glass on the coffee table, making sure to carefully place it on the coaster. "Snoop around? What am I looking for? Besides, I can't do that with her in the house." I kept my voice as low as I could.

"Why not? She won't know what you're doing. She's too busy on the phone."

I pushed to my feet. "Okay, I guess . . . but I don't know what I'm looking for."

Charlotte motioned for me to hurry. "You won't know until you look, now will you?"

I peeked into the kitchen and saw Marie by the window. She didn't notice me as she spoke on the phone. I had to move quickly.

I looked around, unsure of where to start. In the living room, all I saw were knickknacks and a few books. To my left, I noticed a small room off to the side. It contained a desk and a couple chairs.

"That's her office," Charlotte said. "You should look in there."

I glanced over to make sure that Marie wasn't coming. I'd never done anything this risky until Charlotte had come into my life, but I guessed there was a first time for everything. I rushed into the room and weaved around the chairs to reach the desk.

It had one big drawer in the middle and four drawers on each side. I wasn't sure if I would have time to look in all of them, so I started with the few papers on top of the desk.

As it turned out, I wouldn't need to look in the drawers. I discovered a copy of the insurance policy that Bud had taken out on Charlotte.

If Charlotte hadn't been standing right beside me, I would have hidden it from her. But there was no way to keep it from her. "Look at this. It's the insurance policy that Bud had taken out on you."

Her face sank. "Are you sure?"

"Unfortunately, yes. It is the exact paper."

If Marie caught me in her office with the paper, what would she do?

I had no excuse for being in the room. I shoved the paper back under the stack where I'd found it. "We have to get out of here."

Charlotte clutched her fists by her sides. "I can't believe I trusted that woman."

"Do you think she and Bud were in this together?" I asked.

Charlotte grimaced. "Bud doesn't seem smart enough to pull that off. This has Marie written all over it. I bet this was all her idea. He was just stupid enough to go along with it, but he wasn't the one who came up with the plan. No way." Charlotte's voice, usually soft, was flinty with anger. "Marie was conniving behind my back all along. And I was too dumb to even know what was going on. Maybe I wasn't as good in business as I thought."

"You had no way of knowing," I offered.

Charlotte stood a little straighter. "You can't leave that paper here. You need to show it to Detective Valentine."

"You're right. He needs to see the proof." I

rushed back and grabbed the paper. "What do I do with it?"

Charlotte motioned toward my chest. "Put it in your shirt."

I stuffed the paper in my waistband and pulled the shirt over it. "How's that?"

"Perfect." Charlotte glanced at the door. "She's coming."

I rushed out of the room and practically dived onto the sofa where I'd been sitting before. I tried to steady my breath and pretend that nothing was wrong, as if I'd been sitting there all along.

"I will haunt those two for the rest of their lives," Charlotte said.

Marie stepped into the room and eyed me suspiciously. Had she seen me leaving her office? By the look on her face, I knew she had her doubts about my visit.

"Now where were we?" Marie plastered on a fake smile.

"I do have one question," I said as I picked up my glass from its coaster.

"Of course, what is it?" Marie asked through gritted teeth.

"I found a scarf. . . ."

"Was it in the clothing you bought at the estate sale?" she asked.

"No." I chuckled. "This may seem a little wacky, but I have a friend who sometimes goes through trash cans looking for hidden treasures."

Marie scowled as if the very idea was disgusting.

"Anyway, she happened to pass by your garbage can and took a look."

"She was going through my trash?" Marie said, looking offended. "Is that even legal?"

"I don't know. But that's not what I wanted to talk to you about."

Marie said, "Well, what is it then?"

"She found a scarf in your trash."

Marie's face turned red. "I am furious that she would go through my things."

"Well, did you mean to throw it away?" I asked, getting to the point.

Marie objected. "That's not the point. The point is she should stay out of other people's belongings."

"I'll make sure to tell her to stay out of it. Anyway, was that your scarf?"

"Obviously it was mine if it was in my trash." Anger sparked in her eyes.

"Charlotte had a scarf just like that. It was a rare scarf."

Marie said quickly, "Charlotte left the scarf in my car. I had no need for the thing so I threw it away."

That didn't add up. She was anxious to have clothing to remember Charlotte by, yet when she had one of Charlotte's items, she'd tossed it in the trash. I thought she knew what I was thinking.

Charlotte said, "No way. I remember wearing the scarf the moment I was murdered. I was attacked from behind, though, and I couldn't see my killer."

It was hard listening to Charlotte talk and at the same time, conceal my growing panic.

Marie leaned back in her chair and smiled at me, but I knew it wasn't a friendly smile.

"You're not telling me the truth, are you?" I asked.

"You're a smart little Cookie, aren't you?" Marie asked, getting up.

I could hear the rage in her tone.

Chapter 33

Cookie's Savvy Vintage Fashion Shopping Tip

Have fun with vintage clothing!
Make the outfit your own.
After all, it has many years of wear left.

"I am so furious." If Charlotte could have attacked Marie she would have. "Of all the evil and vile things to do. She murdered me," Charlotte yelled. "How could she? What did I ever do to her? I tried to help her as much as I could and this is the thanks I get."

I stood up and faced Marie. "You killed Charlotte, didn't you?" Sweat broke out on my forehead. I couldn't believe I asked her that question. And the bad part was I already knew the answer. "You killed Charlotte Meadows. You were in cahoots with Bud Butler to share life insurance money. And you killed Edward Andersen because he was getting close to finding out what happened."

"Yeah, I did it, and Charlotte deserved it. She treated me as if I wasn't a business partner. I was better at real estate than her. She never let me

have a chance to showcase my skills." Disgust filled
Marie's voice.

I was in serious trouble. I suddenly realized she
wouldn't hesitate to kill me, too.

I needed an escape plan. I looked over her
shoulder and gauged the distance to the front
door. I would have to run past her, which would
allow her to grab me. That would never work. I
thought of my phone in my pocket. If only I could
call Detective Valentine. I definitely needed
backup.

I barely had time to register the fact that Marie
was moving and she was grabbing me. She slammed
my body to the floor and took the scarf from
around her neck. In one movement, she wrapped
it around *my* neck.

Charlotte was frantically trying to move something with her hand in order to distract Marie. She
just didn't have the psychic energy necessary.

I grabbed at the scarf as Marie applied more
pressure. My airway was being compromised. I was
having a hard time breathing, and would soon pass
out. The more I tried to get her off me, the more
she tried to strangle me with the scarf.

I tried to grab her shoulders in order to push
her off, but I didn't have the strength. I reached up
and tried to wiggle my fingers under the fabric of
the scarf to loosen the hold she had on me. If only
I could get some air . . .

A knock sounded on the front door. Marie
looked up but didn't loosen her hold on me.

A crash sounded. Startled, Marie flinched and
loosened her hold. I pushed my fingers under the
material and gasped, breathing in much needed

air. Another crash sounded. Charlotte had managed to knock over two vases of flowers. Her paranormal skills were improving—just when she needed them the most.

The front door rattled, creating the distraction I needed. I pushed Marie off me and grabbed the scarf from around my neck. I wrapped it around her hands and sat on top of her. What I was going to do from this point, I wasn't sure. I had to call the police, but my phone was in my pocket. I needed to get it out without allowing her to get the upper hand again.

"Let her have it, Cookie." Charlotte shook her fist.

What happened next was only what I could call a miracle. The front door burst open and the tall lanky man who had followed me from Cindy's house was in the living room. Even in casual clothing, I recognized him. He pointed a gun at Marie and me. "Freeze. Nobody move," he commanded.

I lifted my hands in the air. "Who the heck are you?"

"Is everyone okay?" he asked.

"Does it look like we are okay? She is a murderer." I pointed to Marie.

"Yeah, I figured that out."

"That still leaves the question as to who you are," I said.

"My name is Vernon Olsen. I'm a private detective hired by the insurance company to find out who murdered Charlotte Meadows."

"Leave it to the insurance company to be the only ones interested in who murdered me," Charlotte huffed.

I wondered if he was telling the truth. "You're the one who followed me. You and another man."

"He's an associate. He was helping me that day."

"Do you think you can stop pointing that gun at me?" I asked, getting off Marie and pulling her to her feet.

He lowered the weapon and gestured at Marie. "Do you need help with her?"

"What do you think?"

He shoved the gun back in its holster and crossed the floor. Marie looked like she was about to make a run for it, so I removed the vintage belt from around my waist and handed it to Vernon.

He restrained her ankles. "There, that should keep her from going anywhere."

Marie's face was red and her eyes slits of rage.

"She killed Edward Andersen, too. Do you know him?"

He placed her in a chair. "Yes, he was an investigator with my agency."

I pulled my phone from my pocket and dialed Dylan's number. As soon as the detective picked up, I said, "I'm at Marie Vance's home and I need you to come here right away. She confessed to both murders."

"I'll be there as quickly as possible. Did she hurt you?"

"I'm okay, but hurry."

The line went dead and I hoped that meant he was on his way. "Why did you come here?" I asked the private detective.

"I was following you. When you came in here I

got nervous. I snooped around the windows, and I saw her on top of you."

"Well, thank-you. . . . It's a little creepy that you were following me, but thank-you."

"It's my job."

Sirens sounded outside and Dylan quickly appeared in the foyer. His gun was aimed at Marie. Worry flashed in his eyes. "You put yourself in a dangerous situation."

Tension eased from my shoulders as relief washed over me. I pushed hair away from my eyes. "I'm fine."

A funny expression crossed his face when he saw the scarf and belt tied around Marie's hands and feet.

"I improvised," I said.

A slight smile crossed his face before he handcuffed Marie and removed the scarf and belt. More uniformed officers entered the room. Dylan stepped over to speak with them while another officer escorted Marie out of the house.

"Get out of my house, Cookie Chanel. You have no right to be here," she yelled as she was hauled past me. Her face was red and her eyes full of rage.

"How did you find yourself in Marie Vance's home with her tied up and making a confession to you?" Dylan asked.

I winked at Charlotte when no one was watching. "I had a little help from a friend."

Charlotte smiled at me.

"Heather found a scarf and I knew that it was a rare collectible. Charlotte had owned one just like it. When Heather said she was Dumpster-diving and found it in Marie's trash, I knew Marie had to know more about Charlotte's murder. So I came here to confront her," I said.

"Leave it to you to solve a murder with fashion," he said with the smallest curve of his lips.

"Fashion is part of our lives more than you realize," I said.

He chuckled. "I guess you're right." He looked over at the man standing in the corner of the room, speaking with another officer.

"That's the private eye who had been following me. Apparently the insurance company hired him. Edward Andersen was with his company, as well." I grinned. "I told you someone was following me. I bet you can confirm that Marie was the one leaving messages on my blog. She admitted that she did it," I said.

"Well, it looks as if you have the whole case wrapped up for us," Dylan said.

"I have to confess that I was in Cindy's home the other day, but I didn't break in. Cindy was there and let me in her house, but for some reason she took off and never come back. The insurance investigators showed up and I hid in the closet." I waited for his reaction.

He waited for me to continue.

I shrugged. "I found a second scarf there, and that helped me figure out that Marie was the murderer."

Dylan shoved his hands into his pockets. "That's strange. Cindy has been telling anyone who will listen that you were at her house and the ghost of Charlotte Meadows was with you."

I attempted a smile. "Well, that is crazy. Why would she say such a thing?"

"I don't know, but she said she saw her plain as I'm looking at you right now."

I thought about telling him that it was true—that Charlotte Meadows was standing beside us, but I decided against it. He probably wouldn't believe me, anyway. Sometimes keeping a secret was the right thing to do. I was just glad that she had helped me and that I'd been able to help her.

What would she do now? Would she leave? Her murder had been solved so there was no reason for her to hang around.

I glanced over to my ghostly friend, but she wasn't there. I wondered if she'd already left this dimension. Surely she would have said good-bye first. But maybe she wasn't given that option. Wherever she went might have called for her with no warning.

"Listen, I have to finish up here, but I'll stop by your shop later, okay? Probably tomorrow," Dylan said.

I noticed he was wearing his vintage shoes. Of course, a wide smile spread across my face. "Yeah, I'll talk to you later."

"That was a close one," Charlotte said from over my shoulder.

I jumped. "Where did you go?"

"I walked outside on the porch to watch the action. It's better than TV."

* * *

Detective Dylan Valentine stepped into It's Vintage, Y'all. I wasn't prepared for what I saw.

"Wow, he looks dapper," Charlotte said.

Yes, he certainly did look sharp in the vintage outfit that I'd picked out for him. "You're wearing the clothes you got here."

"That's what I bought them for," Dylan said. "I thought it would be fun to try out this new look. You know, when I'm off duty? What do you think?"

"I like it."

Wind Song meowed and weaved around his legs.

"She likes it, too."

He reached down and picked her up. "We questioned Marie Vance for three hours last night. She waived the right to counsel and spilled everything. She convinced Bud to take out the insurance policy to set him up as the suspect for Charlotte's murder and avoid suspicion on herself."

"I can't believe they betrayed me like that," Charlotte said.

Dylan set the cat down with a gentle pat. "Marie placed the handkerchief at his home, but she didn't know that she'd lost one out of the set she took from Charlotte's home."

"Why did Marie want Charlotte dead?" I asked.

"Marie had been embezzling money from Charlotte and she knew that Charlotte was close to discovering the truth."

"I should have known," Charlotte said. "Ask him

if he knows why she wanted to buy my clothing from you."

"Why did she want to buy Charlotte's clothing from me?" I asked.

"Because she thought you had the scarf that she had used as the murder weapon," Dylan said.

"Now I remember," Charlotte said as if she'd just had an *ah-ha* moment. "I did confront her about the missing money. She came up from behind, wrapped the scarf around my neck, pulled me back, and the next thing I knew I was dead."

I doubted the courts would allow me to testify on Charlotte's behalf. Her memory would be no good for the case against Marie. It was a good thing Marie had confessed.

"Did Marie say why she killed Edward Andersen?" I asked Dylan.

"He'd figured out she was the murderer. She called him and pretended to be Cindy Johnson and set up the nine AM meeting."

"That's a lot to absorb. It's a good thing I figured out who the killer was," I said.

"How did you figure it out?" he asked.

"I just got lucky." I winked at Charlotte and Wind Song.

"I wonder if you have time later, could we go for that walk?" He flashed a grin.

"I'd like that," I said.

I promised Dylan that I'd stay out of police investigations from now on . . . maybe.

Is Your Cat Psychic?

Take this simple quiz to find out if your cat has supernatural powers. If you answer yes to three or more, your kitty might have a sixth sense.

1. Does your cat have an odd fascination with Ouija boards or tarot cards?

2. Does your cat stare at a wall or ceiling and meow at something you can't see?

3. Does your cat sense when you need attention or love and curl up beside you?

4. Does your cat appear out of nowhere?

5. Can your cat spell?

6. Does your cat know what you're going to do even before you know?

7. Does your cat hiss at certain people, only to seek attention from others?

8. Does your cat warn you when it's about to rain or storm?

Acknowledgments

Huge thanks to my editor, Michaela Hamilton, and to my agents, Becky Vinter and Laura Wood of FinePrint Literary Management. Thanks also to Tammy White for the help and sharing my love for all things vintage.

I can't thank my husband enough for believing in my dream. Without the love of my son, parents, and family, nothing would be possible. Thank you!

Don't miss the next Haunted Vintage mystery
by Rose Pressey

All Dressed Up and No Place to Haunt

Coming from Kensington in 2015

Keep reading to enjoy an excerpt . . .

Chapter 1

Seeing a ghost didn't shock me as much the second time around. Don't get me wrong, it was still strange and a little unnerving, but overall, I thought I handled it quite nicely.

My day had started out to be a fantastic one, but it had gone downhill quickly. A movie was being shot at Fairtree Plantation and I'd been invited to watch. The 1850 antebellum mansion made a gorgeous backdrop for the film. Its three stories loomed at the end of a cobblestone drive lined by tall live oak trees draped in Spanish moss. Maple, oak, magnolia, and dogwood trees covered the twelve-acre estate.

Silence surrounded the set as I watched the actors bring the script to life. The lead characters were embraced in a kiss. Of course, ten seconds ago they had been arguing. But their kiss seemed to have some real passion in it—or was that just because they were good actors?

I'd once watched a movie being filmed while on vacation in New York City, but spectators had been held back by barricades. I'd never been so close to the action before. I had a front row seat because my name was on the production company's special guest list. Apparently, helping the film crew with their vintage costumes had perks. My hometown of Sugar Creek, Georgia, had been abuzz since the director had decided to shoot part of his new movie right outside our little town.

It's Vintage, Y'all, my vintage clothing boutique, is located in the historic Main Street section of town. Since I'd started blogging about my great vintage finds, I'd attracted quite the following of readers. It hadn't taken long before a few movie producers had asked for my advice with their costumes.

Moonlight and Magnolias was the biggest film I'd been involved with so far. Beautiful Nicole Silver and the gorgeous Preston Hart had the lead roles. I'd read in the tabloids that they were dating in real life. Watching their steamy kiss, I could well believe that the sparks between them were real.

I had been beyond excited when asked to help with their costumes.

Nicole's shiny blond hair cascaded to her shoulders and had been styled like Veronica Lake's with a peek-a-boo bang on one side. The black and white Christian Dior dress that I'd picked up at an auction of a late grandmother's belongings hugged her curves in all the right places. Her full red lips seemed to be in a constant pout. The massive diamond on her left-hand ring finger glistened in the sunlight, standing out like a spotlight on a stage.

Preston was tall, dark, and handsome with strong cheekbones and chiseled features. I'd give anything for his thick eyelashes, even my recent score—a vintage Gucci handbag. He wore black trousers and a crisp white shirt with a wide swing tie of small red and ivory paisley.

Fashion is my passion. Coco Chanel once said, "Elegance does not consist in putting on a new dress." I totally agreed—which was why I was wearing a *vintage* dress. Okay, maybe that wasn't exactly what she'd meant, but nevertheless, it was what I'd gotten from the quote. My name happened to be Cookie Chanel. Funny, right? I had no family relationship with her, as far as I knew.

Chanel was a name that came over to Georgia when my Scots-Irish ancestors had settled here, evidently on more than friendly terms with Norman invaders. When I'd shown an avid interest in fashion as a child, my grandmother had started calling me Cookie instead of my given name, Cassandra, because it fit so well with Chanel. Plus, Coco Chanel was my granny's favorite designer. I still use the name Cookie to this day.

The movie took place partly in the forties and partly in the present. I'd had a wonderful time gathering the outfits for the actors. Of course, I had to dress the part, too. After all, vintage was my thing. I wore a rayon-chiffon blend, red and white polka-dot dress. The fitted bodice came down into a princess waist. It had double straps on the shoulders and a pretty red bow in front. I matched it with a red clutch purse and straw wedge heels with a tiny red trim along the edges.

It was hard to look glamorous, though. My hair was plastered to my head from the relentless heat. That was part of life in Georgia. My shoulder-length dark locks had started the day in victory rolls, but they had soon fizzled out. I hoped my bright smile—enhanced by Revlon's Fire and Ice lipstick—would distract others from noticing my bad hair day.

Nicole and Preston finished their scene by disentangling from their embrace. Breathing heavily, they held hands until they parted, walking separate ways. It was the last scene filmed for the day.

While gaffers and other crew members put away their gear, I remained seated. I intended to stay until I absolutely had to leave. My day on the film set had been so exciting that I didn't want it to end.

Shiloh Northcutt, the costume director, approached. Wearing dark blue shorts and a white T-shirt, she had definitely dressed for comfort. Wisps of auburn hair framed her slender face. "Cookie, you've been a lot of help and the costumes were a huge success. I hope you had a fun time today." She looked at her chunky white rhinestone-encrusted watch.

"I had a fantastic time." I'd barely finished the sentence when Shiloh walked off to greet someone else.

Her abrupt departure was a bit rude, but I figured she was just distracted by all the action and decided to take a walk around the property. I'd never been to the plantation before, and I'd always wanted to get a closer look. Once the home of the Abernathy family who had made their fortune in cotton, it was a museum that offered a rare glimpse into a bygone world.

The smell of honeysuckle drifted across the warm summer air as I stepped through the garden. A moss-covered stone path led to a patio surrounded by the aromatic flowering rosebushes.

Beyond, tall boxwood hedges provided a green shield from the rest of the property.

Moving over to a small wooden bench, I sat down and inhaled the sweet floral perfume. The sound of an argument soon caught my attention.

"I saw the way you looked at her," Nicole ground out.

"Baby, it wasn't what it looked like," Preston pleaded.

I leaned to my right, hoping to hear more of the conversation. They lowered their voices and their words became muffled, so I pushed to my feet and headed toward them. Reaching the hedges, I realized the conversation was being held just on the other side. I eased over to the greenery's end and peeked around the corner.

Nicole and Preston were facing each other, still wearing their vintage costumes. Her arms were crossed in front of her waist in a defensive stance. It definitely wasn't a scene from the movie. She glared at him and jerked away when he reached out and touched her arm.

I knew I shouldn't be watching their very private discussion, and getting caught would be embarrassing, so I inched back and hurried toward the front of the plantation and my car.

I ran into a few actors who stopped me to ask questions about the vintage clothing I'd provided for them. After speaking with them for about twenty minutes, I spotted Shiloh again. I'd forgotten to ask her when the garments would be returned. My plan was to auction the items off and donate the proceeds to a scholarship fund to enable a talented local student to attend fashion design school in Atlanta. She was so engrossed in the conversation with the petite blond hairdresser that she didn't see me walking her way.

As I neared them, I heard my name. Since they still didn't notice that I was headed in their direction, I stepped behind a nearby clump of azaleas and listened. Anyone who saw me hiding in the bushes would probably think I'd lost my mind.

"Well, I'm not happy with any of the clothing that she brought," Shiloh said.

My mouth dropped. She'd acted as if she loved the items that I'd brought. Why hadn't she mentioned her dissatisfaction *to me*? If she'd told me earlier, I would have been willing to work with her and get the items that would have suited her.

"I guess there's nothing you can do about it now. I'm sure everything will be fine," the blonde said.

"It'll have to be." Disgust filled Shiloh's voice.

They moved down the path in my direction, so I headed the opposite way. I didn't feel like having a confrontation. If I asked Shiloh why she didn't express her unhappiness, I would have to admit that I had spied on her conversation. I gritted my teeth and thought of an expression my grandpa used to use—*She's lower than a snake's belly in a wagon rut.* At least now I knew her true feelings.

I figured I would walk a bit until they were gone, then hurry back to my car and get the heck out of there. I didn't want to chance any more hiding in bushes. The third time might be one too many. To my right, I noticed a pond on the edge of the plantation's property and walked over to look for wildlife. Maybe a muskrat would streak across its still surface, or a family of ducks would waddle by.

I wasn't sure what made me look to my left, but I noticed the body floating facedown right away.

I knew by the dress that it was Nicole Silver. I pulled out my cell phone. Before I had a chance to dial, I heard a scream behind me. Several panicked people were running toward the pond. The movie director sprinted past me and jumped in the water, dragging Nicole's motionless body from the pond. He laid her on the grass on her stomach and pressed into her back in a steady rhythm, crying, "Come on, Nicole. Breathe!" Tears mingled with the sweat running down his face.

As I stood there watching the frantic resuscitation attempts slow to an end, I heard a woman clear her throat. I looked to my left and saw a willowy figure standing beside me. Her chestnut brown hair was twisted into an updo and she wore a pink dress in a style similar to the one that Nicole wore. It wasn't a dress that I'd given the costume director; I knew that because if it had been, I would remember it. The film crew must have brought the dress with them when they arrived in Sugar Creek.

It was a lovely garment, and I was a little jealous that I hadn't found it myself. The woman wearing it must have been an extra.

"This is just terrible," she said with a shake of her head.

I looked at her. "Were you in the film with her?"

"No, but that's my dress she's wearing," she said matter-of-factly.

Oh no, not again.

An excerpt from Cookie's blog
Movies with Fabulous Vintage Fashions
from the 1920s-1990s

The films listed below were either made in the decade stated or costumes were designed from that era. You'll find great vintage attire in all of these films.

1920s
The Great Gatsby

1930s
Bonnie and Clyde

1940s
The Notebook

1950s
Funny Face

1960s
Breakfast at Tiffany's

1970s
Saturday Night Fever

1980s
Flashdance

1990s
Pretty Woman